Emily Windsnap
Two Magical Mermaid Tales

LIZ KESSLER

illustrations by Sarah Gibb

CANDLEWICK PRESS

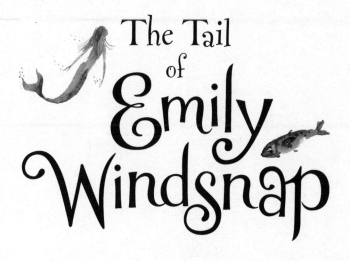

The Tail
of
Emily Windsnap

For Frankie, Lucy, and Emily
And for Dad

Come, dear children, let us away;
Down and away below.
Now my brothers call from the bay;
Now the great winds shoreward blow;
Now the salt tides seaward flow;
Now the wild white horses play,
Champ and chafe and toss in the spray.
Children dear, let us away.
This way, this way!

from "The Forsaken Merman,"
by Matthew Arnold

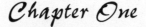

Chapter One

*C*an you keep a secret?

Everybody has secrets, of course, but mine's different, and it's kind of weird. Sometimes I even have nightmares that people will find out about it and lock me up in a zoo or a scientist's laboratory.

It all started in seventh-grade swim class, on the first Wednesday afternoon at my new school. I was really looking forward to it. Mom hates swimming, and she always used to change the subject when I asked her why I couldn't learn.

"But we live on a boat!" I'd say (we actually do). "We're surrounded by water!"

"You're not getting me in that water," she'd reply. "Just look at all the pollution. You know what it's like when the day cruises have been through here. Now stop arguing, and come and help me with the vegetables."

She had kept me out of swimming lessons all the way through grade school, saying it was unhealthy. "All those bodies mixing in the same water." She'd shudder. "That's not for *us*, thank you very much."

And each time I asked her, that would be that: End of Discussion. But the summer before I started middle school, I finally wore her down. "All right, all right," she sighed. "I give in. Just don't start trying to get me in there with you."

I'd never been in the ocean. I'd never even had a bath. Hey, I'm not dirty or anything—I do take a shower every night. But there isn't enough room for a bathtub on the boat, so never in my life had I been totally *immersed* in water.

Until the first Wednesday afternoon of seventh grade.

Mom bought me a special new bag to carry my new bathing suit and towel. On the side, it had a picture of a woman doing the crawl. I looked at the picture and dreamed about winning Olympic races with a striped racing suit and blue goggles just like hers.

Only it didn't happen quite like that.

When we got to the pool, a man with a whistle and white shorts and a red T-shirt told the girls to go change in one room and the boys in the other.

I changed quickly in the corner. I didn't want anyone to see my skinny body. My legs are like sticks, and they're usually covered in scabs and bruises from getting on and off *The King of the Sea.* That's our boat. I admit it's kind of a fancy name for a little houseboat with moldy ropes, peeling paint, and beds the width of a ruler. . . . Anyway. We usually just call it *King.*

Julia Cross smiled at me as she put her clothes in her locker. "I like your suit," she said. It's just plain black with a white stripe across the middle.

"I like your cap," I said, and smiled back as she squashed her hair into her tight, pink swimming cap. I squeezed my ponytail into mine. I usually wear my hair loose; Mom made me put it in a scrunchie today. My hair is mousy brown and used to be short, but I'm growing it out right now. It's a bit longer than shoulder length so far.

Julia and I sit next to each other sometimes. We're not best friends. Sharon Matterson used to be my best friend, but she went to St. Mary's. I'm at Brightport Junior High. Julia's the only person here that I might want to be best friends with. But I think she really wants to be best friends with Mandy Rushton. They hang out together between classes.

I don't mind. Not really. Except when I can't find my way to the cafeteria — or to some of the classes. At those moments, it might be nice to have someone to get lost with. Brightport Junior High is about ten times bigger than my elementary school. It's like an enormous maze, with millions of boys and girls who all seem to know what they're doing.

"You coming, Julia?" Mandy Rushton stood between us with her back to me. She gave me a quick look over her shoulder, then whispered something in Julia's ear and laughed. Julia didn't look up as they passed me.

Mandy lives on the pier, like me, only not on a boat. Her parents run the video arcade, and they've got an apartment above it. We used to be pretty good friends until last year. That's when I accidentally told my mom — who told Mandy's mom — that Mandy had showed me how to win free games on the PinWizard machine. I didn't *mean* to get her in trouble but — well, let's just say I'm not exactly welcome in the arcade anymore. In fact, she hasn't spoken to me since.

And now we've ended up in the same swim class at Brightport Junior High. Fabulous. As if starting a new school the size of a city isn't bad enough.

I finished getting ready and hurried out.

"OK, listen up, 7C," the man with the whistle said. He told us to call him Bob. "Any of you kids totally confident to swim on your own?"

"Of course we can — we're not babies!" Mandy sneered under her breath.

Bob turned to face her. "OK, then. Do you want to start us off? Let's see what you can do."

Mandy stepped toward the pool. She stuck her thumb in her mouth. "Ooh, look at me. I'm a baby. I can't swim!" Then she dropped herself sideways into the water. Her thumb still in her mouth, she pretended to keep slipping under as she did this really over-the-top doggy paddle across the pool.

Half the class was in hysterics by the time she reached the end.

Bob wasn't. His face had reddened. "Do you think that's funny? Get out! NOW!" he shouted. Mandy pulled herself out and grinned as she bowed to the class.

"That was completely out of order," Bob said as

he handed her a towel. "Now I'm afraid you get to sit on the side and watch the others."

"*What?*" Mandy stopped grinning. "That's not fair! What did I do?"

Bob turned his back on her. "We'll start again. Who's happy to swim confidently *and* sensibly?"

About three-fourths of the class raised their hands. I was desperate to get in the pool but didn't dare put mine up. Not after that.

"All right." Bob nodded at them. "You can get in if you want—but walk down to the shallow end."

He turned to the rest of us. We were lined up shivering by the side of the pool. "You guys will be with me. Let's go grab some kickboards."

After he turned his head away, I snuck in with the group making their way down to the shallow end. I'd never swum before, so I shouldn't have, but I couldn't help myself. I just knew I could do it. And the water looked *so* beautiful lying there, still and calm, as though it were holding its breath, waiting for someone to jump in and set it alive with splashes and ripples.

There were five big steps that led gradually into the water. I stepped onto the first one, and warm water tickled over my toes. Another step and the water wobbled over my knees. Two more, then I pushed myself into the water.

I ducked my head under, reaching wide with

my arms. As I held my breath and swam deeper, the silence of the water surrounded me and called to me, drawing my body through its creamy calm. It was as if I'd found a new home.

"Now THAT is more like it!" Bob shouted when I came up for air. "You're a natural!"

Then he turned back to the others, who were squinting and staring at me with open mouths. Mandy's eyes fired hatred at me as Bob said, "That's what I'd like to see you *all* doing by the end of the term."

But then it happened.

One minute, I was skimming along like a flying fish. The next, my legs suddenly seized up. It felt as though somebody had glued my thighs together and strapped a splint on my shins! I tried to smile up at the teacher as I paddled to the side, but my legs had turned to a block of stone. I couldn't feel my knees, my feet, my toes. *What was happening?*

A second later, and I almost went under completely. I screamed, getting a mouthful of water. Bob shouted to everyone to stay put and dove in, in his shorts and T-shirt, and swam over to me.

"It's my legs," I gasped. "I can't feel them!"

He cupped my chin in his big hand and began a powerful backstroke to bring us back over to the side. "Don't worry," he said. "It's just a cramp. Happens to everyone."

7

We reached the big steps at the side of the pool and climbed onto the top one. As soon as I was halfway out of the water, the weird feeling started to go away.

"Let's have a look at those legs." Bob lifted me up onto the side of the pool. "Can you lift your left one?" I did.

"And your right?" Easy.

"Any pain?"

"It's gone now," I said.

"Just a cramp, then. Why don't you rest here for a few minutes? Get in again when you're ready?"

I nodded, and he went back to the others.

But the truth was, I'd felt something that he hadn't seen. And I'd seen something he hadn't felt. And I didn't have a *clue* what it was, but I knew one thing for sure — you wouldn't get me back in that pool for a million dollars.

I sat by the side for a long time. Eventually the whole rest of the class got in and started splashing around. Even Mandy was allowed back in. But I didn't want to sit too near those guys in case I got splashed and *it* happened again. I was even nervous when I went home after school — what if I fell off the pier and into the sea?

The boat docks are all along one side of the

pier. There are three other boats besides *King* tied up at ours: one seriously done-up white speedboat and a couple of bigger yachts. None of the other boats has people living on it, though.

An old plank of wood stretches across to get you from the dock to the boat. Mom used to carry me over it when I was little, but I've been doing it on my own for ages now. Only just then I somehow couldn't. I called out to Mom.

"I can't get across," I shouted when she came up from below deck.

She had a towel wrapped around her head and a satin robe on. "I'm getting ready for book group."

I stood frozen on the dock. Around me, the boats melted into a wobbly mass of masts and tackle. I stared at *King*. The mast rocked with the boat, the wooden deck shiny with sea spray. My eyes blurred as I focused on the row of portholes along the side of the boat, the thin metal bar running around the edge. "I'm scared," I said.

So Mom pulled the dressing-gown cord tighter around her waist and reached her skinny arm out to me. "Come on, sweetie, let's go."

When I had made it across, she grabbed me and gave me a hug. "Dingbat," she said, ruffling my hair. Then she went back inside to finish up.

Mom's always going to some group or another. Last year it was yoga; now it's book group. She

works at the secondhand bookstore on the promenade, and that's where the group meets. It's pretty
cool, actually. At the store, they just opened a café
bar where you can get thick milk shakes with
pieces of real fruit or big chunks of chocolate chip
cookie dough in them. I imagine the book group
is just her latest excuse to meet up and gossip with
her friends—but at least it keeps her focused on
something other than me.

Mystic Millie, who does Palms on the Pier,
comes to stay with me when Mom's out. Not
that I need a babysitter at my age, but Millie's
OK. Sometimes she'll practice her reiki or shiatsu
massage on me. She even brought her tarot cards
once. Apparently they told her that I was about to
achieve academic success and win praise from all
quarters. The next day, I got the lowest grade in
the class on the spelling test and was given three
lunchtime detentions to do extra study. But that's
Millie for you.

Luckily, Millie's two favorite shows were back-
to-back on NBC Wednesdays, so I knew she
wouldn't bother me tonight. I wanted to be left
alone, because I needed time to think. There were
two things I knew for sure. One: I had to figure out
what had happened to me in the pool. And two: I
needed to get out of swimming lessons before it
happened again.

I could hear Mom belting it out all the way from her cabin while I paced up and down in the front room. *"Do ya really love me? Do ya wanna stay?"* She was singing louder than her CD. She always sings when she's getting ready to go out. I don't mind too much — except when she starts doing the video moves. Tonight, I hardly noticed.

I'd already tried asking her right when I got home if I had to go swimming again. She'd gone ballistic. "I hope you're joking," she'd said in that voice that means *she* isn't. "After all the fuss you created, and making me buy you that suit. *No way* are you giving up after only one lesson!"

I paced up to the gas stove in the corner of the saloon. (That's what we call the living room.) I usually get my best ideas when I pace, but nothing was coming to me tonight. I paced past the ratty old sofa with its big orange blanket. Pace, pace, left, right, creak, squeak, think, think. Nothing.

"Better tell me soon, baby. I ain't got all day." Mom's voice warbled out from her room.

I tried extending my pacing to the kitchen. It's called a galley, really. It's got a sink, a tiny fridge, and a countertop that's always covered with empty cartons and bottles. Mom makes us recycle *everything*. The galley's in the middle of the boat, with the main door and a couple of wooden steps opposite. You've got to be careful on those steps when you come in because the bottom one comes loose. I usually jump down from the top one.

I paced through the kitchen and along the corridor that leads to the bathroom and our cabins.

"How do I look?" Mom appeared at the end of the corridor. She was wearing a new pair of Levi's and a white T-shirt with BABE in sparkly rhinestone letters across the middle. I wouldn't have minded much except for the fact that she had bought me a similar shirt at the same time she got hers—and it looked a lot better on her!

"Great." A familiar sharp tap on the roof stopped me from saying any more. The side door opened and Mr. Beeston poked his head through. "It's only me," he called, peering around the boat.

Mr. Beeston's the lighthouse keeper. He comes around to see Mom all the time. He gives me the creeps—he looks at you out of the corners of his eyes when he's talking to you. Plus his eyes are different colors: one's blue; one's green. Mom says he probably gets lonely up in the lighthouse, sitting around looking out to sea, switching the light on and off, only having contact with people by radio. She says we have to be friendly to him.

"Oh, Mr. Beeston, I'm just racing out to my

book group. We're waiting for Millie to show up. Come in for a sec. I'll walk down the pier with you." Mom disappeared down the corridor to get her coat as he clambered through the door.

"And how are we?" he asked, staring sideways into my eyes. His mouth was crooked like the tie he always wore. His shirt was missing a button, his mouth missing a tooth. I shivered. I wish Mom wouldn't leave me on my own with him.

"Fine, thanks."

He narrowed his eyes, still staring at me. "Good, good."

Thankfully, Millie arrived a minute later, and Mom and Mr. Beeston could leave.

"I won't be late, darling," Mom said, kissing my cheek, then wiping it with her thumb. "There's meatloaf in the oven. Help yourselves."

"Hi, Emily." Millie looked at me intensely for a moment. She always does that. "You're feeling anxious and confused," she said—with alarming accuracy for once. "I can see it in your aura."

Then she swept her black Mystic Millie cape over her shoulder and put the kettle on the stove.

I waved good-bye as Mom and Mr. Beeston headed down the pier. At the end of it, Mr. Beeston turned left to walk around the bay, back to his lighthouse. The street lamps lining the promenade were already on, pale yellow spots against an orangey-pink sky. Mom turned right and headed toward the bookshop.

I watched until they were out of sight before joining Millie on the sofa. We had our dinner plates on our knees and laughed together at the weatherman when he flubbed his lines. Then her favorite true-crime show started and she shushed me and went all serious.

I had an hour.

I cleared the plates, then rooted through the pen jar, got a sheet of Mom's fanciest purple writing paper from the living-room cupboard, and shut myself in my cabin.

This is what I wrote:

> *Dear Mrs. Partington,*
> *Please can you let Emily skip swimming lessons? We have been to the doctor, and he says she has a bad allergy and MUST NOT go near water. At all. EVER.*
> *Kindest wishes,*
> *Mary Penelope Windsnap*

I pretended to be asleep when I heard Mom come in. She tiptoed into my room, kissed me on the top of my head, and smoothed the hair off my forehead. She always does that. I wish she wouldn't. I hate having my bangs pushed off my forehead, but I stopped myself from pushing them back until she'd gone.

I lay awake for hours. I've got some fluorescent stars and a glow-in-the-dark crescent moon on my ceiling, and I looked up at them, trying to make sense of what had happened.

Actually, all I really wanted to think about was the silkiness of the water as I sliced through it—before everything went wrong. I could still hear its silence pulling me, playing with me as though we shared a secret. But every time I started to lose myself to the feeling of its creamy warmth on my skin, Mandy's face broke into the picture, glaring at me.

A couple of times I almost fell asleep. Then I suddenly would wake up after drifting into panicky half-dreams—of me inside a huge tank, the class all around me. They were pointing, staring, chanting: "Freak! Freak!"

I could *never* go in the water again!

But the questions wouldn't leave me alone. What had *happened* to me in there? Would it happen again?

And no matter how much I dreaded the idea of putting myself through that terror again, I would never be happy until I knew. More than that, something was simply pulling me back to the water. It was like I didn't have a choice. I HAD to find out—however scary it might be.

By the time I heard Mom's gentle snores coming from her room, I was determined to get to the bottom of it—and before anybody else did, too.

I crept out of bed and slipped into my swimsuit. It was still damp, and I winced and pulled my denim jacket over the top. Then I silently climbed up onto the deck and looked round. The pier was deserted. Along the promenade, guesthouses and shops stood in a silent row of silhouettes against the night sky. It could have been a stage set.

A great big full moon shone a spotlight across the sea. I felt sick as I looked at the plank of wood, stretching across to the dock. *Come on, just a couple of steps.*

I clenched my teeth and my fists—and tiptoed across.

I ran to the pilings at the end of the pier and looked down at the rope ladder stretching beneath me into the darkness of the water. The sea glinted coldly at me; I shivered in reply. Why was I doing this?

I wound my fingers in my hair. I always do that when I'm trying to think, if I don't feel like pacing. And then I pushed the questions and the doubts—and Mandy's sneering face—out of my mind. I had to do it; I had to know the truth.

I buttoned up my jacket. I wasn't getting in there without it on! Holding my breath, I stepped onto the rope ladder and looked out at the deserted pier one last time. I could hear the gentle chatter of halyards clinking against masts as I carefully made my way down into the darkness.

The last step of the rope ladder was still quite a distance from the water because the tide was out. *It's now or never,* I said to myself.

Then, before I had time to think another thought, I pinched my nose between my thumb and forefinger—and jumped.

I landed in the water with a heavy splash and gasped for breath as soon as I came up. At first I couldn't feel anything, except the freezing cold ocean. *What on earth was I doing?*

Then I remembered what I was there for and started kicking my legs. A bit frantically at first. But seconds later, the cold melted away and so did my worries. Instead, a feeling of calm washed over me like the waves. Salt on my lips, hair flat against my head, I darted under the surface, cutting through the water as though I lived there.

And then—*it* happened. I swam straight back to the pier, terrified. *No!* I didn't want this—I'd changed my mind!

I reached out but couldn't get ahold of the ladder. *What had I done?* My legs were joining together again, turning to stone! I gasped and threw my arms around uselessly, clutching at nothing. *Just a cramp, just a cramp,* I told myself, not daring to look as my legs disappeared altogether.

But then, as rapidly as it had started, something changed. I stopped fighting it.

Yeah, so my legs had joined together. And fine, now they had disappeared completely. So what? It was good. It was . . . right.

As soon as I stopped worrying, my arms stopped flailing around everywhere. My head slipped easily below the surface. Suddenly I was an eagle, an airplane, a dolphin — gliding through the water for the sheer pleasure of it.

OK. This is it. You might have guessed by now, or you might not. It doesn't matter. All that matters is that you promise never to tell anyone:

I had become a mermaid.

Chapter Two

*I*t's not exactly the kind of thing that happens every day, is it? It doesn't happen *at all* to most people. But it happened to me. I was a mermaid. A mermaid! How did it happen? Why? Had I always been one? Would I always be one? Questions filled my head, but I couldn't answer any of them. All I knew was that I'd discovered a whole new part of myself, and nothing I'd ever done in my life had felt so good.

So there I was, swimming like—well, like a fish! And in a way, I *was* a fish. My top half was the same as usual: skinny little arms, my bangs plastered to my forehead with seawater, black Speedo swimsuit, and a very soggy jean jacket.

But then, just below the white line that went across my tummy, I was someone else—something else. My suit melted away and, instead, I had shiny scales. My legs narrowed into a long, gleaming, purple-and-green tail, waving gracefully as I skimmed along in the water. I have to say that I had never done anything gracefully in my life, so it was kind of a shock! When I flicked my tail above the surface, it flashed an arc of rainbow colors in the moonlight. I could zoom through the water with the tiniest movement, going deeper and deeper with every flick of my tail.

It reminded me of the time we went to World of Water at summer day camp. We were in a tunnel under the water with sea life all around us. It felt as if we were really in the sea. Only now I really was! I could reach out and touch the weeds floating up through the water like upside-down beaded curtains. I could race along with the fat gray fish that were grouped in gangs, weaving around each other and me as though they were dancing.

I laughed with pleasure and a line of bubbles escaped from my mouth, climbing up to the surface.

It seemed as though I'd only been swimming for five minutes when I realized the sky was starting to grow pink. I panicked as a new thought hit me: *What if I couldn't change back?*

But the second I'd pulled myself out of the water, my tail softened. I dangled on the rope ladder and watched, fascinated, as the shiny scales melted away one by one. As my legs returned, they felt odd, like when your mouth goes numb after you've gotten a filling at the dentist.

I wiggled my toes to get rid of the pins and needles in my feet. Then I headed home with a promise to myself that I would be back — soon.

Bob, the swimming instructor, was standing in front of me, talking into a cell phone. I couldn't hear what he was saying. Somebody grabbed my shoulders.

"This the one, is it?" a snarling voice growled behind my ear. Bob nodded.

I tried to wriggle free from the man's clutches, but he was holding my shoulders too firmly. "What do you want?" my voice squeaked from my mouth.

"As if you didn't know," the snarly voice snapped at me. "You're the freak." He shook my shoulders.

"I'm not a freak," I shouted. "I'm not!"

"Stop pretending," a woman's voice replied.

"I'm not pretending." I wriggled under the hands holding my shoulders. "I'm not a freak!"

"Emily, for Pete's sake," the woman's voice said. "I know you're not really asleep."

My eyes snapped open to see Mom's face inches from mine, her hands on my shoulders, shaking me gently. I bolted upright in my bed. "What's happening?"

Mom let go of me. "What's happening, sleepy-head, is that you're going to be late for school. Now get a move on." She parted the curtain in the doorway. "And don't forget to brush your teeth," she said without turning round.

Over breakfast, I tried to remember my dream and the things I'd been shouting. It had felt so real: the capture, the voices. Had I said anything out loud? I didn't dare ask, so I ate in silence.

It was on the third mouthful that things went seriously wrong.

Mom was fussing around as usual, shuffling through the huge pile of papers stuffed behind the mixer. "What did I do with it?"

"What is it this time?"

"My shopping list. I'm sure I put it down here somewhere." She leaned across to a pile of papers on the table. "Aha, here it is."

I looked up in horror as she picked up a piece of paper. Not just any piece of paper. A sheet of purple writing paper!

"NO-O-O-O-O-O!" I yelled, spitting half a mouthful of cereal across the table and leaping forward to grab the paper. Too late. She was unfolding it.

Her eyes narrowed as she scanned the sheet, and I held my breath.

"No, that's not it." Mom started to fold the paper up. I breathed out and swallowed the rest of my mouthful.

But then she opened it again. "Hang on a sec. That's my name there."

"No, no, it's not. It's someone else, it's not you at all!" I snatched at the paper.

Mom kept it gripped tightly and ignored me. "Where are my reading glasses?" They were hanging around her neck—as they usually are when she's looking for them.

"Why don't I just read it to you?" I said in my very best Perfect Daughter voice. But as I was speaking, she found her glasses and put them on. She studied the note.

I tried to edge away from the table but she looked up on my second step. *"Emily?"*

"Hmm?"

She took her glasses off and waved the note in front of my face. "Want to explain this to me?"

"Um, well, hmm, er, let's see now." I examined

the note with what I hoped was an I've-never-seen-it-before-in-my-life-but-I'll-see-if-I-can-help kind of expression on my face.

She didn't say anything, and I kept staring at the note, pretending I was reading it. Anything to avoid meeting her eyes while I waited for my lecture.

But then she did something even worse than lecture me. She put the piece of paper down, lifted my chin up with her hand, and said, "I understand, Emily. I know what it's about."

"You do?" I squeaked, terrified.

"All those things you were saying in your sleep about being a freak. I should have realized."

"You should?"

She let go of my chin and shook her head sadly. "I've been an idiot not to realize before now."

"You have?"

Then she took my hand between her palms and said, "You're like me. You're afraid of water."

"I am?" I squealed. Then I cleared my throat and twisted my hair. "I mean, I *am*," I said seriously. "Of course I am! I'm scared of water. That's exactly what it is. That's what all this has been about. Just that, nothing more than—"

"Why didn't you tell me?"

I looked down at my lap and closed my eyes tight, trying, if possible, to squeeze a bit of moisture out of them. "I was ashamed," I said quietly. "I didn't want to let you down."

Mom pressed my hand harder between hers and looked into my eyes. Hers were a bit wet, too. "It's all my fault," she said. "I'm the one who's let *you* down. I stopped you from learning how to swim, and now you've inherited my fear."

"Yes." I nodded sadly. "I suppose I have. But you shouldn't blame yourself. It's OK. I don't mind, seriously."

She let go of my hand and shook her head. "But we live on a boat," she said. "We're surrounded by water."

I almost laughed, but stopped myself when I saw the expression on her face. Then a thought occurred to me. "Mom, why exactly *do* we live on a boat if you're so afraid of water?"

She screwed up her eyes and stared into mine as if she was looking for something. "I don't know," she whispered. "I can't explain it, but it's such a deep feeling—I could *never* leave *King*."

"But it doesn't make any sense. I mean, you're scared of water, and we live on a boat in a beach resort!"

"I know, I know!"

"We're miles from anywhere. Even Nan and Granddad live at the other end of the country."

Mom's face hardened. "Nan and Granddad? What do they have to do with it?"

"I've never even seen them! Two cards a year and that's it."

"I've told you before, Em. They're a long way away. And we're not—we don't get along very well."

"But why not?"

"We had a fight. A long time ago." She laughed nervously. "So long ago, I can't even really remember what it was about."

We sat in silence for a moment. Then Mom got up and looked out of the porthole. "This isn't right; it shouldn't be like this for you," she murmured as she wiped the porthole with her sleeve.

Then she suddenly twirled around so her skirt flowed out around her. "I've got it!" she said. "I know what we'll do."

"Do? What do you mean, *do*? I'll just take the note to school, or you could write one yourself. No one will ever know."

"Of course they will! No, we can't do that."

"Yes, we can. I'll just—"

"Now, Emily, don't start with your arguing. I haven't got the patience for it." Her mouth tightened into a determined line. "I cannot allow you to live your life like this."

"But *you* don't—"

"What I do is my own business," she snapped. "Now please stop answering me back." She paused for a second before opening her address book. "No, there's nothing else to do. You need to conquer your fear."

"What are you going to do?" I fiddled with a button on my blouse.

She turned away from me as she picked up the phone. "I'm going to take you to a hypnotist."

"All right, Emily. Now, I want you to breathe nice and deeply. Good."

I was sitting in an armchair in Mystic Millie's back room. I didn't know she did hypnotism, but according to Sandra Castle, she worked wonders on Charlie Hogg's twitch, and that was good enough for Mom.

"Try to relax," Millie intoned before taking a very loud, deep breath. Mom was sitting in a plastic seat in the corner of the room. She had said she wanted to be there, "just in case." In case of what, she didn't exactly explain.

"You're going to have a little sleep," Millie drawled. "When you wake up, your fear of water will have completely gone. Vanished. Floated away . . ."

I had to stay awake! If I fell into a trance and

started babbling about everything, the whole plan would be ruined. Not that I had a plan, as such, but *you* know what I mean. What would Millie think if she found out? What would she do? Visions of nets and cages and scientists' laboratories swam into my mind.

I forced them away.

"Very good," Millie breathed in a husky voice. "Now, I'm going to count down from ten to one. As I do, I'd like you to close your eyes and imagine you are on an escalator, gradually traveling down, lower and lower, deeper and deeper. Make yourself as comfortable as you can."

I shuffled in my seat.

"Ten . . . nine . . . eight . . ." Millie said softly. I closed my eyes and waited nervously for the drowsy feeling to come.

"Seven . . . six . . . five . . ." I pictured myself on an escalator like the one in the mall in town. I was running the wrong way, scrambling up against the downward motion. I waited.

"Four . . . three . . . two . . . You're feeling very drowsy. . . ."

I waited a bit more.

That's when I realized I wasn't feeling drowsy at all. In fact . . .

"One."

I was wide awake! I'd done it—hooray! Millie

was a phony! The "aura" thing had been a fluke after all!

She didn't say anything for ages, and I was starting to get fidgety when a familiar noise broke the silence. I opened my eyes the tiniest crack to see Mom in the opposite corner—fast asleep and snoring like a horse! I snapped my eyes quickly shut again and fought the urge to giggle.

"Now, visualize yourself next to some water," Millie said in a low voice. "Think about how you feel about the water. Are you scared? What emotions are you experiencing?"

The only thing I was experiencing was a pain in my side from trying not to laugh.

"And now think of somewhere that you have felt safe. Somewhere you felt happy." I pictured myself swimming in the sea. I thought about the way my legs became a beautiful tail and about the feeling of zooming along with the fish. I was on the verge of drifting into a happy dream world of my own when—"Nnnnnuuurrrggggghhhh!"— Mom let out a huge snore that made me jump out of my chair.

I kept my eyes closed tight and pretended I'd jumped in my sleep. Mom shuffled in her chair and whispered, "Sorry."

"Not to worry," Millie whispered back. "She's completely under. Just twitching."

After that, I let my mind drift back to the sea. I couldn't wait to get out there again. Millie's voice carried on in the background, and Mom soon started snoring softly again. By the time Millie counted from one to seven to wake me up, I was so relieved I hugged her.

"What's that for?" she asked.

"Just a thank-you, for curing my fear," I lied.

She blushed as she slipped Mom's twenty-dollar bill into her purse. "Think nothing of it, pet. It's a labor of love."

Mom was quiet on the way home. Did she know I hadn't been asleep? Did she suspect anything? I didn't dare ask. We made our way through the town's narrow streets down to the promenade. As we waited to cross the road, she pointed to a bench facing oceanside. "Let's go and sit down over there," she said.

"You OK, Mom?" I asked as casually as I could while we sat on the bench. The tide was out, and little pools dotted the ripply sand it had left behind.

She peered out toward the horizon. "I had a dream," she said without turning around. "It felt so real. It was beautiful."

"When? What felt real?"

She looked at me for a second, blinked, and turned back to the sea. "It was out there, somewhere. I can almost feel it."

"Mom, what are you talking about?"

"Promise you won't think I'm crazy."

"'Course I won't."

She smiled and ruffled my hair. I smoothed it back down. "When we were at Millie's . . ." She closed her eyes. "I dreamed about a shipwreck, under the water. A huge golden boat with a marble mast. *A ceiling of amber, a pavement of pearl . . .*"

"Huh?"

"It's a line from a poem. I think. I can't remember the rest. . . ." She gazed at the sea. "And the rocks. They weren't like any rocks you've ever seen. They used to glisten every color you could imagine—"

"*Used* to? What do you mean?"

"Did I say that? I mean they did—in my dream. They shone like a rainbow in water. It's just, it felt so real. So familiar . . ." Her voice trailed off, and she gave me a quick sideways look. "But I suppose it's sometimes like that, isn't it? We all have dreams that feel real. I mean, you do. Don't you?"

I was trying to figure out what to say when she started waving. "Oh, look," she said briskly, "there's Mr. Beeston." I glanced up to see him marching toward the pier. He comes around for coffee every Sunday. Three o'clock on the dot. Mom makes coffee; he brings honey buns or doughnuts or bear claws. I usually scarf mine down quickly and leave the two of them alone. I don't know what it is about him. He makes the boat feel smaller, some-how. Darker.

Mom put her fingers in the edges of her mouth and let out a sharp whistle. Mr. Beeston turned around. He smiled awkwardly and gave us a quick wave.

Mom stood up. "Come on. Better get back and put the water on." And before I could ask her any-thing else, she was marching back to the boat. I had to run to keep up.

Chapter Three

I snuck out again that night. I couldn't keep away. I swam farther this time. The sea was grimy with oil and rubbish near the shore, and I wanted to explore the cleaner, deeper water farther out.

Looking back across the harbor, Brightport looked so small: a cluster of low buildings, all huddled around a tiny horseshoe-shaped bay, a lighthouse at one end, a marina at the other.

A hazy glow hovered over the town. Blurry yellow street lamps shone, with the occasional white lights of a car moving along between them.

As I swam around the rocks at the end of the bay, the water became clearer and softer. It was like switching from grainy black-and-white film into color. The fat gray fish were replaced by stripy yellow-and-blue ones with floppy silver tails, long thin green ones with spiky antennae and angry mouths, orange ones with spotted black fins—all darting purposefully around me.

Every now and then, I swam across a shallow sandy stretch. Wispy little sticklike creatures as thin as paper wriggled along beneath me, almost see-through against the sand. Then the water would suddenly get colder and deeper as I went over a rocky part. I swished myself across these carefully. They were covered in prickly black sea urchins, and I wouldn't be thrilled to get one of those stuck on my tail.

Soon the water got warmer again as I came to another shallow part. I was getting tired. I came up for fresh air and realized I was miles from home—farther away than I'd ever been on my own. I tried to flick myself along, but my tail flapped lazily and started to ache. Eventually, I made it to a big, smooth rock with a low shelf. I pulled myself out of the water, my tail resting on some pebbles in the sea. A minute later, it went numb. I wiggled my toes and shivered as I watched my legs come back. That part was still *really* creepy!

Sitting back against a larger rock, I caught my breath. Then I heard something. Like singing, but without words. The wet rocks shimmered in the moonlight, but there was no one around. Had I imagined it? The water lapped against the pebbles, making them jangle as it sucked its breath away from the shore. There it was again — the singing.

Where was it coming from? I clambered up a jagged rock and looked down the other side. That's when I saw her. I rubbed my eyes. Surely it couldn't be . . . but it was! It was a mermaid! A real one! The kind you read about in kids' stories. Long blond hair all the way down her back, which she was brushing while she sang. She was perched on the edge of a rock, shuffling a bit as though she were trying to get comfortable. Her tail was longer and thinner than mine. Silvery green and shimmering in the moonlight, it flapped against the rock as she sang.

She kept singing the same song. When she got to the end, she started again. A couple of times, she was in the middle of a really high part when she stopped and hit her tail with the brush. "Come on, Shona," she said sharply. "Get it right!"

I stared for ages, opening and closing my mouth like a fish. I wanted to talk to her. But what exactly do you say to a singing mermaid perched on a rock in the middle of the night? Funnily enough, I've never had that come up before.

In the end, I coughed gently and she looked up immediately.

"Oh!" she said. She gaped open-mouthed at my legs for a second. And then, with a twist and a splash, she was gone.

I picked my way back down the rocks to the water's edge. "Wait!" I shouted as she swam away from me. "I really want to talk to you."

She turned in the water and looked back at me suspiciously. "I'm a mermaid, too!" I shouted. Yeah right, with my skinny legs and my Speedo bathing suit—she'd *really* believe that! "Wait, I'll prove it."

I jumped into the water and started swimming toward her. I still had that moment of panic when my legs stuck together and stiffened. But then they relaxed into their new shape, and I relaxed, too, as I swished my tail and sped through the water.

The mermaid was swimming away from me again, faster now. "Hang on," I called. "Watch!" I waited for her to turn around, then dove under and flicked my tail upward. I waved it as high as I could.

When I came back up, she was staring at me as though she couldn't believe what she'd seen. I smiled, but she ducked her head under the water. "Don't go!" I called. But a second later, *her* tail was sticking up. Not twisting around madly like mine did, more as if she were dancing or doing gymnastics. In the moonlight, her tail glinted like diamonds.

When she came back up, I clapped. Or tried

to anyway, but I slipped back under when I lifted both arms out and got water up my nose.

She was laughing as she swam toward me. "I haven't seen you before," she said. "How old are you?"

"Twelve."

"Me, too. But you're not at my school, are you?"

"Brightport Junior High," I said. "Just started."

"Oh." She looked worried and moved away from me again.

"What's wrong with that?"

"It's just . . . I haven't heard of it. Is it a mermaid school?"

"You go to a mermaid school?" The idea sounded like something out of a fairy tale, and even though I've *totally* grown out of fairy tales, I had to admit it sounded pretty cool.

She folded her arms — how did she do that without sinking? — and said quite sternly, "And what's wrong with that? What kind of school do you *expect* me to go to?"

"No, it sounds great!" I said. "I wish I did, too." I found myself wanting to tell her everything. "I mean. . . I haven't been a mermaid for long. Or I didn't know I was, or something." My words jumbled and tumbled out of me. "I've never even really been in the water, and then when I did get in, it happened and I was scared, but I'm not now and I wish I'd found out years ago."

I looked up to see her staring at me as though I were something from outer space that had washed up on the beach. I stared back and tried folding my arms, too. I found that if I kept flicking my tail a little, I could stay upright. So I flicked and folded and stared for a little while, and she did the same. Then I noticed the side of her mouth flutter a bit and I felt the dimple below my left eye twitching. A second later, we were both laughing like hyenas.

"What are we laughing at?" I said when I managed to catch my breath.

"I don't know!" she answered—and we both burst out laughing again.

"What's your name?" she said once we'd stopped laughing. "I'm Shona Silkfin."

"Emily," I said. "Emily Windsnap."

Shona stopped smiling. "Windsnap? *Really?*"

"Why? What's wrong with that?"

"Nothing—it's just . . ."

"What?"

"No, it's nothing. I thought I'd heard it before, but I guess I couldn't have. I must be thinking of something else. You haven't been around here before, have you?"

I laughed. "A couple weeks ago, I'd never even been swimming in a pool!"

Shona looked serious for a second. "How did you do that thing just now?" she asked.

"What thing?"

"With your tail."

"You mean the handstand? You want me to do it again?"

"No, I mean the other thing." She pointed under the water. "How did you make it change?"

"I don't know. It just happens. When I go in water, my legs kind of disappear."

"I've never seen someone with legs before. Not in real life. I've read about it. What's it like?"

"What's it like having legs?"

Shona nodded.

"Well, it's — it's cool. You can walk, and run. And climb things, or jump or skip."

Shona gazed at me as if I were speaking a foreign language. "You can't do this with legs," she said as she dove under again. This time her tail twisted around and around, faster and faster in an upside-down pirouette. Water spun off as she turned, spraying tiny rainbow arcs over the surface.

"That was fantastic!" I said when she came back up again.

"We've been practicing it in Diving and Dance. We're doing a display at the Inter-Bay competition in a couple of weeks. This is the first time I've been on the squad."

"Diving and Dance? Is that a class you take?" I asked, a wish already forming in my mind.

"Yeah," she went on breathlessly. "But last year, I was in the choir. Mrs. Highwave said that *five* fishermen were seen wandering aimlessly toward the rocks during my solo performance." Shona smiled proudly, her earlier shyness totally vanished. "No one at Shiprock School has *ever* had that many before."

"So that's — that's good, huh?"

"Good? It's great! I want to be a siren when I grow up."

I stared at her. "So all that stuff in fairy tales about mermaids luring fishermen to watery graves — it's all true?"

Shona shrugged. "It's not like we want them to die. Not necessarily. Usually, we just hypnotize them into changing their ways and then wipe their memories so they move away and forget they saw us."

"Wipe their memories?"

"Usually, yes. It's our best defense. Not everyone knows how to do it. Mainly just sirens and those close to the king. We just use it to stop them from stealing all our fish, or finding out about our world." She leaned in closer. "Sometimes, they fall in love."

"The mermaids and the fishermen?"

Shona nodded excitedly. "There're loads of stories about it. It's *totally* illegal — but so romantic, isn't it?"

"Well, I guess so. Is that why you were singing just now?"

"Oh, that. No, I was practicing for Beauty and Deportment," she said, as if I totally would know what she was talking about. "We've got a test tomorrow, and I can't get my posture right. You have to sit perfectly, tilt your head exactly right, and brush your hair in a hundred smooth strokes. It's a pain in the gills trying to remember everything at once."

She paused, and I guessed it was my turn to say something. "Mmm-hmm, yeah, I know what you mean," I said, hoping I sounded convincing.

"I came in first in last semester's final, but that was just hair brushing. This is the whole package."

"It sounds really tough."

"B and D is my favorite subject," she went on. "I wanted to be seventh-grade hairbrush monitor, but Cynthia Smoothflick got it." She lowered her voice. "But Mrs. Sharptail told me that if I do well in this test, maybe they'll give it to me in the spring."

What was I meant to say to that?

"You think I'm a goody-goody, don't you?" she said, watching my face. She started to swim away again. "Just like everybody else does."

"No, of course not," I said. "You're ... you're ..." I struggled to find the right words. "You're ... really interesting."

"You're pretty swishy, too," she said, and let herself float back.

"How come you're out in the middle of the night, anyway?" I asked.

"These rocks are the best ones around for B and D, but you can't really come here in the daytime. It's too dangerous." She stuck a thumb out toward the coast. "I usually sneak out on Sunday nights. Or Wednesdays. Mom's always out like a tide by nine o'clock on Sunday. She likes to be fresh for the week ahead. And she has her aquarobics on Wednesdays and always sleeps more soundly after that. Dad sleeps like a whale every night!" Shona laughed. "Anyway, I'm glad I came tonight."

I smiled. "Me, too." The moon had moved around and was shining down on me, a tiny chink missing from its side. "But I have to get going soon," I added, yawning.

Shona frowned. "Are you going to come back some other time?"

"Yeah, I'd like that." She might be a bit strange, but she was a *mermaid*. The only one I'd ever met. She was like me! "When?"

"Wednesday?"

"Great." I grinned. "And good luck on your test!"

"Thanks!" she shouted. And with a flick of her tail, she was gone.

As I swam around Brightport Harbor in the darkness, the beam from the lighthouse flashed steady rays across the water. I stopped for a moment to watch. Each beam slowly scanned the water before disappearing around the back of the lighthouse. It was almost hypnotic. A large ship silently made its way across the horizon, its silhouette briefly visible with each slow beam of light.

But then I noticed something else. Someone was standing on the rocks at the bottom of the lighthouse. Mr. Beeston! What was he doing? He seemed to be looking out at the horizon, following the ship's progress.

I ducked under the water as another beam came around. What if he'd seen me? I stayed underwater until the light had passed. When I came up again, I looked back at the lighthouse. There was no one there.

And then the light went off. I waited. It didn't come back on.

I tried to imagine what it was like inside. Just Mr. Beeston, all by himself, rattling around in a big empty lighthouse. Footsteps echoing with emptiness whenever he climbed up and down the stone spiral stairs. Sitting alone, looking out at the sea. Watching the light. What kind of a life was that? What kind of a person could live that life? And why hadn't the light come back on?

Dark questions followed me home.

By the time I reached the pier, it was nearly morning. Shivering, I pulled myself up the rope ladder.

I snuck back onto the boat and hung my jacket near the stove. It would be dry by morning. Mom likes the place to be like a sauna at night.

As I crept into bed, I thanked the lucky stars on my ceiling that I'd gotten home with my secret still safe. For now.

Chapter Four

on't forget your things." Mom reached through the side door, holding an object that filled me with dread.

"Oh, yeah." I took my swimming bag from her.

"And get a move on. You don't want to be late, do you?"

"No, of course not." I looked down at the rippled sand between the wooden slats of the dock. "Mom?" I said quietly.

"What, sweetheart?"

"Do I have to go to school?"

"Have to go? Of course you have to go. What crazy idea do you have in your head now?"

"I don't feel well." I clutched my stomach and tried to look like I was in pain.

Mom pulled herself up through the door and crouched on the jetty in front of me. She cupped my chin in her hand and lifted my face to look at hers. I hate it when she does that. The only way I can avoid her eyes is by closing my own, and then I feel like an idiot.

"What is all this about?" she asked. "Is it your new school? Don't you like it?"

"School's fine," I said quickly. "Mostly."

"What is it, then? Is it swimming?"

I tried to move my head away but she held on tight. "No," I lied, looking as far to the side as I could, my head still trapped in her hand.

"I thought we had that all fixed," she said. "Are you worried in case it hasn't worked?"

Why hadn't I thought of that? I couldn't believe how stupid I was! I should have realized that if I let her think I was cured, I'd have to go swimming again!

"I've got a stomachache," I said weakly.

Mom let go of my chin. "Come on, sweet pea, there's nothing wrong with you, and you know it. Now, scoot." She patted my leg and stood up. "You'll be fine," she added, more gently.

"Hmm," I replied, and sloped up the ramp and

along the pier to wait by the promenade for the jitney that drops me off near school.

I slunk into homeroom just as Mrs. Partington was closing the attendance book. She looked at her watch and said, "I'll turn a blind eye, just this once."

She always says that. Everyone laughs when she does because she actually does have a blind eye. It's bright blue, just like her other one, but it doesn't move. It just stares at you, even when she's looking away. It's a bit freaky. You don't know where to look when she's talking to you, so we all try not to get in trouble. She always has the best-behaved class in the school.

I didn't laugh with the others this time, though. I just said, "Sorry," and went to sit down, pushing my hateful swimming bag under the table.

The entire morning was a disaster. I couldn't concentrate at all. In addition to being my homeroom teacher, Mrs. Partington was also my pre-algebra teacher. We were doing some simple equations, and I kept getting x wrong. I was really mad, because I'm good at math, and usually I can solve the bonus questions easily. Mrs. Partington kept giving me sideways looks out of her good eye.

When the bell rang for break, I actually did start to feel sick. Next was swimming. Everyone ran out of the room, but I took ages putting my pens and book away in my backpack.

Mrs. Partington was wiping the board. "Come on, Emily," she said without turning around. "It might be nice to do something on time today."

"Yes, Mrs. Partington," I said, and crawled out of the classroom, reluctantly dragging my swimming bag behind me.

I walked to the gym like a zombie. We were supposed to catch the bus right outside to the Brightport Community Center, where the pool was. It crossed my mind just to keep walking and not stop at all. I'd gotten as far as the double doors when Philip North called me back. "Oy — teacher's pet!" he yelled. Everyone turned to see who he was talking to.

"Teacher's pet? What are you talking about?"

"Come on, we all saw you showing off last week in the pool. Bob couldn't stop going on about how *amazing* you were and how we should all try and be like *you*."

"Yeah. We all heard what he said." Mandy Rushton came up behind Philip. "And we *saw* you."

I glared at her, speechless. She saw me? Saw *what*? My tail? She couldn't have! It hadn't even formed — *had it*?

"I can't help it," I said eventually.

"Yeah, right. *Show-off*," Mandy sneered.

"Shut up."

Mr. Bird, the P.E. teacher, showed up then. "All right, break it up. Come on, you guys."

I found a seat on my own. Julia sat across the aisle from me. "Philip is such a pig," she said, putting her bag on her knee. I smiled at her. "He's only jealous because he doesn't know how to swim."

"Thanks, Ju—"

"Move over, Jules." Mandy plonked herself down next to Julia and flashed me a smarmy smile. "Unless you want to sit with *fish girl*."

Julia went red, and I turned to look out of the window as the bus bumped and bounced down the road. Mandy's words swirled around and around in my head as if they were in a cement mixer. *Fish girl?* What did she know?

The bus stopped in the community center parking lot. "You coming?" Julia hung back while Mandy pushed and shoved to the front with the rest.

"In a sec. I'll catch up with you." I pretended to be tying my shoelaces. Maybe I could hide under the seat until everyone came back, then say I'd fainted or fallen over or something.

I could hear chattering outside the window, then it went quiet. A moment later, there was a huge groan, and people were shouting.

"But *sir,* that's not *fair,*" I heard Philip whine. I snuck a quick peek out of the window. Bob was standing there, talking to Mr. Bird. The kids in the class were just milling around; some had thrown their bags on the ground.

Next thing I knew, somebody had gotten back on the bus. I ducked down again and held my breath. But the footsteps came all the way to the back.

"You're not still tying your shoelaces, are you?" It was Julia.

"Huh?" I looked up.

"What are you doing?"

"I'm just—"

"Doesn't matter anyway." She sat down. "Swimming's canceled."

"What?"

"The pool's closed. Budget cuts. They forgot to tell the school."

"You're kidding!"

"Do I look like I'm kidding?"

I looked at her face; she was totally miserable. I stared down at my lap and shook my head. "God, it's just not fair, is it?" I said, trying hard not to grin. "Wonder what they'll make us do instead."

"That's what Mr. Bird's talking about now with

Bob. They're going to send us on a nature trail, apparently."

"Duh—boring." I folded my arms, hoping I looked in as much of a huff as Julia. Bob soon turned back toward the building, and Mr. Bird announced with a smile that we were going to Macefin Wood.

Mandy glared at me as she sat down across the aisle. I had to sit on my hands to stop myself from punching the air and shouting, "YES!"

I went to bed really early so I could get a few hours of sleep before sneaking out to meet Shona. I easily found my way to the rocks again and was there first this time. A familiar flick of a tail spreading rainbow droplets over the water soon told me she'd arrived.

"Hello!" I called, waving, as soon as she surfaced.

"Hi!" She waved back. "Come on."

"Where are we going?"

"You'll see." She splashed rainbow water in my face with her tail as she dove under.

We seemed to swim for ages. The water reminded me of those advertisements where they pour a ton of melted chocolate into a bar. Warm, and silky smooth. I felt as if I were melting with it as we swam.

Shona was ahead of me, gliding through the water and glancing back from time to time to check whether I was still there. Every now and then, she'd point to the left or right. I'd follow her hand to see a hundred tiny fish swimming in formation like a gymnastics display, or a yellow piece of seaweed climbing up toward the surface like a sunflower. A line of gray fish swam alongside us for a while—fast, smart, and pinstriped, like city businessmen.

It was only when we stopped and came up for air that I realized we'd been swimming underwater the whole time.

"How did I do that?" I gasped, breathless.

"Do what?" Shona looked puzzled.

I looked back at the rocks. They were tiny pebbles in the distance. "We must have swum a mile."

"Mile and a quarter, actually." Shona looked slightly sheepish. "My dad bought me a splish-ometer for my last birthday."

"A *what*?"

"Sorry, I keep forgetting you haven't been a mermaid very long. A splishometer shows you how far you've swum. I measured the distance from Rainbow Rocks yesterday."

"Rainbow what?"

"You know—where we met."

"Oh, right." I suddenly realized I was out of my depth—in more ways than one.

"I wasn't sure if it would be too far for you, but I really wanted to bring you here."

I looked around. Ocean everywhere. What was so special about this particular spot? "Why here?" I asked. "And anyway, you haven't answered my question. How did we do all that underwater?"

Shona shrugged and tossed her hair. "We're mermaids," she said simply. "Come on, I want to show you something." And with that, she disappeared again, and I dove under the water after her.

The lower we went, the colder the water grew. Fish flashed by in the darkness.

A huge gray bruiser with black dots slid slowly past, its mouth slightly open in a moody frown. Pink jellyfish danced and trampolined around us.

"Look." Shona pointed to our left as a slow-motion tornado of thin black fish came toward us, whirling and spiraling as it passed us by.

I shivered as we swam deeper still. Eventually, Shona grabbed my hand and pointed down. All I could see was what looked like the biggest rug I'd ever seen in my life—made out of seaweed!

"What's that?" I gurgled.

"I'll show you." And with that, Shona pulled

me lower. Seaweed slipped and slid along my body, creaking and popping as we swam through it. Where was she taking me?

I was about to tell her that I'd had enough, but then the weeds became thinner. It was as though we'd been stuck in the woods and finally made our way out. Or into a clearing in the center of it, anyway. We'd come to a patch of sand in the middle of the seaweed forest.

"What is it?" I asked.

"What d'you think?"

I looked around me. A huge steel tube lay along the ground; next to it, yards of fishing nets sprawled across the sand, reaching up into the weeds. A couple of old bicycles were propped up on huge rusty springs. "I have absolutely no idea," I said.

"It's like our playground. We're not really meant to come out here. But everyone does."

"Why shouldn't you come here?"

"We're all meant to stick to our own areas — it's too dangerous, otherwise. Too easy to get spotted. And this is really far from where we live." Shona swam over to the tube and disappeared. "Come on," her voice bubbled out from inside it, echoing spookily around the clearing.

I followed her into the tube, sliding along the cold steel to the other end. By the time I came out, Shona was already flipping herself up the fishing net. I scrambled up behind her.

"Like it?" Shona asked when we came back down.

"Yeah, it's wicked."

Shona looked at me blankly. "Wicked?"

"Wicked . . . you know, cool . . ."

"You mean like swishy?"

I laughed, suddenly getting it. "Yeah, I guess so." I looked around me. "Where's all this stuff from?"

"Things fall into the sea — or get thrown away. We make use of it," she said as she pulled herself onto one of the bikes. She perched sideways on it, letting herself sway backward and forward as the spring swung to and fro. "It's nice to have someone to share it with," she added.

I looped my tail over the other one and turned to face her. "What do you mean? What about your friends?"

"Well, I've got *friends*. Just not a *best* friend. I think the others think I'm too busy cramming to be anyone's best friend."

"Well, you do seem to work pretty hard," I said. "I mean, sneaking out at night to study for a test!"

"Yeah, I know. Do you think I'm really dull?"

"Not at all! I think you're . . . I think you're swishy!"

Shona smiled shyly.

"How come there's no one else around?" I asked. "It's kind of creepy."

"It's the middle of the night, gill-brain!"

"Oh, yeah. Of course." I held on to the handle-bars as I swayed forward and back on my swing. "It would be cool to meet some other people like us," I said after a while.

"Why don't you, then? You could come to my school!"

"How? You don't have extra lessons in the middle of the night, do you?"

"Come in the day. Come on Saturday."

"Saturday?"

She made a face. "We have school Saturday mornings. Why not come with me this week? I'll tell them you're my long-lost cousin. It'd be evil."

"Evil?"

"Oops—I mean, wicked. Sorry."

I thought about it. Julia actually had invited me over on Saturday. I could easily tell Mom I was going there and then tell Julia I couldn't make it. But I was only just getting to know Julia—she might not ask me again. *Then* who would I have? Apart from Shona. But then again, Shona was a mermaid. She was going to take me to mermaid school! When else would I get a chance to do *that*?

"OK," I said. "Let's do it!"

"Great! Will your parents mind?"

"You're kidding, aren't you? Nobody knows about my being a mermaid."

"You mean apart from your mom and dad? If you're a mermaid, they must be—"

"I haven't got a dad," I said.

"Oh. Sorry."

"It's OK. I never had one. He left us when I was a baby."

"*Sharks!* How awful."

"Yeah, well, I don't want to know about him anyway. He never even said he was leaving, you know. Just disappeared. Mom's never gotten over it."

Shona didn't reply. She'd gone very still and was just staring at me. "What?" I asked her.

"Your dad left when you were a baby?"

"Yes."

"And you don't know why he went?"

I shook my head.

"Or where?"

"Nope. But after what he did to Mom, he can stay wherever he is, as far as I'm—"

"But what if something happened to him?"

"Like what?"

"Like—like—maybe he got taken away, or he couldn't come back to you or something."

"He left us. And we're fine without him."

"But what if he didn't—"

"Shona! I don't want to talk about it. I haven't

got a dad, OK? End of subject." I watched a shoal of long white fish swim across the clearing and disappear into the weeds. Seaweed swayed gently behind them.

"Sorry," Shona said. "Are you still going to come on Saturday?"

I made a face. "If you still want me to."

"Of course I do!" She swung off her bike. "Come on. We need to head back."

We swam silently back to Rainbow Rocks, my head filled with a sadness stirred up by Shona's questions. Of course they were not so different from the ones I'd asked myself a hundred times. Why *had* my dad disappeared? Didn't he love me? Didn't he want me? Was it my fault?

Would I ever, *ever* see him?

Chapter Five

I waved to Mom as I made my way down the pier. "Bye-bye, darling, have a lovely day," she called.

Go back in, go back in, I thought. "Bye!" I smiled back at her. I walked woodenly along the pier, glancing behind me every few seconds. She was smiling and waving every time I looked.

Eventually, she went inside and closed the side door behind her. I continued up to the top of the pier and checked behind me one last time, just to be sure. Then, instead of turning onto the boardwalk, I ran down the steps onto the beach and snuck under the pier. I pulled off my jeans and shoes and shoved them under a rock. I already had my suit on underneath.

I'd never done this in the daytime before. It felt kind of weird. The tide was in, so I only had to creep a short way under the pier. A few people were milling around on the beach, but no one looked my way. What if they did? For a second, I pictured them all pointing at me: "Fish girl! Fish girl!" Laughing, chasing me with a net.

I couldn't do it.

But Shona! And mermaid school! I *had* to do it. I'd swim underwater all the way to Rainbow Rocks. No one would see my tail.

Before I could change my mind, I ran into the freezing cold water. One last look around, then I took a breath and dove—and was on my way.

I made my way to Rainbow Rocks and hung around at the edge of the water, keeping hidden from the shore. A minute later, Shona arrived.

"You're here!" She grinned, and we dipped under. She took me in a new direction, out across Shiprock Bay. When we came to the farthest tip of the bay, Shona turned to me. "Are you ready for this?" she asked.

"Are you joking? I can't wait!"

She flipped herself over and started swimming

downward. I copied her moves, scaling the rocks as we swam deeper and deeper.

Shoals of fish darted out from gaps in rocks that I hadn't even noticed. Sea urchins clung to the sides in thick black crowds. The water grew colder.

And then Shona disappeared.

I flicked my tail and sped down. There was a gap in the rock. A huge hole, in fact. Big enough for a whale to get through! Shona's face appeared from inside.

"Come on," she said with a grin.

"Into the rock?"

She swam back out and grabbed my hand. We went through together. It was a dark tunnel, bending and twisting. Eventually, we turned a corner and a glimmer of light appeared, growing bigger and bigger until eventually we came out of the tunnel. I stared around me, my jaws wide open.

We were in a massive hole in the rock. It must have been the size of a football field. Bigger! Tunnels and caves led off in all directions, around the edges, above us, below. A giant underwater rabbit warren!

Everywhere I looked, people were swimming this way and that. And they all had tails! Merpeople! Hundreds of them! There were mermaids with gold chains around slinky long tails, swimming along with little merchildren. One had a merbaby on her back, the tiniest little pink tail sticking out from under its sling. A group of mermaids clustered outside one passageway, talking and laughing together, bags made from fishing nets on their arms. Three old mermen sat outside a different tunnel, their tails faded and wrinkled, their faces full of lines, and their eyes sparkling as they talked and laughed.

"Welcome to Shiprock — merfolk style!" Shona said.

"Shona, better get a move on. Don't want to be late." A mermaid with her hair in a tall bun appeared beside us. "Five minutes to the bell." Then she flicked her dark green tail and zoomed off ahead.

"That's Mrs. Tailspin," Shona said. "She's my history teacher. We've got her first thing."

We followed her along a tubelike channel in the rock. At the other end, where it opened up again, mergirls and boys were swimming together in groups, swishing tails in a hundred different shades of blue and green and purple and silver as they milled around, waiting for school to start. A group of girls were playing a kind of skipping game with a long piece of ship's rope.

Then a noise like a foghorn surrounded us. Everyone suddenly swam into lines. Boys on one side, girls on the other. Shona pulled me into a line at the far end. "You OK?"

I nodded, still unable to speak as we swam single file down yet another tunnel with the rest of our line.

Everyone began to take their seats on the smooth round rocks that were dotted around the circular room. It reminded me of the three-hundred-and-sixty-degree dome at the Museum of Science movie theater, where they show films of daredevil flights and crazy downhill skiing. Only this wasn't a film—it was real!

Shona grabbed an extra rock and pulled it next to hers. A few of the other girls smiled at me.

"Are you new?" one asked. She was little and plump with a thick, dark green tail. It shimmered and sparkled as she spoke.

"She's my cousin," Shona answered for me quickly. The girl smiled and went to sit on her rock.

The walls were covered with collages made from shells and seaweed. Light filtered in through tiny cracks in the ceiling. Then Mrs. Tailspin came in and we all jumped off our rocks to say good morning.

Shona put her hand up right away. "Is it all right if my cousin sits in with us, please, ma'am?"

Mrs. Tailspin looked me up and down. "If she's good."

Then she clapped her hands. "Right, let's get

started. Shipwrecks. Today, we're doing the nine-teenth century."

Shipwrecks! That beats pre-algebra!

Mrs. Tailspin passed various objects around the room. "These are all from the *Voyager*," she said as she passed a huge plank of wood to a girl at the front. "One of our proudest sinkings."

Proudest sinkings — what did *that* mean?

"Not a huge amount is known for sure about the wreck of the *Voyager*, but what we do know is that a group of mermaids who called themselves the Siren Sisters were responsible for its great sinking. Through skillful manipulation and careful luring, they managed to distract the entire crew for long enough to bring the great ship down."

Shona passed me a couple of interlocked pieces of chain. I examined them and passed them on.

"Now, the only problem with this sinking was what one or two of the Siren Sisters did. Can any-one think what they might have done?"

Shona thrust her hand in the air.

"Yes, Shona?"

"Ma'am, did they fall in love?"

"Now, how did I know you were going to say that? Ever the romantic, aren't you, Shona?"

A giggle went around the room.

"Well, as a matter of fact, Shona is right," Mrs. Tailspin went on. "Some of these sisters let down the entire operation. Instead of dispersing the crew, they chose to run away with them! Never to be seen again. It's not known whether they attempted to return once they discovered the inevitable disappointments of life ashore. . . ."

I shuffled uncomfortably on my rock.

"Although, as you know," Mrs. Tailspin continued, "Neptune takes a *very* dim view of those who do."

"Who's Neptune?" I whispered to Shona.

"The king," she whispered back. "And you don't want to get on the wrong side of him, believe me! He's got a terrible temper — he makes thunderstorms and typhoons when he gets in a bad mood. Or unleashes sea monsters! But he can calm the roughest seas with a blink. *Very* powerful. And *very* rich, too. He lives in a huge palace, all made of coral and gems and gold —"

"Shona, are you saying anything you'd like to share with the class?" Mrs. Tailspin was looking our way.

"Sorry, ma'am." Shona blushed.

Mrs. Tailspin shook her head. "Now, one rather sorry piece of the *Voyager*'s legacy," she went on, "is that it has become somewhat of a symbol for those who choose to follow their Siren Sisters' doomed path. Instances are rare, but merfolk and humans *have* been caught together here. I needn't tell you that the punishments have been harsh. Our prison is home to a number of those traitors who have attempted to endanger our population in this way."

"You have a prison?" I whispered.

"Of course," Shona replied. "Really scary, from the pictures I've seen. A huge labyrinth of caves out beyond the Great Mermer Reef, near Neptune's palace."

I couldn't concentrate for the rest of the morning. What if they found out that I wasn't a real mermaid, and I ended up in that prison?

Shona grabbed me as soon as lessons finished.

"I've had an amazing thought," she said. "Let's go to the shipwreck. Let's find it!"

"What? How?"

"Don't you remember? Mrs. Tailspin told us the exact location. I thought you were daydreaming then!"

She ran her hand along the side of her tail. Then she did this totally weird thing. She put her hand inside her scales. She felt around for a bit, then pulled something out! It looked like a cross between a compass and a calculator. Her scales closed up as she withdrew her hand.

"What was *that*?" I screeched.

"What?" Shona looked baffled.

I pointed to her tail, where her hand had disappeared.

"My pocket?"

"Pocket?"

"Of course. You have pockets."

"In my denim jacket, yeah. Not in my *body*."

"Really? Are you sure?"

I fumbled round the sides of my tail. My hand slipped through a gap. Pockets! I did have them!

Shona held up the object she'd pulled out. "We can find the shipwreck with my splishometer."

I hesitated. It's true that Mom wasn't expecting me home until four o'clock. Should I go?

"Come on, Emily; it must be such a romantic place!"

I thought for a second. "OK, let's do it—let's go this afternoon!"

Underwater, we made our way slowly out to sea, with Shona checking her splishometer every few yards. After a while, we came up to look around. A lone line of gulls skimmed the surface. Ahead of us, other sea birds shot into the water like white arrows.

We ducked under again. Rays of sun shone in dusty beams under the water. Moments later,

Shona's splishometer beeped. "We're getting close," she breathed as we dove lower.

The sea life was becoming weirder. Something that looked like a peach with tentacles turned slowly around in the water, scanning its surroundings with beady black eyes. Farther down, a see-through jellyfish bounced away from us — a slow-motion space hopper. A rubbery gold crown floated silently upward. Everywhere I looked, fish that could have passed for cartoon aliens bounced and twirled and spun.

Shona grabbed my arm. "Come on," she said, pointing ahead and swimming away again. Lower and lower, the sea grew darker and darker. As we pressed forward, something came into view. I couldn't make out the shape, but it was surrounded by a hazy, golden light. The eerie light grew stronger as we carried on swimming toward it, and bigger. It was everywhere, all around us. We'd found it! The *Voyager!*

We darted along its length, tracing the row of portholes all the way from the back end to its pointy front, then swam away again to take it all in. Long and sleek, the ship lay on a tilt in the sand: still, silent, majestic.

"That is so-o-o amazing." My words gurgled away from me like a speech bubble in a comic strip. It made me laugh, which sent more bubbles floating out of my mouth, up into the darkness.

I couldn't stop staring at the ship. It was like something out of a film — not real life. Especially *my* life! It shone as if it had the sun inside it, as though it were made of gold.

Made of gold? A shipwreck made of gold? A queasy feeling clutched at my insides.

"Shona, the masts —"

"Are you OK?" Shona asked, taking a look at me.

"I need to see a mast!"

Shona pointed up into the darkness again. "Come on."

Neither of us spoke as we skirted around the hundreds of tiny fish pecking away at the ship's sides and swam up to the deck. Yard after yard of wooden slats: some shiny, almost new-looking; others dark and rotting. We swam upward, circling one of the masts, wrapping our tails around it like snakes slithering up a tree, my heart hammering loud and fast.

"What is it?"

"What?"

"What's the mast made of?"

Shona moved back to examine it. "Well, it looks like marble, but that's —"

"Marble? Are you sure?"

A golden boat with a marble mast. No!

I let go of the mast and pushed myself away, scattering a shoal of blue fish as I raced back down to the hull. I had to get away! It wasn't right! It didn't make sense!

"Emily, what's wrong?" Shona was behind me.

"It's—it's—" *What?* What could I say? How could I explain this awful panic inside me? It didn't make sense. I was being ridiculous. It couldn't be—of course it couldn't! I pushed the thought from my mind. Just a coincidence.

"It's nothing," I said, laughing off my unease. "Come on, let's go inside!"

Shona slithered along the hull. Fish nibbled at its sides next to her. I shivered as a silky plant brushed against my arm, swaying with the motion of the sea.

"Found one!" She flapped her tail excitedly.

I slithered over to join her and found myself in front of a broken porthole.

She looked at me for a second, her bright face reflecting the boat's light. "I've never had a real adventure before," she said quietly. Then she disappeared through the empty window. I forced the fear out of my mind. Shona didn't think there was anything to be afraid of. Then I held my arms tight against my sides, flicked the end of my tail, and followed Shona through the porthole.

We were in a narrow corridor. Bits of wallpaper dripped from the ceiling in watery stalactites, swaying with the movement of the sea. Below us, the slanted floor was completely rotten: black and moldy, with random floorboards missing. The walls were lined with plankton.

"Come on." Shona led the way. Long thin fish silently skirted the walls and ceiling. Portholes lined the corridor on our left; doors with paint peeling and cracking all the way down faced them on our right. We tried every one.

"They're all locked," Shona said, wiggling another rotting doorknob and pushing her weight against another stubborn door. Then she raced ahead to the end of the corridor and disappeared. I followed her around the corner. Right in front of our eyes, a white door seemed to be challenging us. It was bigger than the others, shining and glowing, its round brass handle begging to be turned. A big, fat, beady-eyed fish hovered in front of it like a goalie. Shona tossed her head as she leaned forward to try the handle, her hair flowing out in the water. The fish darted away.

The door swung open.

"Swishing heck!" she breathed.

I joined her in the doorway. "Wow!" Bubbles danced out of my mouth as I stared.

It was the grandest room I'd ever seen — and the biggest! Easily as big as a tennis court. At one end, a carpet made out of maroon weeds swayed gently with the sea's rhythm. At the other end was a hard white floor.

"Pearl," Shona said, gliding across its shiny surface.

I swam into a corner and circled one of the golden pillars shining bright light across the room. With every movement, rainbow colors flickered around the walls and ceiling. Bright blue-and-yellow fish danced in the light.

Below huge round windows, benches with velvet seats and high wooden backs lined the walls, large iron tables dotted about in front of them. I picked up a goblet from one of the tables. Golden and heavy, its base was a long skirt, the cup a deep well waiting to be filled with magic.

Above us, a shoal of fish writhed and spun along the yellow ceiling. The ceiling!

"Shona, what's the ceiling made out of?"

She swam up to its surface. "Amber, by the looks of it."

I backed quickly toward the door, flicking my tail as hard as I could. *A ceiling of amber, a pavement of pearl.* No! It couldn't be! It was impossible!

But I couldn't brush away the truth this time.

It was the boat from Mom's dream.

Chapter Six

S hona, we've got to get out of here!" I pulled
at her hand. My fingers shook.

"But don't you want to —"

"We have to get away!"

"What is it?"

"I don't know. Something's not right. *Please,*
Shona."

She looked at my face, and for a moment I saw
shock — or recognition. "Come on," she said.

We didn't speak as we slithered back down the
narrow corridor in silence, Shona following as I

raced ahead. I swam in such a panic that I went straight past the broken porthole and almost all the way to the other end of the boat! I turned and was about to start swimming back when Shona tugged at my arm.

"Look," she said, pointing at the floor.

"What?"

"Can't you see?"

I looked closer and noticed a shiny section of wood, newer than the other floorboards, the size of a manhole. It had a handle on it shaped like a giant pair of pliers.

Shona pulled at the trapdoor. "Give me a hand."

"Shona, I've got a really weird feeling about all this. We really have to —"

"Just a quick look. *Please*. Then we'll go — I promise."

Reluctantly, I pulled at the handle with her, flipping my tail to propel myself backward. Seconds later, it creaked open. A swarm of tiny fish darted out from the gap, shimmering in a flash of silver before disappearing down the corridor.

Shona flipped herself upside down and poked her head into the hole, swishing her tail in my face. "What can you see?" I asked.

"It's a tunnel!" Shona flipped back up and grabbed my hand. "Have a look."

"But you said we could —"

"Five minutes." And she disappeared down the hole.

As soon as we got into the tunnel, the golden light virtually disappeared. Just tiny rays peeping through the odd crack. We felt our way along the sides — which wasn't exactly pleasant. Slimy, rubbery things lined the walls. I decided not to think about what they might be. An occasional fish passed by in the shadows: slow and solitary. The silence seemed to deepen. Inside it, my unease grew and grew. How could it be the same? How *could* it?

"Look!" Shona's voice echoed in front of me.

I peered ahead. We'd reached another door, facing us at the end of the tunnel. "Locked," Shona said quietly. "Hey, but look at—"

Suddenly a luminous fish with huge wide-open jaws sprang out of the darkness, almost swimming into my face.

I screamed and grabbed Shona's arm. "I'm getting out of here!" I burst out, forgetting about the ballroom, the slimy rubbery walls, the trapdoor. All that mattered was getting away from that ship.

We sat on Rainbow Rocks, low down by the water's edge, out of sight from the coast. Water lapped gently against the stones. Shona's tail glistened in the chilly light. Mine had disappeared again, and I rubbed my goosepimply legs dry with my jacket. Shona stared. She obviously found the transformation as weird as I did.

"Do you want to tell me what that was all about?" She broke the silence.

"What?"

"What happened to you back there?"

I threw a pebble into the water and watched the circle around it grow bigger and wider until it disappeared. "I can't."

"You don't want to?"

"No, I mean, I really, actually can't! I don't even know what it's about myself."

Shona fell quiet again. "I understand if you don't trust me," she said after a while. "I mean, it's not like I'm your best friend or anything."

"I haven't got a best friend."

"Me, either." Shona smiled a little bit, her tail flapping on the rock as she spoke.

Then we fell quiet again.

"It's not that I don't trust you," I said after a while. "I do. It's just . . . well, you would think I'm crazy."

"Of course I wouldn't. Apart from the fact that

you're a human half the time and a mermaid who sneaks out to play at night, I haven't met anyone as normal as you in ages!"

I smiled.

"Come on, try me," she said.

So I did. I told her everything; I told her about the swimming lesson and Mystic Millie and about Mom's dream and the ship being exactly the same. I even told her about seeing Mr. Beeston on my way home that first night. Once I'd started letting things out, I couldn't seem to stop.

When I finished, Shona stared at me without speaking.

"What?"

She looked away.

"*What?*"

"I don't want to say. You might get mad, like last time."

"What do you mean? Do you know something? You've got to tell me!"

Shona shook her head. "I don't know anything for sure. But do you remember when we first met, and I thought I'd heard your name before?"

"You said you'd got it wrong."

"I know. But I don't think I did."

"You had heard it?"

She nodded. "I think so."

"Where?"

"It was at school."

"At *school*?"

"I think it was in a book. I never knew if it was true, or just an ocean myth. We studied it in history."

"Studied *what* in history?"

Shona paused before saying in a quiet voice, "Illegal marriages."

"Illegal? You mean—"

"Between merpeople and humans."

I tried to take in her words. What was she trying to tell me? That my parents—

"There'll be something in the library at school. Let's go back." Shona slid down off her rock.

"I thought you finished at lunch time on Saturdays."

"There are clubs and practices and stuff in the afternoon. Come on, I'm sure we can find out more."

I slipped into the water and followed her back to mermaid school, my thoughts as tangled as a heap of washed-up fishing nets.

Back through the hole in the rock, back along the caves and tunnels and tubes until we came to the school playground. It was empty.

79

"This way." Shona pointed to a rocky structure standing on its own, spiral-shaped and full of giant holes and crevices. We swam inside through a thick crack and slithered up through the swirls, coming out into a circular room with jagged rocky edges. A few mergirls and boys sat on mushroom-shaped spongy seats in front of long pieces of scratchy paper that hung from the ceiling. They wound the paper up or down, silently moving their heads from side to side as they examined the sheets.

"What are they doing?" I whispered.

Shona gaped at me. "Reading! What do you think they're doing?"

I shrugged. "Where are the books?"

"It's easier to find stuff on scrolls. Come on. I'll show you where everything's stored." She led me to the opposite side of the room and swam up to the ceiling. We looked through different headings at the top of each scroll: *Shipwrecks, Treasures, Fishermen, Sirens.*

"Sirens—it might be this one," Shona said, pulling on the end of a thick roll. "Give me a hand."

We pulled the scroll down to the floor, hooked it in place on a roller, then wound an old wooden handle around and around, working our way through facts and figures, dates and events. Stories about mermaids luring fishermen into the ocean with songs so beautiful they were almost impossible to hear; of fishermen going mad, throwing themselves into the sea to follow their hearts' desires; mermaids winning praise and riches for their success; ships brought down. We searched the whole scroll. Nothing about illegal marriages.

"We'll never find anything," I said. "I don't even know what we're looking for."

Shona was swimming around above me. "There must be something," she muttered.

"Why is it so illegal, anyway? Why can't people marry who they want?"

"It's the one thing that makes Neptune really angry. Some say it's because he once married a human and then she left him."

"Neptune's married?" I swam up to join her.

"Oh, he's got loads of wives, and hundreds of children! But this one was special, and he's never forgiven her—or the rest of the human race!"

"Shona Silkfin—what are you doing here?" A voice boomed from behind us. We both spun around to see someone swimming toward us. The history teacher!

"Oh, Mrs. Tailspin. I was just, we were—"

"Shona was just trying to help me with my homework," I said with an innocent smile.

"Homework?" Mrs. Tailspin looked at us doubtfully.

"At my school, in — in —"

"Shallowpool," Shona said quickly. "My aunt and uncle live there; that's where she's from."

"And I'm supposed to do a project on illegal marriages," I continued as an idea came to me. Maybe the teacher would know something! After all, Shona did say she heard my name in a history lesson. "Shona said that she'd studied them. She was trying to help me."

Mrs. Tailspin swam down to a mushroomy sponge-seat and beckoned us to do the same. "What do you want to know?"

I paused, glancing at Shona. What *did* I want to know? And — did I want to know at all?

"Emily's doing her project on Shiprock," Shona said, picking up my thread. "That's why she's here. We need to find out if there've been any illegal marriages around here."

"Indeed there has been one," Mrs. Tailspin said, patting the bun on her head. "Rather a well-known incident. Do you remember, Shona? We covered it last term." She frowned. "Or were you too busy daydreaming at the time?"

"Can you tell me about it?" I asked.

Mrs. Tailspin turned back to me. "Very well."

I tried to keep still on my sponge while I waited for her to carry on.

"A group of humans once found out a little

too much about the merfolk world," she began. "There had been a yacht race nearby. A couple of the boats went off course and capsized. Some mermen found them and helped them. They had to have their memories wiped afterward." She paused. "But one was missed."

"And?"

"And she didn't forget. Word spread, both in her world and our own. They started meeting up. Humans and merfolk. At one point, there was talk of them all going off to a desert island to live together. The rumor was that there was even a place where it was already happening."

"Really?" Shona said.

"Like I said, it was a rumor. I don't believe for one moment that it existed, or for that matter, exists. But they kept meeting. As I'm sure you can imagine, Neptune was *not* pleased."

"What happened?" I asked.

"There were storms for weeks. He said that if he ever caught anyone consorting with a human, they would be imprisoned for life. He visited every merfolk area personally."

"He hardly ever does that!" Shona said. "He always stays in his main palace, except when he goes on exotic vacations, or visits his other palaces. He's got them all over the world, doesn't he?"

"That's right, Shona."

"So he came to Shiprock?" I asked.

"He did indeed."

Shona bounced off her seat. "Did you meet him?"

Mrs. Tailspin nodded.

"Really? What's he like?"

"Angry, loud, covered in gold—but with a certain charisma."

"Wow!" Shona gazed at Mrs. Tailspin.

"The preparation took weeks," she continued. "As you know, Neptune can become most unhappy if he is not presented with adequate jewels and crystals when he visits. Our menfolk went on daily searches under the rocks. We made him a new scepter as a present."

"Was he pleased?"

"Very. He gave the town a dolphin as a thank-you."

"So, did the meetings stop?" I asked. "Between the merpeople and the humans?"

"Sadly, no. They continued to meet in secret. I don't know how they lived with themselves, defying Neptune like that."

"And the marriage . . . ?" I asked, holding my breath.

"Yes, there was a merman. A poet. Jake. He married one of the women at Rainbow Rocks—"

Something stirred in the back of my mind;

thoughts that I couldn't quite grasp, like bubbles that burst as soon as you touch them.

Shona didn't look at me. "What was his last name?" she asked, her voice jagged like the library walls.

Mrs. Tailspin patted her bun again. Tutted. Squinted. "Whirlstand? Whichmap? Wisplatch? No, I can't remember."

Looking down, I closed my eyes. "Was it Windsnap?" I asked.

"Windsnap! Yes, that might have been it."

The bubbles turned to rocks and started clogging up my throat.

"And they had a daughter," she continued. "That was when they were caught."

"When exactly was this?" I managed to squeeze out.

"Let's see . . . twelve or thirteen years ago."

I nodded, not trusting myself to speak.

"Gave themselves away with that. The silly woman brought the child to Rainbow Rocks and that was when we got him."

"Got him? What did they do to him?" Shona asked.

"Prison," Mrs. Tailspin said with a proud smile. "Neptune decided to make an example of him. He said Jake would be locked up for life."

"What about the baby?" I asked, swallowing hard while I waited for her to reply.

"Baby? Goodness knows. But we stopped that one." Mrs. Tailspin smiled again. "That's what you'll be doing when you're a siren, Shona. You'll be as good as that."

Shona reddened. "I haven't completely decided what I want to be yet," she said.

"Very well." Mrs. Tailspin glanced around the room. Mergirls and boys were still reading. Some were talking quietly in groups. "Now, girls, if there's nothing else, I must check on my library group."

"Yes. Thanks," I managed to say. I don't know how.

We sat in silence after she'd gone.

"It's me, isn't it?" I said eventually, staring ahead of me at nothing.

"Do you want it to be?"

"I don't know what I want. I don't even know who I am anymore."

Shona swam in front of me and made me look at her. "Emily, maybe we can find out more. He's still alive! He's out there somewhere!"

"Yeah, in prison. For life."

"But at least he didn't want to leave you!"

Perhaps he still thought about me. Perhaps I *could* find out more.

"I think we should go back to the shipwreck," Shona said.

"*What?* No way!"

"Think about it! Your mom's dream, what Mrs. Tailspin said in the lesson. They might have gone there together!"

Maybe she was right. I didn't have any better ideas. "I'll think about it," I said. "Give me a few days."

"Wednesday, then."

"OK."

"Look, I'd better be heading back." I slithered over to the spiral tube.

"Will you be all right?"

"Yeah." I tried to smile. Would I? That was anyone's guess.

I swam home through the silent water, my thoughts as crowded and unfathomable as the sea.

Chapter Seven

"Are you eating that or playing with it?" Mom asked over the top of her glasses as I stirred my cereal, watching the milk turn brown and the flakes fade into a soggy beige.

"What? Huh? Oh, sorry." I took a mouthful, then stirred some more.

Mom had the *Times* spread out in front of her. She flicked through the pages, tutting every now and then, or frowning and pushing her glasses farther up her nose.

How was I ever going to find out what was going on? It's not exactly the kind of thing that crops up naturally at Sunday breakfast: "Oh, by the way, Mom, I've been meaning to ask. I don't suppose you married a merman, had his child, and then never saw him again? OR THOUGHT TO TELL YOUR DAUGHTER ABOUT IT? *HUH???*"

I squelched my cereal against the side of the bowl, splashing milk onto the table.

"Be careful, sweetie." Mom wiped off a splash from the edge of her paper with her hand. Then she looked at me. "Are you all right? It's not like you to ignore your breakfast."

"I'm fine." I got up and emptied my bowl into the sink.

"Emily?"

I ignored her as I sat back down at the table and pulled at my hair, winding it around my fingers.

Mom took her glasses off. That meant it was serious. Then she folded her arms. Double serious. "I'm waiting," she said, her mouth tight, her eyes small. "*Emily,* I said I'm—"

"Why do you never talk about my dad?"

Mom jerked in her seat as though I'd punched her. "*What?*"

"You never talk about my father," I said, my voice coming out quieter this time. "I don't know anything about him. It's as though he never existed."

Mom put her glasses back on; then she took them off again and got up. She turned on one of the gas burners, put the kettle on it, and gazed at the flickering flame. "I don't know what to *say*," she muttered eventually.

"Why not start by telling me something about him?"

"I want to. Darling, of course I want to."

"So how come you never have?"

Her eyes had gone all watery, and she rubbed them with the sleeve of her sweater. "I don't know. I just can't—I can't do it."

If there's one thing I can't *bear*, it's Mom crying. "Look, it's OK. I'm sorry." I got out of my seat and put my arms around her shoulders. "It doesn't matter."

"But it does." She wiped her nose with the edge of the tablecloth. "I want to tell you. But I can't, I can't, I—"

"It's OK, Mom, honest. You don't have to tell me."

"But I want to," she sobbed. "I just can't remember!"

"You can't remember?" I let go and stared at her. "You don't remember the man you married?"

She looked at me through bloodshot eyes. "Well, yes—no. I mean, sometimes I think I remember things. But then it goes again. Disappears."

"Disappears."

"Just like he did," she said quietly, her body shaking, her head in her hands. "I can't even remember my own husband. Your father. Oh, I'm a terrible mother."

"Don't start that," I sighed. "You're a great mother. The best."

"Really?" She smoothed down her skirt against her lap. I forced myself to smile. She looked up and stroked my cheek with her thumb. "I must have done something right to get you," she said weakly.

I stood up. "Look, just forget it. It doesn't matter. OK?"

"You deserve better than—"

"Come on, Mom. It's all right," I said firmly. "Hey, I think I'll go over to the arcade, OK?"

She pinched my cheek. "Munchkin," she sniffed. "Pass me my purse."

She handed me two dollars, and I headed up the stairs.

I dawdled as I made my way past the video arcade. Not fair. Nothing was fair. I couldn't even waste a quarter on the Skee-Ball. On top of everything else, I didn't need Mandy turning up and going after me just for being there.

I bought some cotton candy from the end of the pier and wandered down to the boardwalk, my head filled with thoughts and questions. I didn't notice Mr. Beeston coming toward me.

"Watch yourself," he said as I nearly walked into him.

"Sorry. I was miles away."

He smiled at me in that way that always gives me weird shivers in my neck and arms. One side of his mouth turned up, the other reached down, and his crooked teeth poked out through the dark gap in between.

"How's Mom?" he asked.

That's when I had a thought. Mr. Beeston had been around a long time. He was kind of friendly with Mom. Maybe he'd know something.

"She's not doing that great, actually," I said as I took a bite, the pink fluff melting into sugar in my mouth.

"Oh? Why not?"

"She's a bit sad about . . . some things."

"Things? What *things*?" he said quickly, his smile gone.

"Just . . ."

"Is she ill? What's the matter?" Mr. Beeston's face turned hard as he narrowed his eyes at me.

"Well, my father . . ." I pulled at my cotton candy and a long piece came away like a loose thread from a fluffy pink ball of mohair yarn. I folded it over into my mouth.

"Your *what*?" Mr. Beeston burst out. What *was* his problem?

"I was asking her about my father, and she got upset."

He lowered his voice. "What did she tell you?"

"She didn't tell me anything."

"Nothing at all?"

"She said she couldn't remember anything. Then she started crying."

"Couldn't remember anything? That's what she said?"

I nodded.

"You're quite sure now? Nothing at all?"

"Yes. Nothing."

"All right, then." Mr. Beeston breathed out hard through his nose. It made a low whistling sound.

"So, I wondered if you could help me," I continued, trying to sound casual.

"Me? How on earth can *I* help you?" he snapped.

"I just wondered if she'd ever talked to you about him. With you being her friend and everything."

He examined my face, squeezing his eyes down to narrow slits as he stared. I wanted to run away. Of course he wouldn't know anything. Why would she talk to him and not me? I tried to hold his eyes but he was staring at me so hard I had to look away.

He took hold of me by my elbow and pointed up the promenade with his other hand. "I think it's time you and I had a little chat," he said.

I tried to shake my elbow away as we walked, but he held it tighter and walked faster. We'd gotten all the way to the end of the boardwalk before he let go and motioned for me to sit down on a bench.

"Now, listen to me and listen well, because I'll tell you this once and once only."

I waited.

"And I don't want you bothering your mother with it afterward. You've upset her enough already."

"But I—"

"Never mind, never mind." He raised his hand to stop me. "You couldn't have known."

He wiped his forehead with a hankie. "Now then," he said, shifting his weight onto his side as he put his hankie away. His trousers had a hole just below the pocket. "Your father and I, we used to be friends. Best friends. Some folks even thought we were brothers; that's how close we were."

Brothers? Surely Mr. Beeston was lots older than my father? I opened my mouth to speak.

"He was like a kid brother to me. We did every-thing together."

"Like what?"

"What?"

"What things did you do? I want to know what he was like."

"All the things young boys get up to," he snapped. "We went fishing together. Went out on our bikes—"

"Motorbikes?"

"Yes, yes, motorbikes, mountain bikes—all of that. We were best friends. Chased the girls together, too."

Imagining Mr. Beeston chasing girls, I shuddered.

He cleared his throat. "Then, of course, he met your mother and things changed."

"Changed? How?"

"Well, one might say they fell in love. At least, she did. Very much so."

"And what about my dad?"

"He did a very good impression of love, for a while. He certainly didn't want to fool around with cars anymore."

"I thought you said he liked bikes."

"Cars, bikes—whatever. He wasn't interested. They spent all their time together."

Mr. Beeston stared into the distance, his hands in his pockets. He looked as though he was struggling with something. Then he jingled his coins and said, "But of course it didn't last. Your father turned out not to be the gentleman we all had believed he was."

"What do you mean?"

"This is rather a delicate matter. But I shall tell you. Let us say he wasn't the most *responsible* person. He was happy enough to lead your mother up the garden path, but not prepared to stay by her side when they got to the gate."

"Huh?"

His face reddened. "He was content to sow but not reap."

"Mr. Beeston, I don't know what you're talking about."

"Good grief, child. I'm talking about responsibility," he snapped. "Where do you think *you* came from?"

"Do you mean he got my mom pregnant with me and then ran off?"

"Yes, yes, that is what I mean."

Why didn't you say so, then? I wanted to say — but didn't dare. Mr. Beeston looked so angry. "So he left her?" I asked, just to make sure I'd got it right.

"Yes, he left her," he replied through tight lips.

"Where did he go?"

"That's just it. No one ever heard from him again. The strain was obviously too much for him," he said sarcastically.

"What strain?"

"Fatherhood. Good-for-nothing slacker. Never willing to grow up and take responsibility." Mr. Beeston looked away. "What he did—it was despicable," he said, his voice becoming raspy. "I will never forgive him." He got up from the bench, his face hard and set. "Never," he repeated. Something about the way he said it made me hope I'd never get on his wrong side.

I followed him as we carried on along the boardwalk. "Didn't anybody try to find him?"

"Find him?" Mr. Beeston looked at me, but it was as though he were seeing right through me. His eyes wouldn't meet mine. "Find him?" he repeated. "Yes—of course we tried. No one could have done more than I did. I traveled around for weeks, put up posters. We even had a message on the radio, begging him to come home and meet his—well, his . . ."

"His daughter?"

Mr. Beeston didn't reply.

"So he never even saw me?"

"We did everything we could."

I looked down the wide boards of the

promenade, trying to take in what I'd heard. It *couldn't* be true. Could it? A young couple ambled toward us, the man holding a baby up in the air, the woman laughing, a spaniel jumping up between them. Farther down, an elderly couple were walking slowly against the wind, arms linked.

"I think I need to go now," I said. We'd walked all the way around to the lighthouse.

Mr. Beeston pulled me back by my arm. "You're not to talk to your mother about this, do you hear me?"

"Why not?"

"You saw what happened. It's far too painful for her." He tightened his grip, his fingers biting into my arm. "Promise me you won't mention it."

I didn't say anything.

Mr. Beeston looked hard into my eyes. "People can block things out completely if the memory is too much to cope with. That's a scientific fact. There'll be all sorts of trouble if you try to make her talk about this." He pulled on my arm, his face inches from mine. "And you don't want trouble — do you?" he said in a whisper.

I shook my head.

"*Do* you?" he repeated with another yank on my arm.

"No — of course not," my voice wobbled.

He smiled his wonky smile at me and let go of my arm. "Good," he said. "Good. Now, will I be seeing you when I come over this afternoon?"

"I'm going out," I said quickly. I'd think of something to do. I couldn't cope with Sunday coffee with Mom and Mr. Beeston. Especially now.

"Very well. Tell your mother I'll be over at three o'clock."

"Yeah."

We stood by the lighthouse. For a moment, I had a vision of him throwing me inside and locking me in! Why would he do that? He'd never done anything to hurt me — before today. I rubbed my arm. I could still feel the pinch of his fingers digging into my skin. But it was nothing compared with the disappointment I felt in my chest. Jake wasn't my father, after all, if Mr. Beeston was to be believed. And he had no reason to lie — did he? Nothing made sense anymore.

"Now, let's see, where's the, hmm . . ." Mr. Beeston talked to himself as he fumbled with his keys. He had about five key rings rattling on a long chain. But then he gasped. "What — where's my . . ."

"What's wrong?"

He ignored me. "It can't be missing. It can't be." He felt in his pants pockets, pulling the insides out and shaking out his handkerchief. "It was here. I'm sure it was."

"The lighthouse key?"

"No, not the lighthouse key, the —" He stopped fumbling and looked up at me, as if he'd only just remembered I was there, his eyes dark and hard. "You're still here," he said. "Go on. Leave me alone. But don't forget our chat. It's between you and me. Remember, you don't want to cause any *trouble*." Then he unlocked the lighthouse door. "I've got some important things to do," he said. Squinting into my eyes, he added, "I'll see you again soon." For some reason, it sounded like a threat.

Before I had a chance to say anything else, he'd slipped inside and shut the door behind him. A second later, a bolt slid across.

As I turned to leave, I kicked something up in the dust. It glinted at me. A key ring. I picked it up. There was a brass plate on the ring with crystals around the edges. There was a picture of a pitch-fork or something engraved on one side.

Two keys hung from the ring: one big chunky one, the other a little metal one, same as Mom has for our suitcase. A tiny gold chain hung from the plate; a clasp at its other end was broken and open.

I banged on the lighthouse door and waited. "Mr. Beeston!" I called. I banged once more.

Nothing.

I looked at the key ring again, running my fingers over its crystal edge. Oh, well. I could always give it back another time.

I buttoned the key ring into my pocket and headed home.

Chapter Eight

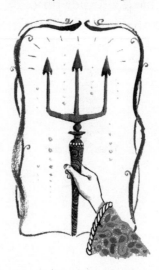

*T*his was it. The moment I'd been dreading. The school board had only gone and reopened the pool! Apparently some parents made a fuss. So here we were again. I stepped through the trough of icy cold water on the way to the pool. Back at the gym, I had tried telling Mr. Bird I had a planter's wart on my foot, but he just gave me a couple of rubber socks to put on. So now the game was up, *plus* I looked ridiculous. Great. What was I going to do? Five more minutes and my secret would be revealed. Everybody would know I was a freak!

"Come on, people; we haven't got all day." Bob clapped his hands together as I walked slowly to the side of the pool and joined the rest of the class. "It'll be time to get out again before you set foot in the water."

My heart thumped so loud I could feel it in my ears.

"OK, those who can swim already can jump right in," he said. *Please, please don't remember that I can swim,* I prayed silently. Time was running out.

"That means you." Mandy Rushton elbowed Julia and pointed to me. "What's up, *fish girl*?" she sneered. "Have you gotten water shy all of a sudden?"

I tried to ignore her, but Bob was looking our way. "What's going on over—" Then he recognized me. "Oh, yeah. You're the one who got a cramp, aren't you?"

I stepped back toward the wall, hoping it might swallow me up and then I could disappear forever. I couldn't do it—I couldn't!

"You can get in when you're ready." *Yeah, right—no way.* "Take it easy, though. We don't want the same thing to happen again." He turned back to the others. "Come on, you guys. Let's get on with it, shall we?"

"Let's all see how the *fish girl* does it!" Mandy said loudly, and everyone turned around to look at us. Then she pushed me forward and I lost my footing. Tripping on the slippery floor, I went flying into the pool with a loud SPLASH!

For the tiniest moment, I forgot all about Mandy. She wasn't important. All that mattered was that I was in the water again, losing myself to its creamy smoothness, wrapping myself up in it as if it were my favorite dressing gown, keeping me safe and warm.

Then I remembered where I was!

I swam to the surface and looked up to see thirty pairs of eyes facing my way—at least one of them glinting nastily at me, waiting for my *freakness* to be revealed!

I had to fight it—I had to—but it was starting already! My legs were going numb, joining together. And, like an idiot, I'd swum halfway across the pool!

I heaved myself through the water, splashing and dragging my body along, keeping my legs as still as possible to try to stop my tail from forming. Bit by bit, I propelled myself to the side, my arms working like a windmill. I *had* to get there before it happened. Hurry, hurry!

Gasping and panting, I finally heaved myself out of the pool—*just* in time! The second I dragged my body over the side, my legs started to relax. Wheezing and breathless, I pulled myself out of the pool and sat on the side.

Bob was over in a second. "Have you hurt yourself?" He stared down at me, and I suddenly had an idea. I grabbed my foot.

"It's my ankle," I said. "I think I've sprained it."

Bob narrowed his eyes. "How did that happen?"

I was about to say I'd fallen in when I saw Mandy's face. Sneering and jeering at me. Why should I let her off the hook? "Mandy pushed me," I said.

"OK, well, there'll be no swimming for either one of you this week," he said. "You can sit in the corner for the rest of the lesson," he said sternly to Mandy. Then he turned to me. "And you put that ankle up and rest it."

He clapped his hands as he went back to the class. "That's it, people, show's over. Let's do some swimming!"

It wasn't the cold that made me shiver as I limped back to the changing room. It had more to do with Mandy's words, hissed at me through clenched teeth so quietly no one else could hear.

"I'll get you back for this, fish girl," she said. "Just wait."

I hung back while Shona swam ahead, my tail flapping as we drew closer to the shipwreck. The night was crunchy with a million stars, but no moon.

"We're nearly there." Shona dove under the water. I followed her, trailing a few yards behind.

Soon, the golden light was filtering through weeds and rocks, pulling us toward the ship.

"Shona, we can't do it!" I blurted out. "There's no point."

Shona swam back to me. "But you agreed—"

"It's no good. He's not my father."

She stared at me.

"My father left us. Just like I thought he had." I told her what Mr. Beeston had said—and about his strange threat.

"Are you sure?" she asked when I'd finished.

Why would Mr. Beeston bother to lie? I'd asked myself that question so many times over the last three days. I still wasn't sure I believed him—but it was better than building up false hopes.

"I was so certain. . . ." Shona looked over her shoulder at the ship. "Look—why don't we go anyway? We're nearly there."

"What's the use?"

"What have we got to lose? And there was something I wanted to show you. Something about the door in that passageway."

What did it matter? If the ship didn't have

anything to do with me, there was nothing to fear. "OK," I said.

We slithered along the dark corridor, feeling our way back down those slimy walls. I tried hard not to make eye contact with the open-jawed fish that had followed us down.

"So what did you want to show me?" I asked as we swam.

"There was a symbol on the door. I completely forgot about it after everything that happened."

"What symbol?"

"A trident."

"What's a trident?"

"Neptune's symbol. He carries it everywhere with him. It's what he uses to create thunder-storms—or islands."

"Islands? He can create whole islands?"

"Well, that's only when he's in a good mood—so it doesn't happen much. More often he makes the biggest storms out at sea!" Shona's eyes had that wide shiny look they always did when she talked about Neptune.

"Some merfolk say he can turn you to stone with his trident. His palace is filled with stone ani-mals. I heard that they were all animals who had disobeyed him at one time. And he can make ships disappear, just by waving it at them — or produce a feast for a hundred merpeople, or create volcanoes out of thin air."

"Cool!"

We'd arrived at the door. "Look." She pointed at the top corner of the door. A brass plate. An engraving. Quite faint — but there was no mistaking what I was looking at.

The picture from Mr. Beeston's key ring.

"But — but that's —" I pulled at my pocket. "It's impossible. It can't be!"

"What?" Shona swam up to my side. I handed her the key ring. "Where did you get this?" she asked.

"It's Mr. Beeston's."

"Sharks!" Shona breathed. "So do you think . . ." Her words trailed away into the watery darkness. What did I think? I didn't think anything anymore.

"Shall we try it?" Shona took the key from me.

I watched in amazement as it turned smoothly in the lock.

The door slid open.

Silently, we slithered inside. We were in a small office. It had a desk stacked about a yard high with laminated folders and papers held down by rocks, and a stool nailed to the floor in front of it. Shona swam to the desk and pulled on something. A second later, an orange glow burst out above me. I blinked as I got used to the sudden glare, then looked up to see where the light had come from. A long slimy creature with a piece of string on its tail clung to the ceiling.

"Electric eel," she explained.

We looked at each other in silence. "What about the other key?" she said eventually, swimming over to a metal filing cabinet in the corner. I tried the drawers, but they wouldn't pull out. I almost closed my eyes as I tried to put it in the lock at the top. *Please don't fit, please don't fit,* I said to myself. What would I find if it did?

I couldn't even get it halfway in.

I let out a huge breath and was suddenly desperate to get out of there. "Shona, maybe this is all a big mistake," I said, backing out of the office. But then I knocked my tail against the stool and slipped backward. A swarm of tiny black fish escaped from under the table, spinning out of the room and away from us.

"Emily!" Shona tugged my sleeve and pointed at something under the table.

I leaned forward to get a closer look. There was a wooden chest; quite big, with brass edging and a chain looped all around it. It was like something out of *Treasure Island*. I swam under the table, and Shona helped me drag it out. "Flipping fins," she said quietly, staring at something dangling at the front of the chain. A brass padlock.

As I slipped the key easily into the lock and the brass hook bounced from the tumbler, I wasn't even surprised. A line of silver fish pecked at the chest as I opened it. It was full of files. I grabbed a handful of them. The colors changed from blue to green as I lifted them toward me. Rummaging through the pile, I tried to pull the rest of them out. Then I came to a folder that was different from the others. For one thing, it was thicker. For another thing, it looked newer.

And for another, it had my name on it.

Chapter Nine

I don't know how long I looked at the file. I realized at some point that my hand had almost gone numb from clutching it so tightly.

"What is it?" Shona came to look over my shoulder at the files. That's when I noticed another one at the bottom of the chest. I reached down to get it. It had my mom's name on it. Below that was another. I almost didn't dare to look. I shut my eyes as I picked it up. When I opened them, I was looking at a name I'd been dreaming about for a week: Jake Windsnap.

I traced the words with my fingertips. Jake Windsnap. I said his name over and over, wondering if there was any way it could be a mistake or a practical joke or something. "Jake *is* my father,"

I said out loud. Of course he was. I'd known it in my heart from the first time I'd heard his name. It just took seeing it in writing to convince my brain.

I opened the file, my hands shaking so much I almost dropped all its contents. The sheets inside it were plastic. And they all had the pitchfork image at the top: Neptune's trident.

"But what in sharks' name does Mr. Beeston have to do with any of this?" Shona asked.

"Maybe he knows where my dad is, after all. I mean, if they were best friends, maybe he's trying to help him. Maybe they've been in touch all along." My words came out in a rush, none of them convincing me — or Shona, by the look on her face.

"There's only one way to find out," she said.

I held the files out in front of me. Once I'd looked inside, there would be no going back. I couldn't pretend I hadn't seen whatever was in there. Maybe I didn't want to know. I pulled at my hair, twiddling, twisting it around and around. I had to look. Whatever it said, I needed to know the truth.

I opened the file with my name on it. A scrappy bit of paper with a handwritten note scrawled across it fell on the floor. I picked it up, Shona looking over my shoulder as I read.

> EW One: All clear.
> Nothing to report. No mer-gene identified.
> Possibly negative. (50% chance.) Scale detection nil.

"What in the ocean is that supposed to mean?" asked Shona.

I shook my head, pulling a bigger sheet out of the file.

> EW Eight: Moment of truth?
> Subject has requested swimming lessons again.
> (See MPW file for cross-ref.) CFB present to
> witness request. Denied by mother. Unlikely to
> be granted in near future. Needs careful
> attention. Almost certainly negative mer-gene
> but experiment MUST NOT be abandoned.
> Continued observation—priority.

"Subject!" I spluttered. "Is that me?"
Shona winced.
Careful watch? Had he been stalking me? What if he was watching us now? I shuddered and swam over to close the office door. A lone blue fish skimmed into the room and over my head as I did.

We scanned the rest of the file. It was all the same: subjects and initials and weird stuff that didn't make sense.

I picked up my mom's file.

MPW Zero: Objectives.

MPW — greatest risk to merworld detection. Constant supervision by CFB. M-drug to be administered.

Shona gasped. "M-drug. I know what that is! They're wiping her memory!"

"*What?* Who is?"

"Mr. Beeston is. He must work for Neptune!"

"Work for Neptune? But how? Then he'd be a . . . I mean, he *can't*. Can he?"

Shona rubbed her lip. "They usually send people away after they've been memory wiped."

"Why?"

"It can wear off if you go near merfolk areas. We learned all about it in science last term."

"So you think they did it to my mom?"

"They probably still are. One dose is usually enough for a one-time incident—but not for a whole series of memories. They must be topping it up somehow."

Topping it up? I thought about all Mr. Beeston's visits. He wasn't lonely! He was drugging my mom!

We looked all the way through Mom's file. Page after page noting her movements. He'd been spying on us for years.

"I feel sick," I said, closing the file.

Shona picked up Jake's file. There was a note stuck on the front with something scribbled on it. East Wing: E 930. We read in silence.

JW Three: Bad influence.
JW continuing to complain about sentence. Sullen and difficult.
JW Eight: Improvement.
Subject has settled into routine of prison life. Behavior improved.
JW Eleven: Isolation.
Operation Desert Island discussed openly by prisoner. Isolation—three days.

"Operation Desert Island!" Shona exclaimed. "So it's true after all. There *is* a place! Somewhere merfolk and humans live together!"

"How do you know that's what it is?" I asked. "It could be anything."

We read on.

"None of it makes any sense," I said, swimming backward and forward across the room to help me think.

Shona continued flicking through the file. "It's all numbers and dates and weird initials." She closed the file. "I can't make fin or tail of it." She grabbed another file from the chest. "Listen to this," she said. "'Project Lighthouse. CFB to take over Brightport Lighthouse until completion of Windsnap problem. Ground floor adapted for access. Occasional siren support available with unreliable beam. Previous lighthouse keeper: M-drug and removal from scene.'" Shona looked up.

"What are we going to do?" I whispered.

"What *can* we do? But, hey — at least you've found your dad."

My dad. The words sounded strange. Not right. Not yet. "But I *haven't* found him," I said. "That's just it. All I've found is some stupid file that doesn't make any sense."

Shona put the file down. "I'm sorry."

"Look, Shona, we know Jake's my — my father, don't we?"

"Without a doubt."

"And we know where he is?"

"Well, yes."

"And he can't come out. He's locked away. And he didn't *choose* to leave me. . . ."

"I'm *sure* he never wanted to —"

"So we'll go to him!"

Shona looked at me blankly.

I shoved the files back in the chest, locked it firmly. "Come on, let's go!"

"Go? Where?"

"The prison." I turned around to face her. "I've got to find him."

Shona's tail flapped gently. "Emily, it's *miles* away."

"We're mermaids! We can swim for miles, no problem!"

"Maybe *I* can, but it's definitely too far for you. You're only half mermaid, remember?"

"So you're saying I'm not as good as you?" I folded my arms. "I thought you were supposed to be my friend. I thought you might even have been my best friend."

Shona's tail flapped even more. "Really?" she said. "I want you to be my best friend, too."

"Well, you've got a funny way of showing it. You won't even help me find my father."

Shona winced. "I just don't think we'd make it there. I'm not even sure exactly where it *is*."

"But we'll never know if we don't try. Please, Shona. If you were *really* my best friend, you would."

"OK," she sighed. "We'll try. But I don't want you collapsing on me miles out at sea. If you get tired, you have to tell me, and we'll come back, OK?"

I shoved the chest back under the table. "OK."

I don't know how long we'd been swimming; maybe an hour. I started to feel as if I had heavy weights attached to each arm; my tail was practically dropping off. Flying fish raced along with us, bouncing past on both sides. An occasional gull darted into the sea, like a white dart piercing the water.

"How much farther is it?" I gasped.

"We're not even halfway." Shona looked back. "Are you all right?"

"Fine." I tried not to pant while I spoke. "Great. No problem."

Shona slowed down to swim alongside me, and we carried on in silence for a bit. "You're not OK, are you?" she said after a while.

"I'm fine," I repeated, but my head slipped under the water while I spoke. I coughed as a mouthful of water went down the wrong way. Shona grabbed me.

"Thanks." I wriggled away from her. "I'm all right now."

She looked at me doubtfully. "Maybe we could both do with a rest," she said. "There's a tiny island about five minutes' swim from here. It's out of our way, but it would give us a chance to get our breath back."

"OK," I said. "If you really need a rest, I don't mind."

"Fine." Shona swam off again. "Follow me."

Soon, we were sitting on an island barely larger than the flat rock that had become our meeting place. It was hard and gravelly, but I lay down the second I dragged myself out of the sea, the water brushing against me as my tail turned back into legs.

It seemed only seconds later that Shona gently shook my shoulder. "Emily," she whispered. "You'd better get up. It's starting to get light."

I sat up. "How long have I been asleep?"

Shona shrugged. "Not long."

"Why didn't you wake me? We'll never get there now. You did it on purpose!"

Shona squeezed her lips together and scrunched up her eyes. I thought about her pretending she needed a rest, and about taking me to her school and everything. "I'm sorry," I said. "I know why you did it."

"It's too far. It's probably even too far for me, never mind you."

"I'm *never* going to see him. I bet he doesn't even remember he's got a daughter!" I felt a drop of salty water on my cheek and wiped it roughly away. "What am I going to do?"

Shona put her arm around me. "I'm sorry," she said.

"I'm sorry, too. I shouldn't have been mean to you. You've been amazing. Really helpful."

Shona made a face at me, as if she was trying not to smile but couldn't stop a little grin from slipping out through her frown.

"And I know you're right," I added. "There's no way I could get there tonight, not if we're only halfway."

"Not even that. Look." She pointed out to the horizon. "See that big cloud that looks like a whale spurting water—with the little starfish-shaped one behind it?"

I looked up at the sky. "Um, yeah," I said uncertainly.

"Just below that, where the sea meets the sky, it's lighter than the rest of the horizon."

I studied the horizon. It looked an awfully long way away!

"That's it. The Great Mermer Reef. It's like a huge wall, bigger than anything you've ever seen in your life, made of rocks and coral in every shape and color you could imagine—and then about a hundred more. The prison's a mile beyond it. You have to go through the reef to get there."

My heart felt like a rock itself—dropping down to the bottom of the sea. "Shona, it's absolutely *miles* away."

"We'll work something out," Shona said. "I promise." Then she scrabbled around among the rocks and picked up a couple of stones. She handed one to me.

"What's this?" I looked at the stone.

"They're friendship pebbles. They mean that we're best friends—if you want to be."

"Of course I want to be!"

"See? They're almost exactly the same." She showed me her pebble. "We each keep ours on us at all times. It means we'll always be there for each other." Then she said, more quietly, "And it's also a promise that we'll find your dad."

I washed my pebble in the water; it went all shiny and smooth. "It's the best present anyone's ever given me."

Shona slipped hers into her tail, and I put mine in my jacket pocket. I didn't want it to disappear when my legs returned! I looked at the patch of light that was spreading and growing across the horizon.

"Come on." Shona slid back into the sea. "We'd better get going."

We slowly made our way back to Rainbow Rocks.

"See you Sunday?" I asked as we said good-bye.

Shona's cheeks reddened a touch. "Can we make it Monday?"

"I thought you couldn't get out on Mondays."

"I will. I'll make sure of it. It's just that the Diving and Dance display is Monday morning, and I don't want to be too tired for the triple flips."

"Monday night, then." I smiled. "And good luck."

By the time I got home, I was so tired I could have fallen asleep standing up. But my head was spinning with thoughts and questions. And sadness. I'd found out where my father was, but how would we ever get there? Would we really find him? It felt like I was losing him all over again. I'd virtually lost my mom as well. If only I could make her remember!

As I tried to get to sleep, something Shona had said swam into the corner of my mind. *Sometimes it doesn't work at all, especially if you go near merfolk areas.*

Of course!

I knew *exactly* what I was going to do.

Chapter Ten

*M*om always sleeps in on Sundays. She says even God had a day of rest, and she doesn't see why she can't. I'm not allowed to disturb her until she says it's morning—which usually isn't until around noon.

I paced up and down the boat, willing her to wake up. What if she slept right through the afternoon and woke up at coffee time? Disaster! I couldn't take the risk of Mr. Beeston showing up before I'd spoken to her. So I broke a golden rule. I crept into her room and sat on the bed.

"Mom," I stage-whispered from the end of the bed. She didn't stir. I inched farther up and leaned toward her ear. "Mom," I croaked a bit louder.

She opened one eye and then closed it again. "Whadyouwan?" she grumbled.

"You have to get up."

"Whassamatter?"

"I want to go out."

Mom groaned and turned over.

"Mom, I want us to go out together."

Silence.

"Please get up."

She turned back to face me and opened her eyes a crack.

"We never do anything together," I said.

"Why now? Why can't you leave me in peace? What time is it, anyway?"

I quickly turned her alarm clock around so she couldn't see it. "It's late. Come on, Mom. *Please.*"

Mom rubbed her eyes and lay on her back. "I don't suppose you're going to give me any peace until I do, are you?"

I smiled hopefully.

"Just leave me alone, and I'll get up."

I didn't move. "How do I know you won't go back to sleep the minute I leave?"

"Emily! I said I'll get up, and I will. Now leave me alone! And if you want to get back in my good graces, you can make me a nice cup of tea. And then I might forgive you."

Mom took a bite of her toast. "So, where do you imagine we're going, now that you've ruined my Sunday morning?"

I knew *exactly* where we were going. Shiprock Bay. The nearest you could get to Rainbow Rocks by road. I'd been studying the bus routes, and there was one that took us almost all the way there. We could get off on the coast road and walk along the headland. It must be worth a try. I had to jog her memory somehow.

"I just thought we could have a day trip around the coast," I said casually as I popped a piece of toast and strawberry jelly in my mouth.

"What about Mr. Beeston?"

"What about him?" I nearly choked on my toast.

"We'll have to be back by three. We can't let him down."

"Oh, Mom! Can't you break your date with him for once?"

"*Emily*. Mr. Beeston is a lonely man and a good friend. How many times do I have to tell you that? You know I don't like letting him down. He has not broken our arrangement once in all these years, and I'm not about to do it to him now. And it is *not* a date!"

"Whatever." This wasn't the time to tell her what I knew about the "lonely man." What *did* I know, anyway? Nothing that made any sense. I swallowed hard to get my toast down. My throat was dry. We'd still have time to get there. Maybe we could accidentally-on-purpose miss the bus back. I'd think of something. I *had* to!

"This is really nice, actually." Mom looked out of the window as we bumped around the coast road. It had started to turn inland, and I was trying to figure out which stop would be best for us to try. The ocean looked completely different from this angle. Then I saw a familiar clump of rocks and decided to take a chance. I got up and rang the bell. "This is our stop," I said.

"You know, I think I'm almost glad you woke me up," Mom said as we got off the bus. "Not that that's an excuse to do it every week!" She walked over to a green bench on the headland that looked out to sea and sat down. "And you've picked such a nice spot, too."

"What are you doing?" I asked as she reached into her bag and brought out the sandwiches.

"We're having a picnic, aren't we?"

"Not *here*!"

Mom looked around. "Why not? I can't see anywhere better."

"Mom, we're right by the road! Let's walk out toward the water a bit."

She frowned.

"Come on, just a little way. *Please.* You promised."

"I did no such thing!" she snapped. But she put the sandwiches back anyway, and we headed along a little headland path that led out toward the beach.

After we'd been walking for about fifteen minutes, the path came to an abrupt end. In front of us was a gravelly climb down the cliff.

"Now what?" Mom looked around.

"Let's go down there."

"You must be joking. Have you seen my shoes?"

I looked at her feet. Why hadn't I thought to tell her not to wear her platform sandals? "They're OK," I said.

"Emily. I am *not* going to break my ankles just so you can drag me off down some dangerous cliff." She turned around and started walking back.

"No, wait!" I looked around desperately. She couldn't leave — she had to see the rocks. A winding path lay almost hidden under brambles, stony and rough but not nearly as steep as the other one. "Let's try here," I said. "And look — it gets flat again over there if we can just get down this part."

"I don't know." Mom looked doubtfully down the cliff.

"Come on; let's try it. I'll go first and then I can cushion your fall if you trip and go flying." I tried an impish smile, and she gave in.

"If I break my legs, you're bringing me breakfast in bed every day until I'm better."

"Deal."

I picked my way through the brambles and stones, checking behind me every few seconds to make sure Mom was still there. We managed to get down to the rocks in one piece.

Mom rubbed her elbow. "Ouch. Thorns." She pulled up a piece of seaweed and rubbed it on her arm. I gazed in front of us. Just a few yards of water separated us from Rainbow Rocks. I couldn't help smiling as I watched the sea washing over the flat rocks, rainbow water caressing them with every wave.

"Mom?"

"Hmm?"

I took a deep breath. "Do you believe in mermaids?" I asked, my throat tight and strained.

Mom laughed. "Mermaids? Oh, Emily, you do ask some silly—"

But then she stopped. She dropped the seaweed on the ground. Looking out to sea, her face went all hard.

"What is it, Mom?" I asked gently.

"Where are we?" she whispered.

"Just by the coast. I just thought it'd be nice to go out for—"

"What is this place?"

I hadn't actually thought about what I'd say once we got here! What would she do if she knew—not just about Jake but about me, too? What if she only half remembered? She might think we were *both* freaks. Maybe she'd be ashamed of us. Why hadn't I thought this through?

I cleared my throat. "Um, it's just some rocks," I said carefully. "Isn't it?"

Mom turned to me. "I've been here before," she said, her face scrunched up as if she was in pain.

"When?"

"I don't know. But I know this place."

"Shall we go farther down?"

"No!" She turned back the way we'd come. "Emily. We have to go back. Mr. Beeston will be expecting us."

"But we just got here. Mr. Beeston won't be around for ages yet."

"I can't stay here," Mom said. "I've got a bad feeling about it. We're going home." She started walking back so quickly I could hardly keep up.

We ate our sandwiches on that green bench on the headland, after all. A bus went whizzing past just as we were approaching the road, so there was nothing to do but wait for the next one. We ate in silence: me not knowing what to say, Mom gazing into space.

I kept wanting to ask her things, or tell her things, but where could I start?

Eventually another bus came, and we rode home in silence as well. By the time we got back to Brightport Pier, it was nearly four o'clock.

"Are you angry with me?" I asked as we let ourselves into the boat.

"Angry? Why? You haven't done anything wrong, have you?" Mom searched my face.

"I wanted to have a nice day out and now you've gotten all sad."

Mom shook her head. "Just thoughtful, sweetheart. There was something about that place. . . ." Her voice trailed off.

"What? What was it?"

"It was such a strong memory, but I don't even know what it was." She shook her head again and took her coat off. "Listen to me, talking drivel as usual."

"You're not talking drivel at all," I said urgently. "What was the memory?"

Mom hugged her coat. "Do you know, it wasn't a memory of a *thing*. More a feeling of something. I felt an overwhelming feeling of . . . love."

"Love?"

"And then something else. Sadness. Enormous sadness." Mom took her coat down to the engine room to hang it up. "I told you I was talking nonsense, didn't I?" she called. "Now get that teakettle on, and I'll go and give Mr. Beeston a shout. I'll bet he's wondering where we've been."

I glanced out of the window as I filled the kettle. Mr. Beeston was on his way up the pier! My whole body shivered. He was striding fast and didn't look happy.

POUND! POUND! POUND! He banged on the roof as Mom came back in the galley.

"Oh, good. He's here." Mom went to let him in. "Hello." She smiled. "I was just coming to—"

"Where have you been?" he demanded.

"We've been out for a little adventure, haven't we Emily? Just up along the—"

"I was here at three o'clock," he snapped, stabbing a finger at his watch. "I waited a whole hour. What's the meaning of this?" His head snapped across to face me. I swallowed hard.

Mom frowned at us both. "Come on, there's no need to get upset," she said. "Let's have some coffee." She went to get the cups and saucers. "What have you got for us today, Mr. B.? Some lovely cinnamon buns? With vanilla glaze?"

"Doughnuts," Mr. Beeston said without taking his eyes off me.

"I haven't done anything," I said.

"Of course you haven't, Emily. Who said you did? Now, won't you please join us?" Mom held a cup out to Mr. Beeston as he finally turned away. He took his jacket off and folded it over the back of a chair.

"No, thanks." I lay on the sofa and eaves-dropped, waiting for Mr. Beeston to try to inject her with the memory drug. I had to catch him in the act, to prove to Mom that he wasn't really her friend. But what if he got to me first? What if he injected *me* with the memory drug, too?

But he didn't do anything. As soon as he sat down with Mom, he acted as though nothing had happened. They just drank their coffee and munched doughnuts and chatted about condo owners and the price of mini golf.

They'd barely finished eating when Mr. Beeston glanced at his watch. "Well, I've got to move along," he said.

"You're going?" But he hadn't drugged her yet! Maybe he didn't do it every week. Well, I'd be waiting for him as soon as he tried!

"I have a four-forty-five appointment," he growled, the left side of his mouth twitching as he spoke. "And *I* don't like to keep people waiting."

I didn't say anything.

"Good-bye, Mary P." He let himself out.

Mom started clearing the cups away, and I grabbed a hand towel.

"So you were saying earlier," I began as Mom handed me a saucer to dry.

"Saying?"

"About our outing."

"Oh, of course—the little trip to the headland," Mom smiled. "Lovely, wasn't it?"

"Not just the headland," I said. "The rocks."

Mom looked at me blankly.

"Rainbow Rocks . . ." The words caught in my throat as I held my breath.

"Rainbow what?"

"Mom—don't tell me you've forgotten! The rocks, the rainbow colors when the sea washed over them, the way you felt when we were there. Love. And sadness and stuff?"

Mom laughed. "You know, Mrs. Partington told me at our last parent-teacher conference that you had a good imagination. Now I know what she means."

I stared at her as she bustled around the galley,

straightening the tablecloth and brushing crumbs off chairs with her hands.

"What?" She looked up.

"Mom, what do you think we were talking about before Mr. Beeston came around?"

Mom shut one eye and rubbed her chin. "Heck—give me a minute." She looked worried for a moment, then laughed. "You know—I can't remember. Gone! Never mind. Now bring me the broom and dustpan. We can't leave the carpet like this."

I continued to stare at her. She'd forgotten! He *had* drugged her, after all! But how? And when?

"Come on, shake a leg. Or do I have to get them myself?"

I fetched the broom and pan out of the cupboard and handed them to her.

"Mom . . ." I tried again as she swept under the table. "Do you *really* not remem—"

"Emily." Mom sat up on her knees and spoke firmly. "A joke is a joke, and any joke is usually not funny after a while. Now, I don't want to hear any more nonsense about multicolored rocks, if you don't mind. I've got more important things to do than play along with your daydreams."

"But it's not a—"

"EMILY."

I knew that tone of voice. It meant it was time to shut up. I picked up the doughnut bags from the table and went to throw them away. Then I noticed some writing on one of the bags: *MPW.*

"Why does this one have your initials on it?" I asked.

"I don't know. Probably so he knows which doughnuts are mine."

"What difference does it make?"

"Come on, Emily, everybody knows I've got a sweet tooth. I always get the ones with more sugar."

"But can't you tell which ones have more sugar just by looking at them?"

"Emily, why are you being so difficult today? And what do you have against Mr. Beeston? I *won't* have you talking about him like this. I'm not listening to another word."

"But I don't understand! Why can't he just look in the bag?"

Mom ignored me. Then she started whistling, and I gave up and went back to my cabin. I took the bags with me. They held some kind of answer, I was sure of it—if only I could figure out what it was.

I stared so hard at her initials that my eyes started to water.

And then, as the letters blurred under my gaze, it hit me so hard that I nearly fell over. Of course! The memory drug!

He gave it to her in the doughnuts.

Chapter Eleven

hen I got home from school on Monday, I slumped on the sofa and threw my backpack on the floor. Mom was reading. "Did you have a nice day?" she asked, folding over the corner of the page and putting her book down.

"Mm." I got a glass of milk out of the fridge.

I could hardly stand to look at her. How was I ever going to make her believe me? Somehow I had to make her see for herself what Mr. Beeston was up to. *Plus* I still had to find my father.

A gentle rap on the roof startled me out of my thoughts. I clenched my fists. If that was Mr. Beeston, I'd—

"Hello, Emily," Millie said in a mysterious kind of way as she unwrapped herself from her large black cloak.

"Are you going out tonight?" I asked Mom.

"It's the Bay Residents' Council meeting. I told you last week."

"You did?"

"Nice to see I'm not the only one around here with the memory of a goldfish." She tweaked my cheek as she passed me.

I checked my watch. "But it's only six o'clock!"

"I need to get there early to open up. It's at the bookshop," she called from down the corridor. "Thanks for this, Millie," she added as she came back in with her coat. "Get out the sofa bed if I'm late."

"I might just do that," Millie replied. "My energy is a little depleted today. I think it's the new ginkgo biloba tablets on top of my shiatsu."

"Sounds likely," Mom said, doing up her coat. Another knock on the roof made me jump again.

"Heavens to Betsy, Emily, you're a bit twitchy tonight, aren't you?" Mom ruffled my hair as Mr. Beeston's face appeared at the door.

I froze.

"Only me," he said, scanning the room without coming in.

"You didn't tell me *he* was going," I whispered, grabbing at her coat while Mr. Beeston waited outside.

"Of course he's going—he's the chairman!"

she whispered back. "And he's offered to help me set up," she added. "Which is nice of him, by the way."

"Mom, I don't want you to go!"

"Don't want me to go? What on earth are you talking about?"

What could I say? How could I get her to believe me? She wouldn't hear a word against Mr. Beeston—the sweet, kind, lonely man. Well, I'd prove to her that he wasn't anything of the kind!

"I just—"

"Come on, now. Don't be a baby." She pried my fingers from her sleeve. "Millie's here to look after you. I'm just up at the shore if you need me urgently. And I mean *urgently.*" She gave me a quick peck, rubbed my cheek with her thumb—and was gone.

"How come you don't go to the Bay Residents' meetings, Millie?"

"Oh, I don't believe in all that democratic fuss and nonsense," she said, shifting me up the sofa so she could sit down.

We sat silently in front of the television. Once her first show had finished, I waited for her to tell me it was bedtime. But she didn't. I looked across at the sofa; she lay on her side, her eyes closed, mouth slightly open.

"Millie?" I whispered. No reply. She was fast asleep! When would I get an opportunity like this again? I had to do it.

The Great Mermer Reef might be too far to swim—but it wouldn't be too far by boat! And now was the perfect time. In fact, it might be my only chance.

Could I do it? *Really?* I looked at the clock. Half past eight. Mom wouldn't be back for ages yet, and Millie was fast asleep.

I grabbed the engine key from the peg and crept outside. There was probably another half an hour or so before it was dark. I could handle the darkness now anyway; I'd gotten used to the sea at night.

But would I remember how to operate the boat? I'd only done it a few times. We have to go around to Southpool Harbor every couple of years to get the hull checked out, and Mom usually lets me take it some of the way. We hardly ever use the sail. I don't know why we have it, really.

The pier was quiet except for all the masts clinking and chattering in the wind. I pulled at my hair, twisting it frantically around my fingers. I probably looked like somebody about to take their first bungee jump. But I simply had to do it, however dangerous or scary or insane it might be.

Uncoiling the ropes, I had one last look down the pier. Deserted . . .

Almost.

Someone was coming out of the arcade. I ducked below the mast and waited. It was Mandy's mom! She was heading down the pier, probably to the meeting. And a figure was standing in the doorway of the arcade. Mandy!

I ducked down again, waited for her to go back inside. Had she seen me?

The rope slackened in my hands—I was drifting away from the jetty. Close enough to jump back and pull the boat in again—but floating farther away by the second. *What should I do?* There was still time to abandon the whole thing.

Then a breeze lifted the front of the boat off the water and, without any more thinking on my part, the decision was made. I glanced back. She'd gone. I hurled the rope onto the jetty and turned the ignition key.

Nothing happened.

I tried again. It started this time, and I held my breath as its familiar *dunka dunka dunka* broke into the silence of the evening.

"HEY!"

I turned around.

"Fish girl!"

It was Mandy! She stepped onto our dock.

"What d'you think you're doing?" she called.

"Nothing!" *Nothing?* What kind of a stupid thing was that to say?

"Oh, I know. Are you running away now that Julia doesn't want to be your friend?"

"What?"

"She doesn't want to know you anymore, after you blew her off last weekend. Lucky she had me there to make her see *someone* cares about her feelings." Mandy paused as she let an evil smile crawl across her face. "Your mom knows you're taking the boat out, I assume?"

"Of course!" I said quickly. "I'm just moving it over to Southpool."

"Yeah. Shall we check?" She waved her cell phone in front of her.

"You wouldn't!"

"No? Want to make a bet? You think I haven't been *waiting* for an opportunity like this? Little miss goody-goody two shoes, making out like you're soooo sweet and innocent."

The boat bobbed farther away from the dock. "Why do you hate me so much?" I called over the engine.

"Hmm. Let me think." She put her finger dramatically to her mouth and looked away, as though talking to an audience. "She gets me grounded, steals my best friend, turns the swimming teacher against me. She's a great big fat SHOW-OFF!" Mandy looked back at me. "I really don't know."

Then she turned and started walking back up the jetty, waving her phone in the air.

"Mandy, don't! Please!"

"Maybe I will, maybe I won't," she called over her shoulder. "See ya."

What should I do? I couldn't go back. I *couldn't*. This was probably my one and only chance to find my father. And Mandy Rushton was NOT going to ruin it. I forced her words out of my mind. She wasn't going to stop me — she *wasn't*!

I turned my attention back to my plan.

Minutes later, I was edging away from the pier, holding the tiller and carefully navigating my way out of the harbor. I went over what I'd done when I'd driven the boat to Southpool — and tried hard to convince myself that what I was doing now really wasn't very different.

As I sailed out to sea, I looked back at Brightport Bay. The last rays of the sun winked and glinted on the water like tiny spotlights. Ocean spray dusted my hair.

I closed my eyes for a second while I thought about what I was doing. I had to find the Great

Mermer Reef. Based on the time Shona and I had gotten halfway there, I knew more or less where it was, so I studied the horizon and aimed for the section that was lighter than the rest. The part that would shimmer a hundred colors when I got close by.

It got dark very suddenly as we sliced slowly through the water. *King* never does anything in a hurry. My hand was getting cold, holding on to the tiller. And I was getting wet. *King* bounced on the water, gliding along with the swells, then rising and bumping down over the waves. It had been quite calm when I set off. The farther out I got, the more hilly the sea became.

Above me, stars appeared, one by one. Soon, the night sky was packed. A fat half-moon sat among them, its other half a silhouette, semivisible as though impatient for its turn to come.

King swayed from side to side, lumbering slowly through the peaks and troughs. Was I getting anywhere? I looked behind me. Brightport was miles away! If I closed one eye and held up my hand, I could hide the whole town behind my thumbnail.

Up and down we went, climbing the waves, bouncing on the swells, inching ever closer to the Great Mermer Reef.

My eyes watered as I strained to keep them on the patch of light on the horizon, shimmering and glowing and coming gradually closer. I let myself dream about Jake — about my dad.

I'd get into the prison, and we'd escape. Hiding him in the boat, we'd cruise back to the pier before anyone even realized he was gone. Then Mom would come home from the meeting. Dad would be waiting in the sea at the end of the pier, and I'd ask Mom to come for a walk with me. Then I'd leave her there on her own for a minute, and he would appear. They'd see each other, and it would be like they'd never been apart. Mom would remember everything, and we'd all live happily ever after. *Excellent* plan.

Excellent daydream, anyhow. A "plan" was something I didn't exactly have.

"EMILY!" A voice shattered my thoughts. I spun around, searching the night sky. There was a shape behind me — a long way away but coming nearer. A boat, one of those little motorboats with outboard engines that they hire out in the summer. As it got closer, I could see an outline of two people, one leaning forward in the front, one in the back at the tiller.

"Emily!" A woman's voice. And not just any woman. Mom!

Then I recognized the other voice.

"Come back here, young lady! Whatever you think you are doing, you had better stop it—and *now*!"

Mr. Beeston!

I shoved the tiller across and quickly swapped sides as the boat changed direction, pushing the throttle as far forward as it would go. *Come on, come on,* I prayed. The boat sputtered and chugged in reply but didn't speed up.

"What are you doing here?" I shouted over the engine and the waves.

"What am *I* doing here?" Mom called back. "Emily, what are YOU doing?"

"But your meeting!"

The motorboat edged closer. "The meeting got canceled when Mrs. Rushton's girl phoned in a state. She thought you might be in danger."

I should have known she'd do it! I don't know how I could have thought even for a moment that she wouldn't.

"I'm sorry, Mom," I called. "I've got to do this. You'll understand, honestly. Trust me."

"Oh, please come back, darling," Mom called. "Whatever it is, we can sort it out."

King's engine sputtered again and seemed to be slowing down. Seawater soaked my face as we bounced on the waves, rolling and peaking like a mountain range.

145

"Look what you're doing to your mother," Mr. Beeston shouted. "I won't have it, do you hear me? I won't allow it."

I ran my sleeve over my wet face. "You can't tell me what to do," I shouted back, anger pushing away my fear — and any desire to keep my stupid promise to Mr. Beeston. "It's not like you're my father or anything."

Mr. Beeston didn't reply. He was concentrating hard and had almost caught up with me. Meanwhile, the shimmering light on the horizon was glowing and growing bigger all the time. I could almost see the different colors. *Come on, King,* I said under my breath. *It's not much farther now.* I looked back at the motorboat. Mom was covering her face with her hands. Mr. Beeston held the tiller tight, his face all pinched and contorted.

"You remember my father?" I called to him. "You know, your 'best friend.' What kind of a person lies to their best friend's wife for years? *Huh?*"

"I don't know what foolish ideas you've gotten into your head, child, but you had better put an end to them right now. Before I put an end to them for you." Mr. Beeston's eyes shone like a cat's as he caught mine. "Can't you see how much you are upsetting your mother?"

"Upsetting my mother? Ha! Like *you* care!"

"Emily, *please*," Mom called, her arms stretched out toward me. "Whatever it is, we'll talk about it. Don't blame Mr. Beeston. He's only trying to help."

"Come *on, King!*" I said out loud as the engine crackled and popped. "Mom." I turned to face her. They were only a couple of yards away from me now. "Mr. Beeston isn't who he says he is. And he's *not* trying to help you."

Then the engine died.

"What's the *matter* with this thing?" I shouted.

"You know we never keep much diesel on board," Mom called. "It's a fire hazard."

"What? Who told you that?" I was in despair.

"I did," Mr. Beeston called. "Don't want you injuring yourselves, do I?" He smiled his creepy smile at me.

That was it. I stood up and lurched forward to grab the mast. I'd have to sail the rest of the way!

I uncleated the mainsheet to free the boom— that's the wooden pole that runs along the bottom of the sail. Then I undid the main halyard (the rope at the base of the mast) and hoisted the mainsail.

As a gust of wind filled the sail, the boom swung out wildly over the water. I grabbed for the mainsheet—that's the rope that controls the boom—but the gust sent its whole length running right out of the cleat and out of reach. I watched helplessly as my last hope unraveled with it.

"Oh, Emily, please stop it," Mom shouted as the boat lurched to the side. "You don't need to upset yourself like this. I know what it's about."

"*What?* If you know, what are you doing in there with him?"

"It's natural for you to feel like this, darling. Mr. Beeston told me about you being a little jealous, and how that might make you try to turn me against him. But he's just a friend. There's no need for you to go fretting like this."

The shimmering was really close now. I could see colors and lights dancing on the surface of the water. It was like a fireworks display. I groaned. "Mom, it's not—"

I broke off when I saw Mom's stricken face. It looked like those performance artists on the boardwalk who pretend to be statues. In a soft voice that I barely recognized, she said, "No one could ever take the place of your father." She was gazing wide-eyed at the lights on the water.

"*My father?*"

For a moment, everything stood completely still, like a photo. The sea stopped moving; Mr. Beeston let go of the tiller; my mom and I locked eyes as though seeing each other for the first time.

Then Mr. Beeston leaped into action. "That's it," he yelled. "I'm coming aboard."

"Wait!" I shouted as a wave caught the side of the boat. *King* lurched sideways, the sail swinging across to the other side.

Mr. Beeston had just pulled himself aboard when—*thwack!*—the boom swung back again and knocked him flying.

"Aaarrrgghh!" He clutched his head as he fell backward. Crashing to the deck with a thump, he lay flat on his back without moving.

Mom screamed and stood up. The motorboat rocked wildly.

"Mom—be careful!" I ran to the side and leaned over. "Get on," I shouted. She was alongside *King*.

Mom didn't move.

"You have to get on board. Come on, Mom." I held an arm out. "I'll help you."

"I—I can't," she said woodenly.

"You can, Mom. You've *got* to." I scrabbled around in the bench seat and pulled out a life jacket. *King* rocked like the coin-operated bucking bronco at the arcade. The sail was still waving off to the side, the mainsheet dangling hopelessly out of reach. Holding tight to the railing, I threw the life jacket to Mom. "You'll be fine," I called. "Just get on board fast before you drift away."

She stared at me.

"Do it!"

Mom stood up in her rocky boat, the life jacket on, and suddenly lunged for the steps. I grabbed her hand as she pulled herself onto the deck.

"Oh, Emily," she said. "I'm so sorry."

"What for?"

"It's all my fault," Mom said, holding on to me with one hand and the railing with the other as we swayed from side to side.

"Of course it's not your fault, Mom. If it's anyone's fault, it's Mr. Beeston's. He's not what he seems, Mom; he's been—"

Mom put her finger over my lips. "I know why we're here."

"You—you—"

"I remember." Mom pulled me toward her and held me tight. Over her shoulder, I could see the water shimmering and sparkling like an electric light show. The Great Mermer Reef.

I wriggled out of Mom's grasp. "You remember—what?"

Mom hesitated. "It's all a bit hazy," she said.

All at once, the sky exploded with light. "Look!" I pointed behind her. Pink lights danced below the water while a dozen colors jumped in the air above it.

"I know this place," Mom said, her voice shaking. "He—he brought me here."

"Who? Mr. Beeston?" I glanced nervously across at him. He still hadn't moved. Mom clutched the railing as the boat tilted again, and I made my way over to join her. Her face seemed to be covered in spray from the sea, but when I looked more closely, I realized it wasn't seawater at all. It was tears. "On our first anniversary," she said.

She'd been here with my dad?

"He told me this was where they would take him when they caught him."

"*Who* would take him?"

"If they ever found out about us. He knew they'd get him in the end. We both knew it, but we couldn't stop. Because we loved each other so much."

Mom's body sagged; I put my arms around her.

"I'm going to find him," I said, holding her tighter. "That's why I took the boat. I did it for all of us."

"I can't bear it," she said. "I can remember everything now. How could I have forgotten him? He was taken away because he loved me, and I forgot all about him. How can I ever forgive myself?"

"Mom, it's not your fault! You didn't just *forget* him."

"I did," she gulped. "You know I did. You asked about him, and I didn't even know. I couldn't remember anything."

"But you weren't to blame."

Mom wiped a curtain of wet hair off her face and looked at me. "Who was, then?"

I nodded a thumb behind me. "Mr. Beeston," I whispered.

"Oh, Emily. Don't start with that claptrap again!"

"It's NOT claptrap!" I tried to keep my voice down. I didn't want him to wake up and ruin everything. "It's true," I whispered. "He's not what he seems."

"Emily, please don't make this worse than it is."

"Mom, *listen* to me," I snapped.

She caught my eyes for just a second, but then looked at Mr. Beeston. "We should see how he is." Mom shook herself free from my grasp and stumbled along the deck to him.

"He'll be fine," I said. "Don't worry about him."

Mom ignored me and crouched down next to him. I crouched down beside her as she leaned over his chest and listened. Then she looked up at me, her face paler than the million stars shining above us.

"Oh, my God," she said. "I think we've killed him."

Chapter Twelve

*T*here's no heartbeat," Mom said, rocking back on her heels.

I opened my mouth. What could I say? A second later, the side door suddenly swung open with a bang. Mom and I grabbed each other's arms.

Millie's face appeared in the doorway.

"Do you think there's anything either of you would like to share with me?" she asked as she hitched up her long skirt and clambered out onto the deck.

Mom and I looked at each other.

"I'm sensing some . . . disorientation."

"No time now," Mom said, beckoning Millie over. "We have to do something. Mr. Beeston has had an accident. I think he's dead." She clapped a fist to her mouth.

Millie struggled over to join us, slipping and swaying on the wet deck. "Let's have a look," she said, kneeling down beside Mr. Beeston. She undid his coat and lifted up his sweater. He was wearing a thick, padded jacket of some sort underneath. I flinched as I noticed a picture of Neptune's trident sewn onto a pocket.

"Armored vest?" Millie murmured. "Now why in the blinking cosmos would he need something like that?"

I didn't say anything.

"Well, that's your answer, anyway, Mary P." Millie turned to Mom. "You wouldn't hear a ten-ton truck through that."

Just then, the boat jolted to the side. I slid across the deck and bumped against the bench seat.

"Emily, get the tiller!" Millie ordered, suddenly in charge.

I did what she said, not that it made much difference. The boat dipped and swayed helplessly in the waves.

Millie reached under Mr. Beeston's back and unbuckled the vest. Lifting it off, she bent over him, her ear to his chest. Mom came over and grabbed my hand while we waited.

"Absolutely fine," Millie announced a few seconds later.

"Oh, thank heavens." Mom hugged me. "I'd never have forgiven myself if anything had happ—"

"He just needs his chakras realigned," Millie continued. "A bit of reflexology should do it."

She pulled off Mr. Beeston's shoes and socks and settled herself at his feet. Placing her hands across her large chest, she closed her eyes and breathed in deeply. Then she lifted his right foot and started to massage it. A moment later, his foot twitched. She carried on massaging. He twitched again, this time his leg jerking about in the air. The twitching and jerking spread up his body until it reached his face, and he started giggling. He was soon laughing loudly. Eventually, he leaped up, screaming, "Stop, stop!"

Millie released his foot and stood up. "Never fails," she said, wiping her hands on her skirt and heading back inside. "Give me a minute or two. Reflexology always drains my chi."

Mom went over to Mr. Beeston. "Thank heavens you're all right."

Mr. Beeston straightened his coat as he glanced at me. "Just a scratch," he said. "No harm done." A red path was worming its way down the side of his head.

My hand tightened on the tiller. "No harm done? Do you *think*?"

"Emily, this is no time to start your nonsense again. What on earth have you got against the poor man?"

"What have I got against the poor man? Where do you want me to start?" I looked him in the eyes. "Is it the fact that he's been wiping your memory since the day I was born, or the fact that he's been spying on us *forever*?"

Mom didn't speak for a second. Then she laughed. "Oh, Emily, I've never heard such—"

"It's true." Mr. Beeston spoke, his eyes still locked onto mine. "She's right."

"What?" Mom held tightly on to the mast with one hand; with the other, she clutched her chest.

"It's too late, Mary P. I can't pretend anymore. And I won't. Why should I?"

"What are you talking about?" Mom looked from Mr. Beeston to me. I didn't say anything. Let him explain it.

Mr. Beeston sat down on the bench opposite me. "It was for your own good," he said. "All of you." His hands were still clutching his head, his hair all mangled and tangled up with blood and sweat and seawater.

"What was for my own good?" Mom's face hardened and grew thinner as she spoke.

"The two worlds — they don't belong together. It doesn't work." He leaned forward, his head almost between his knees. "And I should know," he added, his voice almost a whisper. "You're not the only one to grow up without a father." He spoke to the floor. "Mine disappeared the minute I was born, he did. Just like all the others. Fishermen. All very nice having an unusual girlfriend, isn't it? Taming a beautiful siren. Show off to your friends about that, can't you?"

A tear fell from his face onto the deck. He brushed his cheek roughly. "But it's a bit different when your own son sprouts a tail! Don't want to know then, do you?"

"What are you saying?" Mom's voice was as tight as her face, her hand still gripping the mast. The sea lifted us up and down; the sail still flapped uselessly over the water.

"You can't put humans and merfolk together and expect it to work. It doesn't. All you get is pain." Finally, Mr. Beeston raised his head to look at us. "I was trying to save you from that. From what I've been through myself."

The boat shook violently as another wave hit

us. I clutched the tiller more tightly. "I told you he wasn't really your friend," I hissed to Mom, the wind biting my face.

"Friendship?" he spat. "Loyalty is all that matters. To Neptune and the protection of the species. That is my life." He held up a fist across his chest. Then he glanced at Mom. His fist fell open. "That's to say," he faltered, "I mean—look, I never wanted to . . ." His voice trailed away, his chin dropping to his chest.

Mom looked like she'd been hit over the head herself. Her face was as white as the sail and her body had gone rigid. "I often wondered why they got a new lighthouse keeper so suddenly," she said. "No one ever did quite explain what happened to old Bernard. You just appeared one day. And something else I've never really thought about—you never invited me in. Not once in twelve years. Not like Bernard. We used to go up there all the time when I was younger, up on the top deck, looking all around with binoculars and telescopes. But you—my *friend*—you always kept the door closed to me. And to think I actually felt sorry for you."

The boat was starting to career up and down, the sea getting wilder as we held the tiller together. She put her hand on my arm. "He saw you once," she said quietly to me in the darkness. "At Rainbow Rocks. Held you against his chest at the water's edge. I wouldn't let him take you in the water. Maybe if he had . . ." Her words slipped away as she looked at me, her hair plastered across her face with seawater. "I've lost twelve years."

I bit my lip, tasting salty water.

"Hidden from my own mind like everything else." She stood up and inched over toward Mr. Beeston. "You stole my life from me," she said, anger creeping into her voice. "You're nothing but a thief! A nasty, rotten, scheming THIEF!"

"Hey now, hold on a minute!" Mr. Beeston stood up. "I've been *good* to you. I've looked *after* you. You should hear what some of them wanted to—"

"You had no right." Mom shook his arm, tears rolling down her cheeks. "He is my husband. Who do you think you are?"

"Who do I think I am? I know *exactly* who I am! I'm Charles—" He stopped. Glanced briefly at Mom and took a breath. Then he suddenly thrust out his chin, his eyes clear and focused for a brief moment. "I am Charles Finright Beeston, adviser to Neptune, and I have conducted my duties with pride and loyalty for twelve years."

"How dare you!" Mom snapped. "All these years, pretending to be my friend."

"Now, wait a minute. I wasn't—I mean, I *am* your friend. You think I didn't care about you? It's for your own good. We had to put a stop to it. It's wrong, unnatural—dangerous, even—don't you see?"

Mom paused for a moment, then flew at him, bashing her fists against his chest. "All I can see is a beast. A despicable worm!" she screamed.

Mr. Beeston backed away from her. As she went for him, Mom tripped and nearly fell flat on her face. She stopped herself by clutching a rope tied onto the mast. The rope ripped loose in her hand, tearing the canvas that held the boom in place. All three of us watched as the boom drifted away from us and the sail flapped over the water even more uselessly than before.

We'd never get *anywhere* now.

I tried to hold the tiller steady as the boat lurched again. The waves were getting choppier, throwing us all over the deck. "We need to do something," I said, my voice quivering.

"I'll fix it," Mr. Beeston said, his words slow and deliberate, his eyes cold and determined. Then he turned and walked along the side of the boat to the door, holding the railing as the boat rocked.

"Mom, what are we going to do?" I asked as the waves rolled us from side to side again. Mom's steely eyes followed Mr. Beeston down the boat.

"Forget him," I said. "We need to think of

something or we'll never get home again — never mind seeing Jake."

"Oh, Emily, do you really think we're going to find—"

"I know where he is," I said. "We can do it. We're nearly there!"

Mom pulled her eyes away from Mr. Beeston. "OK. Come on," she said, snapping into action. She lifted the lid up off the bench, rummaged through hose pipes and foot pumps. "Put this on." She passed me a life jacket that was much too small for me.

"Mom. I don't need one."

"Just to be on the safe—" She stopped and looked at my legs. "Oh, golly," she said. "You mean you can . . . you're a—"

"Didn't you know?" I asked. "Didn't you ever suspect?"

She shook her head sadly. "How could I have? Maybe somewhere in the back of my mind, but I . . ." A massive wave crashed over the side, washing away the rest of her sentence and drenching us both.

"Mom, I'm scared," I yelped, wiping the spray off my face. "It's too far even for me to swim back from here. We'll never make it."

As I spoke, the boat gave one more enormous lurch to the side. I fell to the floor, slipped across the deck. As I clutched the railing and tried to pull myself up again, I noticed a shape in the sea in front of us. A fin! That was it, then. The boat was going to capsize; we'd be eaten by sharks!

Mom has never been religious, and she's always said it's up to me to make my mind up when I was ready. I never was before. Until then.

Without even wondering what to say, I put my hands together, closed my eyes, and prayed.

Chapter Thirteen

*M*y lips moved soundlessly behind my hands, scanning all the words I could summon up: half-remembered prayers from half-listened-to visits to friends' churches. *Why didn't I pay more attention?* I asked myself. When I got to, "Thy will be done on earth as it is in heaven," I couldn't for the life of me think what came next.

"Emily!" Mom was tugging at my arm.

I shook her off. "I'm busy."

Mom tugged again. "I think you should take a look."

I opened my fingers wide enough to sneak a peek between them. It was hard to see anything, actually; the boat was careening up and down so much. I felt even more giddy and reached out for the railing. That was when I heard it—someone calling my name! I looked at Mom even though I knew it hadn't been her. Holding the railing beside me, she pointed out to the mountainous waves with her free hand.

"Emily!" a familiar voice called again. Then a familiar head poked out above the waves, bobbing up and down in the swell. It was Shona! She grinned and waved at me.

"What are you doing here?" I shouted.

"It's Monday. You didn't show up at the rocks. I've been looking for you."

"Oh, Shona, I'm so sorry."

"When you didn't come, I had a funny feeling you'd be doing something like this!"

"I've messed it all up," I called, my throat clogged up. "We're never going to get there now."

"Don't be too sure!" she called back. "Throw me a rope. I'll see if I can tow you."

"But the boat must weigh a ton!"

"Not in water it doesn't, so long as I can get some momentum going with my tail. We do it in P.E. all the time."

"Are you sure?"

"Let's just give it a try, OK?"

"OK," I said uncertainly, and with a flick of her

tail, she was gone. Shona's tail! Of course! Not a shark fin at all!

I made my way up to the front deck, untied a rope and threw it down. Mom came with me. I tried to avoid looking at her, but I could feel her eyes boring into the side of my face. "What?" I asked without turning to her.

"Is she a . . . friend of yours?" Mom asked carefully.

"Mmm-hmm."

Mom sighed. "We've got a lot of catching up to do, don't we, sweetie?"

I carried on looking ahead. "Do you think I'm a freak?"

"A freak?" Mom reached over to pick up one of my hands. "Darling, I couldn't be more proud."

Still holding my hand, she put her other arm around me. The boat had leveled out again, and I snuggled into Mom's shoulder; wet, cold, and frightened. Neither of us spoke for a few minutes while we watched Shona pull us ever nearer to the prison — and Jake.

A few moments later, Mom and I caught each other's eyes, the same thought coming into our minds. *Where is Mr. Beeston?*

"He might be hiding," Mom said.

"I think we should check it out."

Mom stood up. "I'll go."

"I'm coming with you."

She didn't argue as we stood up and edged our way down the side of the boat. The deck was still soaking, and it was a slippery trip to the door.

I pushed my head inside. Mr. Beeston was standing by a window in the saloon, his back to us, the window pushed open and a large shell in his hands.

"A conch? What on earth is he doing with that?" Mom whispered.

Mr. Beeston put the shell to his mouth.

"Talking to it?" I whispered back.

He muttered quietly into the shell.

"What's he saying?" I looked at Mom.

She shook her head. "Stay here," she ordered. "Crouch down behind the door. Don't let him see you. I'll be back in a second."

"Where are you going?" But she'd slid back outside. I hunched low and waited for her to return.

Two minutes later, Mom was back with a huge fishing net in her arms. "What are you doing with—"

Mom shushed me with a finger over her lips and crept inside. She beckoned me to follow.

Mr. Beeston was still leaning out of the window, talking softly into his conch. Mom inched toward him, and I tiptoed behind her. When we were right behind him, she passed me one end of the net and mouthed, "Three . . . two . . ."

When she mouthed, "One," I threw my side of the net over Mr. Beeston's head. Mom did the same on her side.

"What the—" Mr. Beeston dropped the conch and fell back into a chair.

"Quick, wrap it around him," Mom urged.

I ran in a circle around him, dragging the net with me. Mr. Beeston struggled and lashed out, but we kept wrapping, like when someone's dog runs up to you in the park and knots your ankles together with its leash. Only better.

Mom pushed him back into his chair and lifted his legs up. "Get his feet," she demanded, dodging his kicks. I slipped under his legs with the net. There was still tons of net left over, so I ran around him again, fastening him to his chair. Mom grabbed my end of the net and tied it securely to hers, and we stood back to admire our work.

"You won't get away with this, you know," Mr. Beeston said, struggling and trying to kick out. All he managed to do was make the chair wobble on its legs.

"I wouldn't do that if I were you," a voice suddenly boomed from the other side of the saloon.

We all turned to see Millie clambering up off the sofa. She stood majestically in the center of the room, arms raised as though waiting for a voice from heaven.

"I put my back out for weeks once, falling backward off a chair. Had to see a chiropractor for six months. And they're not cheap, I can tell you." She swept into the galley. "OK, who's ready for a nice, hot cup of tea?" she asked. "I'm parched."

The sea had calmed down, and the three of us drank our tea on the front deck. The sky sparkled with dancing colors. As we watched, the lights danced faster and faster. Pink, blue, green, gold—every color you could imagine, in a million different shades, jumping around, stabbing at the water as though it were too hot for them to settle. It seemed as though the lights were speaking—in an alien language that I had no chance of understanding.

Millie looked at them intently for a while, then sniffed her cup of tea. "I don't know what they put in this," she said, draining the cup and heading back inside, "but I'll have to get some."

Mom buttoned up her coat, her eyes fixed on the lights.

"All of this," she whispered. "I remember it all."

"Do you remember my dad?" I asked nervously, recalling what happened last time I had tried to find out about him.

"We never meant it to happen," she said, her eyes misting over. "He told me right from the start how dangerous it would be. It was after the regatta."

"The regatta?"

"We used to hold it every year, but that was the last one. I don't know how we went so wrong, but we did. I went with Mrs. Brig, who used to run the Sea View B and B. She had a little two-person yacht. We got into trouble on the rocks. That was when I met Jake." She looked at me for the first time. "Your father," she added before looking away again. "I don't know what happened to Mrs. Brig. She moved away soon afterward. But Jake and I — well, I couldn't help it. I went back to Rainbow Rocks every night."

"Rainbow Rocks?"

"Well, near enough. I waited by those rocks you took me to. You know?"

"Yes. I know."

She smiled sadly. "You knew more than I did. But not anymore. I remember it all."

"So did he come?"

She shook her head. "I waited every night. Then one night I told myself I'd give it one last try before giving up for good. I just wanted to thank him." She turned to face me again. "He saved my life, Emily."

"And he came?"

She smiled. "He'd been there every night."

"Every night? But you said—"

"He had hidden himself. But he had seen me every time I went. Said he couldn't keep away either, but he couldn't bring himself to talk to me."

"Why not?"

"You know, that first time, when he helped us . . . he never got out of the water." Mom laughed. "I thought at the time, what an amazing swimmer!"

"So you didn't know . . ."

"He thought I'd be shocked, or disgusted or something."

I took a deep breath. "And were you?"

Mom put her hand out to me, cupped my chin. "Emily, when I saw his tail, when I knew what he was—I think that was the moment I fell in love with him."

"Really?"

She smiled. "Really."

"So then what happened?"

"Well, that was when I left home."

"Left home? You mean Nan and Granddad used to live here?"

Mom swallowed hard. "I remember why we argued, now. They wouldn't believe me. They thought I was crazy. They tried to make me see a psychiatrist."

"And you wouldn't."

She shook her head. "So then they sold off everything and moved away from the ocean for good. They gave me an ultimatum—either I came with them, or . . ."

"Or they didn't want to know anything about you." I finished her sentence for her.

"The boat was your granddad's. He didn't want anything more to do with it—or me. Said he'd had enough of the sea to last him a lifetime."

"He gave it to you?"

She nodded. "I like to think the gesture meant that a part of him knew it was true. That he knew I wasn't crazy."

"And what about Jake?"

"I used to sail out to sea to meet him, or around to Rainbow Rocks."

"Was that where they caught him?"

She dabbed the edge of her eye with the palm of her hand. "I never believed it would happen," she said. "Somehow, I thought everything would be all right. Especially after you were born."

"How come they didn't make you move away?"

"Maybe they wanted to keep an eye on us."

"On me, you mean?"

She pulled me close, hugging me tight. "Oh, Emily," she whispered into my hair. "You only saw him once. You were so tiny."

"I'm going to see him again, Mom," I said, my voice coming out in a squeak. "I'm going to find him."

She smiled at me through misty eyes.

"I *am*."

A moment later, I noticed Shona swimming around to the side of the boat. "We're nearly there," she called. "Are you coming in?"

I looked at Mom. "Is it OK?" I asked.

For an answer, she pulled me tighter—then she let me go.

I ran inside and changed into my swimsuit. Millie came back out with me. I perched on the edge of the boat. "See you." I smiled.

Mom swallowed hard and held Millie's hand as I jumped into the water. Within seconds I felt my tail form. My legs melted and stretched, spreading warmth through my whole body. I waved to Mom and Millie as they watched me from the front deck.

"Look!" I shouted, then ducked under the water. I flicked my tail as gracefully as I could, waving it from side to side while I stretched out in a downward handstand. When I came back up,

Mom was clapping. "Beautiful," she called, wiping her hand across her eye. She blew me a kiss as I grinned at her. Millie's eyes widened. She shook her head, then picked up Mom's cup of tea and finished that one off, too.

"Are you ready?" Shona asked.

"As ready as I'll ever be," I replied, and we set off.

The Great Mermer Reef isn't like anything you're ever likely to see in your life. It's the highest, widest, longest wall in the world—in the universe, probably—made out of rainbow-colored coral, miles and miles from anywhere, smack in the middle of the sea.

You don't realize what it is at first. It feels like the end of the world, stretching up and down and across, farther than you can see in every direction. I shielded my eyes from the brightness. It reminded me of the school dance we had at our graduation at the end of last year. They'd borrowed a machine that threw disco lights across the room, swirling around and changing color in time to the music. The Great Mermer Reef was a bit like that, but about a million times bigger and brighter, and the colors swirled and flashed even more.

And somehow, we had to get past it! It was the only way to the prison.

As we got closer, the swirling lights became laser-beam rays, shooting out at every angle from jagged layers of coral heaped upon coral.

Sharp, spiky rocks were piled all the way up to the surface and higher, with soft, rubbery bushes buried in every crevice in the brightest purples and yellows and greens you've ever seen. A moving bush like a silver Christmas tree flapped toward us. Two spotted shrimp dragged a starfish along the seabed. All around us, fish and plants bustled and rustled about. But we were stuck — in a fortress of bubbles and bushes and rocks. We couldn't even climb over the top; it was way too high and rough. Above the water, the coral shot diamond rays where it sparkled with stones like cut glass. I was never, ever going to find him.

"It's hopeless," I said, trying desperately not to cry. It was like that darn game about going on a bear hunt. You keep coming across things that you've got to get past. "We can't get over it; we can't get under it."

Shona was by my side, her eyes bright like the coral. "We'll have to go through it!" she exclaimed, her words gurgling away in multicolored bubbles. "There's bound to be a gap somewhere. Come on." She pulled at my arm and dove deeper.

We weaved in and out of spaghetti-fringed tubes and swam into bushes with tentacles that opened wide enough to swim inside. But it was the same thing every time: a dead end.

I perched on a rock, ready to give up, while Shona scaled the coral, tapping it with her fingers like a builder testing the thickness of a wall. A huge shoal of fish that had been sheltering in a cave suddenly darted out as one, writhing and spinning like a kaleidoscope pattern. I stared, transfixed.

"I think I've found something." Shona's voice jolted me out of my trance. She was scratching at the coral, and I swam closer to see what she'd found.

"Look!" She scrabbled some more. Bits of coral crumbled away like dust in her fingers. She pulled me around and made me look closer. "What can you see?" she asked.

"I can't see anything."

"Look harder."

"At what?"

Shona pushed her face close to mine and pointed into the jagged hole she'd scraped away at. She pushed her fist into it and pulled out some more dust; it floated away, dancing around us as she scraped.

"It's a weak point," she said. "This stuff's millions of years old. I'm sure they have people who check the perimeter and maintain it and stuff, but there's always going to be a bit of it that they miss."

I pushed my own hand into the hole and scrabbled at it with my fingertips as though I were digging a hole into sand. It felt different from the rest of the wall. Softer. I pushed farther.

Scrabbling and scraping, we'd soon scooped all the way up to our shoulders, white dust clouds billowing around us.

"Now what?" I asked.

"Make it wider. Big enough to swim into."

We worked silently at the hole. The coral didn't glint and glisten with colors once we got inside it. We scraped and scratched in darkness.

Eventually, as my arms were going numb and my whole body was aching and itching from the dust particles swirling all around us, Shona grabbed my arm. I looked up and saw it. The tiniest flicker of light ahead of us.

"We're through," I gasped.

"Nearly. Come on."

Filled with hope, I punched my fist deep into the hole, scratching my hand as I pulled at the wall. The hole grew bigger and rounder, eventually large enough to get through. I turned to Shona.

"Go on. You first," she urged. "You're smaller than me."

I scrunched my arms tightly against my body and flicked my tail gently. Then, scratching my arms and tail on the sides, I slid through the hole.

Once on the other side, I turned and carried on scraping so Shona could get through as well. But nothing came away in my hands. No dust. I cut my fingers against jagged rock.

"I can't make it bigger," I called through the hole.

"Me, neither," Shona replied, her voice echoing inside the dark cavern I'd left behind.

"Try to squeeze through."

Shona's head came close to the hole. "It's my shoulders. I'm too big," she said. "I'll never manage it."

"Should I pull you?"

"I just can't do it." Shona backed away from the gap. "I'll get stuck—and then you won't be able to get back through."

"I can't do it without you." My voice shook as it rippled through the water to her.

"I'll wait here!"

"Promise?"

"Promise. I'll wait at the end of the tunnel."

I took a deep breath. "This is it, then," I said, poking my head into the opening.

"Good luck."

"Yeah." I backed away from the hole again. "And thanks," I added. "For everything. You're the bestest best friend anyone could want."

Shona's eyes shone brighter in the darkness. "*You* are, you mean."

There was *no way* I'd been as good a friend as she had. I didn't tell her that, though—I didn't want her to change her mind!

Then I turned away from the hole. Leaving the Great Mermer Reef behind me, I swam toward a dark maze of caves covered in sharp, jagged pieces of coral.

"I'm going to see my dad," I whispered, trying out the unfamiliar thought, and desperately hoping it could be true.

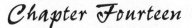

Chapter Fourteen

I swam cautiously away from the reef, glancing nervously around me as I moved ever closer to the prison. A solitary manta ray slid along the ground, flapping its fins like a cape. Small packs of moody-looking fish with open jaws threaded slowly through the silent darkness, glancing at me as they passed. Ahead of me, a barrel of thick blackness rotated slowly. Then suddenly, it parted! Thousands of tiny fish scattered and reformed into two spinning balls. Beyond them, a dark gray shadow, bigger than me and shaped like a submarine, moved silently between them.

I held my breath as the shark passed by.

As I drew nearer to the prison, the water grew darker. Dodging between rocks and weeds, I finally reached the prison door. It looked like the wide-open mouth of a gigantic whale, with sharp white teeth filling the gap. In front of the door, two creatures silently glided from side to side, slow and mean, with a beady eye on each side of their mallet-shaped heads. Hammerhead sharks.

I'd *never* get past them. Maybe there was another entrance.

I remembered the note in Dad's file. "East Wing," it had said. It was a shame there wasn't one of those *You are here* signs, like you get at the mall.

I figured I'd been heading west since I'd set off from Brightport, because I'd been chasing the setting sun all the way. Shona and I had turned right from the boat to head toward the reef, which meant I should now be facing north.

I turned right again to go east. In front of me was a long tunnel attached to the main cave. It reminded me of those service stations on the highway — the kind on the median that join the two sides together. Apart from the fact that this was made of rock, that is, and it didn't appear to have any windows, and was about fifty feet under the sea. The East Wing?

Swimming carefully from one lump of coral to another and hiding behind every rock I could find, I made it to the tunnel. But there was no entrance. I swam all the way along it, right to the end. Still no opening.

The front gate must be the only way in. I'd come this far for nothing! There was *no way* I'd get past those sharks.

I started to swim back along the other side of the tunnel. Perhaps there'd be a doorway on this side.

But as I made my way along the slimy walls, I heard a swishing noise behind me. The sharks! Without stopping to think, I flicked my tail and zoomed straight down the side so I was underneath the tunnel itself. Pressing myself up against the wall, I wrapped a huge piece of seaweed around my body. Two hammerheads sliced past without stopping, and I inched my way back up again, scaling the edge with my hands and looking around me all the way. A minute later, I noticed something I hadn't seen earlier. There was a gap. I could see an oval shape about half my height and slightly wider than my shoulders with three thick, gray bars running down it. They looked like whalebone. The nearest thing I'd found to a way in — it had to be worth a try.

I tugged at the bars. Rock solid. I tried to swim between them. I could get my head through, but my shoulders were too big to follow. This wasn't going to work.

Unless I swam through on my side. . . .

I tried again, coming at the bars sideways. But it was no good. I couldn't squeeze my face through the gap. I never realized my nose stuck out that much!

I held on to the bars, flicking my tail as I thought. Then it hit me. How could I have been so stupid? I turned to face them. Just like before, I edged my head through the bars, as slowly and carefully as I could. All I needed to do now was flip onto my side and pull the rest of my body through.

But what if I got stuck—my head on one side, my body on the other, caught forever with my neck in these railings?

Before I had time to talk myself out of it, I swiveled my body onto its side. I banged my chin, and my neck rubbed on the bars—but I'd done it! I swished my tail as gently as possible and gradually eased my body through the gap.

I thought back to the time when we were changing to go swimming and how I hadn't wanted anyone to see my skinny body. Maybe being a little sticklike wasn't such a bad thing, after all.

I rubbed my eyes as I got used to the darkness. I'd landed in a tiny round bubble of a room, full of seaweed mops hanging on fish hooks all around me.

I swam to the door and turned a yellow knob. The door creaked open. Which way? The corridor was a long, narrow cave. Closing the door behind me, I noticed a metal plate in the top corner. *NW: N 874.* North Wing? I must have gotten my calculations wrong!

I swam along the silent corridor, passing closed doors on either side. *N 867, N 865.* Each one was the same—a big round plate of metal, like a submarine door; a brass knob below a tiny round window in the center. No glass, just fishbone bars dividing each window into an empty game of tic-tac-toe.

Should I look through one?

As I approached the next door, I swished up to the window and peeked in. A merman with a huge hairy stomach and long black hair in a ponytail swam over to the window. "Can I help you?" he asked, an amused glint in his eye. He had a ship tattooed on his arm; a fat brown tail flickered behind him.

"Sorry!" I flipped myself over and darted away. This was impossible! I wasn't even in the right wing. And there were scary criminals behind those doors! Which was only to be expected, I suppose. This was a prison, after all.

Suddenly, I heard a swooshing noise. Hammerheads! Coming nearer. I flicked my tail as hard as I could and swam to the end of the corridor. I had to get around the bend before they saw me!

With one last push of my tail, I zoomed around the corner—into an identical tunnel.

Identical except for one thing. The numbers all started with *E*. The East Wing!

I swam carefully up to the first door. *E 924*. I tried to remember the number from that note in Mr. Beeston's files. Why hadn't I written it down?

An old merman with a beard and a raggedy limp tail was inside the cell, facing away from me. I moved on. *E 926, E 928*. Would I ever find him?

Just then, two mallet-shaped heads appeared around the corner. I hurled myself up against the next door, frantically twisting the brass knob. To my amazement, it wasn't locked! The door swung open. Banking on the odds that whoever occupied it would be less scary than the sharks, I backed into the room and quietly shut the door. The whooshing noise came past the moment I'd closed it. I leaned my head against the door in relief.

"That was a lucky escape."

Who said that? I swung around to see a merman sitting on the edge of a bed made of seaweed. He was leaning over a small table and seemed to be working on something, his sparkly purple tail flickering gently.

I looked at him, but I didn't move from the door. He appeared to put the end of a piece of thread in his mouth and then tied a knot in the other end.

"Got to keep myself busy somehow," he said somewhat apologetically.

I slunk around the edges of the bubble-shaped room, still keeping my distance. The thread he was sewing with looked as if it was made of gold, with beads of some kind strung on it in rainbow colors.

"You're making a necklace?"

"Bracelet, actually. Got a problem with that?" The merman looked up for the first time, and I backed away instinctively. *Don't make fun of criminals whose cells you've just barged into,* I told myself. Never a good idea if you're planning to get out again in one piece.

Except he didn't look like a criminal. Not how I usually imagine a criminal to look, anyway. He didn't look mean and hard. And he *was* making jewelry. He had short black hair, kind of wavy, a tiny ring in one ear. A white vest with a blue prison jacket over it. His tail sparkled as much as the bracelet. As I looked at him, he ran his hand through his hair. There was something familiar about the way he did it, although I couldn't think what. I twiddled with my hair as I tried to —

I looked harder at him. As he squinted back at me, I noticed a tiny dimple appear below his left eye.

It couldn't be . . .

The merman put his bracelet down and slithered off his bed. I backed away again as he came toward me. "I'll scream," I said.

He stared at me. I stared back.

"How in the sea did you find me?" he said, in a different kind of voice from earlier. This one sounded like he had molasses blocking up his throat or something.

I looked into his face. Deep brown eyes. My eyes.

"Dad?" a tiny voice squeaked from over the other side of the cell somewhere. It might have been mine.

The merman rubbed his eyes. Then he hit himself on the side of the head. "I knew it would happen one day," he said, to himself more than me. "No one does time in this place without going a little bit crazy." He turned away from me. "I'm dreaming, that's all."

But then he turned back around. "Pinch me," he said, swimming closer. I recoiled a little.

"Pinch me," he repeated.

I pinched him, and he jumped back. "Youch! I didn't say pull my skin off." He rubbed his arm and looked up at me again. "So you're real?" he said.

I nodded.

He swam in a circle around me. "You're even more beautiful than I'd dreamed," he said. "And I've dreamed about you a lot, I can tell you."

I still couldn't speak.

"I never wanted you to see me in this place." He swam around his cell, quickly putting his jewelry things away. He picked up some magazines off the floor and shoved them into a crack in the wall; he threw a vest under his bed. "No place for a young girl."

Then he swam back and came really close to me; he held his hand up to my face, and I forced myself not to move.

He cradled the side of my face in his palm, stroking my dimple with his thumb, and wiped the tears away as they mingled with the seawater.

"Emily," he whispered at last. It was him. My dad!

A second later, I clutched him as tightly as I could, and he was holding me in his strong arms. "A mermaid as well," he murmured into my hair.

"Only some of the time," I said.

"Figures."

He loosened his arms and held me away from him. "Where's your mother?" he asked suddenly. "Is she here? Is she all right?" He dropped his arms to his sides. "Has she met someone else?"

I inched closer to him. "Of course she hasn't met anyone else!"

"My Penny." He smiled.

"Penny?"

"My lucky penny. That's what I always called her. Guess it wasn't too accurate in the end." Then he smiled. "But she hasn't forgotten me?"

"Um . . ." How was I supposed to answer that! "She still loves you." Well, she did, didn't she? She must, or she wouldn't have been so upset when she remembered everything. "And she hasn't *really* forgotten you — at least, not anymore."

"Not anymore?"

"Listen, I'll tell you everything." And I did. I told him about the memory drugs and Mr. Beeston and about what had happened when I took Mom to Rainbow Rocks. And about our journey to the Great Mermer Reef.

"So she's here?" he broke in. "She's that close, right now?"

I nodded. He flattened his hair down, spun around in circles, and swam away from me.

"Dad." *Dad! I still couldn't get used to that.* "She's waiting for me. She can't get into the prison." I followed him over to his table. "She can't swim," I added softly.

He burst out laughing as he turned to face me. "Can't swim? What are you talking about? She's the smoothest, sleekest swimmer you could find—excluding mermaids, of course."

My mom? A smooth, sleek swimmer? I laughed.

"I guess that disappeared along with the memory," he said sadly. "We swam all over. She even took scuba lessons so she could join me underwater. We went to that old shipwreck. That's where I proposed, you know."

"She definitely still loves you," I said again, thinking of the poem and even more sure now.

"Yeah." He swam over to the table by his bed. I followed him.

"What's that?" I asked. There was something pinned onto the wall with a fish hook. A poem.

"That's mine," he said miserably.

"'The Forsaken Merman'?" I read. I scanned the lines, not really taking any of it in—until I came to one stanza that made me gasp out loud. *A ceiling of amber, a pavement of pearl.*

"But that's, but that's—"

"Yeah, I know. Soppy old stuff, isn't it?"

"No! I know those lines."

Jake looked up at me. "Have you been to that shipwreck yourself, little 'un?"

I nodded. "Shona took me. My friend. She's a mermaid."

"And your mother?"

"No—she doesn't even know *I've* been there."

Jake dropped his head.

"But she knows those lines!" I said.

I pulled the poem off the wall, reading on. "She left lonely forever the kings of the sea," I said out loud.

"That's how it ends," he said.

"But it's not!"

"Not what?"

"That's not how it ends!"

"It does; look here." Jake swam over, took the poem from me. "Those are the last lines."

I snatched it back. "But that's not how *your* story ends! She never left the king of the sea!"

Jake scratched his head. "You've lost me now."

"*The King of the Sea*. That's our boat! That's what it's called."

His eyes went all misty like Mom's had earlier. "So it is, love. I remember when we renamed it.

I forget what her father had called it before that. But you see —"

"And she could never leave it! She told me that. And now I know why. Because it's you! She could never leave *you*! You're not the forsaken merman at all!"

Jake laughed. "You really think so?" Then he pulled me close again. He smelled of salt. His chin was bristly against my forehead.

"Look — you'll need to go soon," he said, holding me away from him.

"But I've only just found you!"

"The dinner bell is about to ring, and we need to get you out of here. I don't know how you got your way into this place, little gem, but you sure as sharks don't want to get caught here. Might never get out again."

"Don't you want me?"

He held my hands and looked deep into my eyes, locking us into a world of our own. "I want you alive," he said. "I want you free, and happy. I don't want you slammed up in some stupid place like this for the rest of your life."

"I'll never see you again," I said sadly.

"We'll find a way, little gem." I liked how he called me that. "Come on," he said, looking quickly from side to side. "We need to get you out of here." He opened his door and looked down into the corridor.

"How come you can do that?" I asked. "Aren't you supposed to be locked up in here?"

He pointed to a metal tag stapled to the end of his tail.

"Does that hurt?"

"Keeps me in my place. If I take it across the threshold"—he pointed at the doorway—"and I know what I'm talking about—it's like being slammed between two walls."

"You tried it?"

He rubbed his head as though he'd just bashed it. "Not to be advised, I tell you."

I giggled. "Why *have* doors then?"

He shrugged. "Extra security—they lock 'em at night." He swam back toward me. "You understand, don't you?"

"I think so." I suddenly remembered Mr. Beeston's words, how he said my dad ran off because he didn't want to be saddled with a baby. But Mr. Beeston had lied about *everything*. Hadn't he?

"What is it, little 'un?"

I looked down at my tail, flicking rapidly from side to side. "You didn't leave because . . . It's not that you didn't want me back then?" I said.

"*What?*" He suddenly swam over to his bed. I'd

192

totally scared him off. I wished I could take the words back.

He reached under the bed. "Look at this." He pulled a pile of plastic papers out. "Take a look. Any of them."

I approached him shyly. "Go on," he urged. "Have a look." He passed me one. It was a poem. I read it aloud.

> *"I never thought I'd see the day,*
> *They'd take my bonny bairn away.*
> *I long-ed for her every day.*
> *Alas, she is so far away."*

"Yeah, well, it was an early one," he said, pulling at his ear. "There's better than that in here."

I couldn't take my eyes off the poem. "You . . ."

"Yeah, I know. Jewelry, poetry. What next, eh?" He made a face.

But before I could say anything else, a bell started ringing. It sounded like the school fire alarm. I clapped my hands over my ears.

"That's it. Dinner. They'll be here soon." He grabbed me. "Emily. You have to go."

"Can I keep it?" I asked.

He folded the poem up and handed it back to me. Then he held my arms tightly. "I'll find you," he said roughly. "One day, I promise."

He swirled around, picked up the bracelet from his bedside table, and quickly tied a knot in it. "Give this to your mother. Tell her—" He paused. "Just tell her, no matter what happens, I never stopped loving her, and I never will. Ever. You hear me?"

I nodded, my throat too clogged up to speak. He hugged me one last time before swirling around again. "Hang on." He pulled the poem off his wall and handed it to me. "Give her this as well, and tell her—tell her to keep it till we're together again. Tell her to never forsake me."

"She won't, Dad. Neither of us will. Ever."

"I'll find you," he said again, his voice croaky. "Now go." He pushed me through the door. "Be quick. And be careful."

I edged down into the corridor and held his eyes for a second. "See you, Dad," I whispered. Then he closed the door and was gone.

I wavered for a moment in the empty corridor. The bell was still shrieking—it was even louder outside the cell. I covered my ears, flicked my tail, and got moving: back along the corridors, into the cleaning cupboard, through the tiny hole, out across the murky darkness, until I found the tunnel again.

Shona was waiting at the end of it, just like she'd said she would be. We fell into each other's arms and laughed as we hugged each other. "I was so worried," she said. "You were gone ages."

"I found him," I said simply.

"Swishy!" she breathed.

"Tell you all about it on the way. Come on." I was desperate to see Mom. I couldn't wait to see her face when I gave her Dad's presents.

"So tell me again." Mom twirled her new bracelet around and around on her wrist, watching the colors blur and merge, then refocus and change again, while Millie looked on jealously. "What did he say, exactly?"

"Mom, I've told you three times already."

"Just once more, darling. Then that's it."

I sighed. "He says he's always loved you and he always will. And he had stacks of poems that he'd written."

She clutched her poem more tightly. "About me?"

I thought of the one in my pocket. "Well, yeah. Mostly."

Mom smiled in a way I'd never seen before. I laughed. She was acting just like the women in those horrible, gooey romantic films that she loves.

"Mom, we have to see him again," I said.

"He's never stopped loving me, and he never will," she replied dreamily. Millie raised her eyebrows.

A second later, a huge splash took the smile off her face. We ran outside.

"Trying to get one over on me?" It was Mr. Beeston! In the water! How did he get past us? "After everything I've done for you," he called, swimming rapidly away from us as he spoke.

"What are you going to do?" I shouted.

"I warned you," he shouted, paddling backward. "I won't let you get away with it." Then in a quiet voice, his words almost washed away by the waves, he added, "I'm sorry it had to end like this, Mary P. I'll always remember the good times."

And then he turned and swam toward the Great Mermer Reef. Mom and I looked at each other. Good times?

Millie cleared her throat. "It's all my fault," she said quietly.

Mom turned to Millie. "What?"

"I loosened the ropes." Millie pulled her shawl around her. "Only a tiny bit. He said they were hurting."

Mom sighed and shook her head. "All right, don't worry, Millie," she said. "There's nothing we can do now, is there?"

As we watched Mr. Beeston swim off into the

distance, Shona appeared in the water below us. "What's up?" she called. "I thought I heard something going on."

"It's Mr. Beeston," I said. "He's gone!"

"Escaped?"

"He went over there." I pointed toward the prison. "I think he's up to something."

"Should we go after him?"

"You girls are not going back there!" Mom said. "Not now. It's too dangerous."

"What, then?" I asked. "How will we get back? We don't have any fuel; the sail's broken. Shona can't tow us all the way back to the harbor."

"We could radio the coast guard," Mom said.

"Mom, the radio's been broken for *years*. You always said you'd get it fixed at some point—"

"But I kept forgetting," Mom finished my sentence with a sigh.

"We could always meditate on it," Millie offered. "See if the answer comes to us."

Mom and I both glared silently at her. Ten seconds later, the decision was taken out of our hands. A loud voice wobbled up from below the surface of the sea. "You are surrounded," it gurgled. "You must give yourselves up. Do not try to resist."

"Who are you?" I shouted. "I'm not afraid of—"

"Emily!" Mom gripped my arm.

The voice spoke again. "You are outnumbered. Do not underestimate the power of Neptune."

Before I could think about what to say next, four mermen in prison-guard uniforms appeared on the surface of the water. Each one had an upside-down octopus on his back. In perfect formation, they leaped from the water, their tails spinning like whirlpools. They flipped on their sides, the octopus legs swirling above their backs like rotary blades, and headed toward us. Between them, they plucked Millie, Mom, and me from the deck, spun themselves around, and held us under their arms as they plopped back into the water.

"I can't swim," Mom yelped.

For an answer, she was dragged silently under the water. Gulping and gasping, we were shoved roughly into a weird tube-thing. My legs started turning into a tail right away—but, for once, I hardly noticed.

We slid along the tube, landing on a bouncy floor. The entrance we'd slipped through instantly closed, leaving us staring at the inside of a white, rubbery bubble. Two masks hung from the ceiling. They looked like the things they show you when you go on a plane.

I grabbed hold of them and helped Mom and Millie put them on. Then we sat in silence as we bumped along through the water. Millie pulled some worry beads out of her pocket and twirled them furiously around her fingers.

Mom clutched my fingers, holding them so tight it hurt.

"We'll be fine," I said, putting my arm around her. Then in an uncertain whisper, I added, "I'm sure we will."

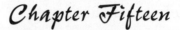

Chapter Fifteen

*T*he good news: they didn't keep us in that
tiny, wobbly cage forever. The bad news: they
separated us and threw us each into an even tinier
one. This time it was more like a box. Five small
tail spans from side to side and a bed of seaweed
along one edge. It was all Mr. Beeston's fault. How
could he have done this to us?

I sat on my bed and counted the limpets on
the rocky wall. Then I counted the weeds hanging down from the ceiling. I looked around for

something else to count—all I could find were my miserable thoughts. There were plenty of them.

A guard swam in with a bowl of something that looked nothing like food but that I suspected was my dinner.

"What are you going to do with—"

He shoved the bowl into my hands and disappeared without answering.

"It's not fair!" I shouted at the door. "I haven't done anything!"

I examined the contents of the bowl. It looked like snail vomit. Green, slimy trails of rubbery goo spread on top of something flaky and yellow that looked suspiciously like sawdust. Gross. I pushed the bowl away and started counting the seconds. How many of them would I spend in here?

The next thing I knew, I was lying on my side on my horrible bed. Someone was shaking me and I slipped around on the seaweed.

"Mom?" I jumped up. It wasn't Mom. A guard lifted me up by my elbows. "Where are you taking me?" I asked as he clipped a handcuff onto my wrist and fastened the other one onto his own.

But of course he didn't answer. He just pulled me out of the cell and slammed the door behind us.

"Strong, silent type, are you?" I quipped nervously as we swam down long, tunnel-like corridors and around curvy corners then down more long corridors. We soon arrived at a mouthlike entrance with shark teeth across it like the prison door.

The guard knocked twice against one of the teeth, and the jaw opened wider. He pushed me forward.

Once inside, another guard swam toward us. I was attached to a different-but-similar wrist and whisked along a different-but-similar set of corridors.

And then I was thrown into a different-but-similar cell.

Super.

I'd only gotten as far as counting the limpets when they came back for me this time. And this journey took us somewhere different-but-different. *Very* different.

We reached the end of another long corridor. When the guard pushed me through the door, there were no more tunnels. I was looking out at the open ocean again. For a moment, I thought he was setting me free, except I was still attached to his wrist.

The sea grew lighter and warmer. Something was coming into view. Color—and light. Not dancing and jumping around like the Great Mermer Reef, but shimmering and sparkling from the depths of the sea. As we drew closer, the lights emerged into a shape. Like a big house. A huge house! Two marble pillars so tall that they seemed to reach from the seabed to the surface stood on either side of an arched gateway, a golden sea horse on a plinth in front of each pillar. Jewels and crystals glinted all the way across the arch.

"In there." The guard gestured toward the closed doorway, nodding at two mermen stationed on either side. They both had a gold stripe down one side of their tails. As the mermen moved apart, the gates slowly opened.

We swam toward the arch. Long trails of shells dangled from silver threads above us, clinking with the movement of the water.

"What is this place?" I asked as we swam inside. We were in some sort of lobby—the fancy kind they have in really expensive hotels, only even more lavish, and kind of dome-shaped.

Chandeliers made from glasslike crystals hung from the ceiling, splashing mini rainbows around the walls. In the center of the room, a tiny volcano shot out clouds of bright green light—an underwater fountain. The light flowed over the top of the rocky cauldron, bubbling and frothing and turning blue as it melted onto the floor.

"Don't you know anything?" the guard grunted. "This is Neptune's palace." He pushed me forward.

Neptune's palace! What were we doing *here*? I thought about all the things Shona had told me about him. What was he going to do to me? Would he turn me to stone?

We swam across the lobby. Two mermen with long black tails passed us, talking hurriedly as they swam. A mermaid looked up from behind a gold pillar as we came to the back of the lobby. Reaching into his tail, the guard pulled out a card. The mermaid nodded briskly and moved aside. There was a hole in the wall behind her.

"Up there." The guard swam into the hole, pulling me along. Around and around, spiraling upward through tubes, we climbed the upside-down super-slide till we came to a trapdoor. The guard opened it with one push and nudged me through.

We came out into a rectangular room with glass walls. A giant fish tank—except the fish were on the outside! All brightly colored yellows and blues, darting around, looking in as the guard led me to a line of rocks along one edge and told me to sit down. A notice in front of my row had a word written in capital letters: ACCUSED.

Accused? What had I *done?*

In front of me, there were rows of coral seats. Merpeople were loitering here and there, dressed in suits.

One wore a jacket made of gold reeds with a trident on his chest. I watched him flick through files, talking all the time to a mermaid by his side. A merman on the row behind them in a black suit was whispering frantically to a mermaid next to him as he, too, shuffled through files.

At the front, a mermaid facing the court sat at a coral desk examining her nails. Behind her was a low crystal table — and behind that, the most amazing throne: all in gold, the back of the seat tapered upward into three prongs filled with pearls and coral, downward into a solid gold block. The round seat was marble, with blue ripples carved outward from the center to the edges. A golden sea horse stood on either side of the throne: each arm a sea horse body, each leg its tail, stretching downward and curling into a mass of diamonds at its base.

The throne towered over the court — powerful and scary, even when it was empty!

Every now and then, the mermaid in front of the throne rearranged the items on her desk. She had a row of reeds in a line across the top edge, with some plastic papers beside them. On top of these was a sign saying CLERK. A huge pile of files was balanced in one corner. In the other, a grumpy-looking squid sat with its tentacles folded into a complicated knot.

The mermaid kept glancing backward at a gateway behind the throne, which was gold and arched and covered with jewels, like the palace entrance. The gates within it were closed.

A splashing noise opposite me drew my eyes away from the front of the court. Two guards were opening a door in the ceiling; they had someone in between them.

Mom! The guards unhooked a mask from the ceiling, like the ones she and Millie had when we were captured. Mom clumsily strapped it over her face, a tube leading from her mouth up through the top of the box.

She looked around the court with frightened eyes. Then she noticed me and her face brightened a tiny bit. She tried to smile through her mask, and I tried to smile back.

Outside the fish tank, a row of assorted merpeople were taking their seats. A portly mermaid undid a velvety eel from around her neck as she sat down. She made the others all move up so she could make a seat for an enormous jewel-encrusted crab.

Another huddle of merpeople with notebooks and tape recorders chatted to each other as they sat down. Reporters, I guessed. Along the back of the court, a line of sea horses stood in a silent row. They looked like soldiers.

Then a hush fell on the room as a sound of thunder rumbled toward us.

As the noise grew louder, the water started swishing around. The clerk grabbed her table; people reached out to grip the ledges in front of them. *What was happening?* I glanced around as I held on to the coral shelf. No one else looked worried.

The waves grew heavier, the thunder louder, until the gates at the front of the court suddenly opened. A fleet of dolphins washed into the room—a gold chariot behind them, filled with jewels and crystals. The chariot carried a merman into the room. At least seven feet tall, he had a white beard that stretched down to his chest and a tail that looked as if it was studded with diamonds. It shot silver rays across the room as the merman climbed out of the chariot. Sweeping his long tail under him, he slid into the throne. In his hand, a gold trident.

It was Neptune! Right in front of me! In real life!

A sharp rap of the trident on the floor, and the dolphins swiftly left the courtroom, whisking Neptune's chariot away. Another rap and the gates closed behind them. A third, and the water instantly stopped moving. I fell back on my seat, thrown by the sudden calm.

"U-U-P!" a voice bellowed from the front.

Neptune was pointing his trident at me! I

jumped back up, praying silently that I hadn't just doubled whatever sentence I was about to get.

He leaned forward to talk to the clerk, gesturing toward me. The clerk looked up at me too, then picked up one of her reeds. Poking the squid with the reed, she wrote something down in black ink. The squid shuffled grumpily on the edge of the desk and refolded its tentacles.

Eventually, Neptune turned back to the courtroom. He stared angrily around. Then, with another rap of his trident, he shouted, "DOWN!"

Everyone took their seats again as the sea horses at the back split into two rows and swam to the front of the court. They formed a line on either side of Neptune.

The merman in the gold jacket stood up. He bowed low.

"APPROACH!" Neptune bellowed.

The merman swam toward him. Then he ducked down and kissed the base of Neptune's tail. "If it please Your Majesty, I would like to outline the prosecution's case," he began, straightening himself up.

Neptune nodded sharply. "On with it!"

"Your Majesty, you see before you a mermaid and a . . . *human*." He screwed up his face as he said the word, as though it made him feel sick. Pulling at his collar, he continued. "The pair of them have colluded and connived. They have planned and plotted—"

"How DARE you waste my time!" Neptune shouted. He lifted his trident. "FACTS!"

"Directly, Your Majesty, directly." The merman shuffled through a few more files and cleared his throat. "The child before you today has forced an entry into our prison, damaged a section of the Great Mermer Reef in the process—and assaulted one of your own advisers."

"AND? Is there more?" Neptune's face had turned red.

"It's all in here, Your Majesty." The merman handed a file to Neptune, who snatched it and handed it to the clerk without looking at it.

The merman cleared his throat again. "As for the *human*"—he forced the word out—"the same charges apply."

Neptune nodded curtly. "Once again, Mr. Slipreed, will that be ALL?"

"Absolutely, Your Majesty." The merman bowed again as he spoke. "If I could allude to one outstanding area of this case . . ." Neptune clenched his fist around his trident. The merman spoke quickly. "In apprehending the accused, a merchild, acting with the help of another *human*"—he cleared his throat and swallowed loudly—"was discovered in the vicinity."

Millie and Shona! I slapped my hand over my mouth to stop from gasping out loud.

"Both merchild and the other human are being held awaiting instructions from the court."

"From the COURT, Slipreed? ANY old court is that?"

"Your Majesty, they await your divine ruling."

"THANK you, Mr. Slipreed!" Neptune boomed.

"If I may now call upon my first witness . . . Mr. Charles Finright Beeston."

As Mr. Beeston entered the court, I folded my arms. I tried to cross my legs, but remembered they were a tail so I couldn't. He looked different, somehow. As he swam toward Neptune, I realized what it was. I'd never seen him as a merman before!

Mr. Beeston bowed low and kissed Neptune's tail. He avoided looking at me or Mom. "If I may refer to my notes . . ." A line of bubbles escaped from his mouth and floated up through the water as he spoke.

To your lies, you mean, I said to myself.

"Your Majesty, last night I was tricked into a rescue operation involving a yacht and a small motorboat. I was beaten around the head with a boom and tied up while the accused—" He looked quickly at Mom, then at me. Suddenly breaking his flow for a moment, he looked away again and

210

coughed quietly before continuing. "Before they carried out their unlawful plans. Thankfully, the accused were amateurs and not equipped to deal with a high-ranking professional such as myself." He paused and turned toward Neptune.

"BEESTON—do not presume to look to me for compliments! CONTINUE!"

Mr. Beeston's face reddened. "Of course, Your Majesty. And so, I disembarked and sought the strong fin of the law."

"You swam for the guards?"

"Indeed I did, Your Majesty."

"Thank you." Neptune banged his trident on the floor. "DEFENSE!" he bellowed. "Mr. Thinscale? Your first witness?"

The merman in the black suit jumped up. "Thank you, Your Majesty."

I looked around the court, wondering who his first witness was going to be. "Get up," the guard next to me grunted. "You're on." Then he pulled me out of my seat and pointed toward the throne. I swam nervously toward Neptune. Taking my cue from the others, I bent to kiss his diamond-studded tail.

Neptune pulled on his beard and leaned down. "You understand the charges?" he asked in a slightly quieter voice.

"I think so."

"Speak, then!" he snapped. "Do you HAVE anything to say in your defense?"

"Well, I—" I stopped and looked around the courtroom, and at the merpeople watching on all sides. Some were staring at me. Others were talking quietly or laughing—at me, probably. My tail turned to jelly, and I was about to say, "No," when I caught Mom's eyes. She removed her mask for a second and forced herself to smile.

"Do not make me wait," Neptune growled.

That was when I realized what I had to do.

"Um, sir, Mr.—"

"Do I LOOK like a *sir*? A *Mr.*? Do I?"

I flicked my tail a little, propelling myself higher than my three feet eight inches (presuming my tail was as long as my legs—I had never checked), and looked nervously around at the courtroom. "Your Majesty," I corrected myself. "I know this might sound weird, but, well, it's actually kind of nice to be here."

A murmur flickered through the room and along the rows outside it. The reporters scribbled furiously on their pads.

"'Nice,' did she say?" I heard someone ask.

"Is she being sarcastic?" another one replied.

"It's what I've always wanted," I added quickly. "Not being in court about to get locked up for the rest of my life, obviously. But being here. With all of you. It feels right."

I glanced at Mom. "I mean, I know I'm part human, and my mom's fantastic. She raised me all on her own and everything. But my dad's great, too. Not just because he's a merman, so I get to be part mermaid." I paused and looked Neptune in the eyes. "Although that part's absolutely wicked," I said.

Neptune leaned forward. He scowled, narrowing his eyes at me.

"I mean, it's fantastic — it's swishy! But more than anything, I'm proud of him because of his belief in love." I pulled the poem he'd written out of my pocket and held it out. "My dad might have been locked away, but his feelings weren't."

I glanced at Neptune. A tic was beating in his cheek, a glare shone in his eyes, but his body had softened a little; the grasp on his trident had loosened. "You can't make people stop loving each other just because a law says it's wrong," I said.

The dolled-up mermaid with the pet crab wiped her eel across her cheek. Another took a hankie out of her coat pocket. A few merpeople were nodding. I heard someone at the back say, "She's got a point, you know."

Neptune let out a thunderous sigh and a huge mock yawn.

"My dad fell in love. So what? What did *I* do to deserve to grow up without a father?" I continued.

Tutting noises were spreading through the spectators' seats. A couple of them shook their heads.

"I wanted to see my dad, that's all. Is that so wrong?" I paused and looked at Mom. "If it really is so terrible, if love is such a horrible crime, then fine, lock me up. Lock up my mom, too." I turned back to Neptune. "Your Majesty. That merman"—I pointed to the first one who'd spoken—"he wants us imprisoned because of laws that were written centuries ago. Things have changed. Humans aren't all bad, you know."

As I looked around the courtroom, I paused on Mr. Beeston's face. Neptune remained silent. "Hey, even one of your top advisers had one for a father," I said. Mr. Beeston lowered his eyes as people turned to look at him. "If it can produce such loyal, devoted merfolk as Mr. Beeston, can it really be so wrong?"

I let my question hang in the air for a moment before turning back to Neptune. I couldn't think of anything else to say. "I only wanted to see my dad," I said finally.

Neptune held my eyes for a few seconds. Then he banged his trident on the floor. "I will NOT be told my laws are wrong! How DARE you presume!"

He got up from his throne, banging his trident again. Everyone instantly rose to their tails.

The gates behind him opened. His chariot was waiting outside. "Court will adjourn," he barked as the dolphins swam into the courtroom. Then he leaped into his chariot and swept out of the court.

I slumped back on my rock and waited to hear my fate.

Chapter Sixteen

*n*o one spoke for the first few minutes. Then, gradually, everyone started whispering to each other, like at the doctor's when you have to act like it's a crime to talk. Maybe it was a crime, here. Everything else was, it seemed.

I returned to my seat and looked up nervously to see if I could catch Mom's eye. She was sitting with her head in her hands. Was she mad at me?

We sat like that for ages, the court almost silent while we waited. Some people left; a few took out lunch boxes and munched on seaweed sandwiches.

Then the gates at the front of the court opened. Neptune was coming back in. Everyone leaped up.

Neptune waved us down impatiently with his trident.

He waited for the court to be absolutely silent before he spoke.

"Emily Windsnap." He looked at me and indicated sharply for me to get up. I flicked my tail and stood as straight as possible. He looked at Mom and pointed upward again. "Mary Penelope Windsnap," he read from the card in front of him, and Mom stood up. "You have both defied ME, and MY laws!"

I swallowed hard.

"My kingdom has held by these laws very well for many generations. *I* invent them; *you* abide by them. That's how it works!"

I tried to get used to the idea of living in a cell with a bed of seaweed and limpets on the wall.

"Do you DARE say I am wrong?" he continued, his voice rising with every word. "Do you think you know better than ME? You do NOT!"

He leaned forward to stare at me. What would I get? Ten years? Twenty? Life?

He paused for ages. When he spoke again, a gentleness had fought its way into his voice. He spoke so quietly, I had to hold my breath to hear him.

"However . . ." he said, then stopped. He stroked his beard. "However," he repeated, "you have touched on something today. Something beyond laws." His voice softened even more. "And therefore, beyond punishment."

I held my breath as he paused, tapping the side of his trident.

"You will both be released!" he boomed eventually.

A gasp went through the court, followed by a stream of murmuring. Neptune lifted his trident and glared around the room. The chattering stopped instantly.

"You defied my laws," he went on. "But why? Shall I pretend I do not understand? Or that I have never felt that way? NO! I am no hypocrite! And I shall NOT punish you for love. I shall NOT! Mrs. Windsnap." He turned to Mom. A long deep sigh, his breath rumbling out from his throat. Then— "Your husband is also to be released."

Another gasp whizzed through the court.

"On one condition," he continued. "The three of you will join a community on an island with a secret location. This will be your home from now on. If you break this condition, you will be punished most severely. Do you understand?"

He stared at us both. I nodded vigorously. Had I heard right? Was I *really* going to see my dad again?

The gold-jacketed merman suddenly rose from his seat. "Your Majesty, forgive me," he said, bowing low. "But the other merchild? You know, there could be trouble if—"

"Just get them all out from under my tail," Neptune barked. "She can join them, for all I care. Discuss it with her parents. Either that or a memory wipe."

"Very well, Your Majesty." He sat down again.

Neptune scanned the court. "And perhaps you can all tell your kinfolk that your king is not only a firm ruler, but also a just and compassionate one." His eyes landed on me. "One who will no longer punish folk merely for loving."

Then he got up from his throne and banged his trident on the floor. "Case closed," he bellowed, and left the court.

It all happened so quickly after that. The room erupted in noise. People were clapping and cheering; others gossiped among themselves. A few came over to the dock to shake my hand.

"Can I go now?" I asked the guard. He nodded curtly and pointed to the exit as he undid my handcuffs.

Outside the court, a mermaid with her hair in a bun took my hand. "Your mom will be escorted separately; she'll meet you in a bit," she said. "Let's get you out of here."

"Who are —" I began, but she'd turned around and was pulling me toward a boat that looked like a cross between a limousine and a submarine. It was white and long, with gold handles on the doors.

A crowd was waiting by the limo boat. "Emily, can you tell me how you feel?" one of them asked, a black reed poised above her notebook. I recognized her as one of the reporters from the court.

"Emily doesn't want to talk at the moment," the mermaid said. "She has to —"

"I feel great," I said. "I just can't wait to see my mom and dad together."

"Thanks, Emily." The reporter scribbled furiously as I was bundled into the boat. There was someone else inside.

"Shona!"

"Emily!"

We hugged each other tight.

"We're going to an island!" I said. "My dad's coming!"

"Seat belts," the mermaid instructed from the driver's seat. Then we shot forward like a bullet. As we sped through the water, I told Shona everything that had happened. "And they said you might be able to come, too!" I finished off. I didn't mention the other option. Surely her parents would agree?

"Swishy!" Shona laughed.

"Going up," the mermaid called from the front as we tipped upward, gradually climbing until we came to a standstill. Then she opened a door in the ceiling. "Your stop," she said to me, holding out her hand. I shook it, feeling rather stupid. "Good luck, Emily," she said. "You're a brave girl."

"See you soon," Shona said. She giggled, and we hugged each other before I climbed out. I stood on top of the boat.

Blinking in the daylight, I tried to adjust to the scene. *King* was moored just in front of me. A group of mermen waited in the water in front of it, holding on to two thick ropes. Mom was leaning right over the side, reaching down to someone in the sea. She was holding his hands.

I stood on tiptoe so I could see who it was. For a moment, I thought I must be imagining things. It couldn't have happened this quickly, surely! A mop of black hair, sticking up where it was wet, a pair of deep brown eyes. Then he noticed me, and the dimple below his left eye deepened as he let go of Mom's hands and swam toward me.

"Dad!" Without thinking, I jumped into the sea—and into his arms.

"My little gem," he whispered as he hugged me

tight. Then he took my hand, and we swam back to the side of the boat together. Mom reached down with both arms, and we held each other's hands: a circle, a family.

A second later, a series of splashes and shouting exploded behind us. A bunch of reporters were heading our way.

"Mr. Windsnap." One of them shoved a microphone shaped like a huge mushroom in my dad's face. "Simon Watermark, Radio Merwave. Your story has melted Neptune's heart. How does it feel to have made history?"

"Made history?" Dad laughed. "At the moment, my only feelings about history are that I want to go back twelve years and catch up with my wife and daughter."

The reporter turned to Mom. "Mrs. Windsnap, is it true that your babysitter helped with your plan?"

That was when I noticed Millie sitting on a plastic chair at the front of the boat. One of the mermen was perched on the deck opposite her, his tail dangling over the side, the pair of them frowning at a pack of tarot cards spread out between them.

"We couldn't have done it without her," Mom said.

The reporter turned to me. "Emily, you were a brave girl to do what you did. You must have had some help along the way. Is there anyone you'd like to say a special thank-you to?"

"Well, I'd like to thank my mom for being so understanding. I'd like to thank my dad for believing in us." He kissed my cheek. "And Millie for falling asleep at the right time."

The reporter laughed.

"And I'd like to thank Shona. My best friend. I could never have done this without her."

But out of the corner of my eye, I saw a familiar figure. Merpeople were talking and laughing in groups all around us, but he was on his own. He looked up and smiled a shaky, crooked smile at me, his head tilted in what looked almost like an apology.

And I forgave him.

Almost.

There was just one thing he could do for me first.

He jumped a little as I swam over to him. I whispered my favor in his ear.

"A mass memory wipe?" he blurted out. "That's ridiculous — not to mention dangerous."

"Please, Mr. Beeston," I begged. "Think about all the nice things I said in there. After everything that's happened, I should hate you forever. But I won't. Not if you do this one little thing for me."

He looked at me hard. What did he see? A girl

he'd known all her life? Someone he perhaps cared about, just a tiny little bit?

"Very well," he said eventually. "I'll do it."

I kept my head down as we stood by the side of the pool. Everyone around me chatted in groups. Julia was with Mandy, giggling together in the corner. Fine. I didn't need Julia. I had Shona and no one could be a better best friend than her.

My heart thumped in my ears, blocking out everything else.

Bob arrived. I stepped forward, put my hand up. "Please, sir — I'd like to show you something."

Bob frowned.

"I've been practicing."

He waved a hand out. "All right then," he said with half a smile. "Let's have it."

I stepped toward the edge of the pool.

"Look at *fish girl*," Mandy sneered from the corner. "Showing off again."

"That's right," I said, looking her right in the eyes. "Fish girl is showing off."

I glanced up to the window. Too high. I couldn't see outside, but I knew he'd be there. He promised.

I had five minutes. Five minutes to be proud

instead of scared. Five minutes to be free, to be myself. But mostly, I had five minutes to give Mandy Rushton the biggest shock of her life!

And so I dove in. Piercing the surface as gently as I could, I swam underwater all the way to the opposite end of the pool.

"Big deal!" Mandy snorted. "So fish girl can do a length underwater. Whoop-de-do!"

As she mocked me, something was happening under the water. My tail was starting to form. The familiar feeling filled me with confidence. This was it!

I dove straight down. And then I flicked my tail up in the air. Spinning around and around under the water, I could feel my tail swirling and dancing, faster and faster. I couldn't wait to see Mandy's face!

I swam up to the surface, wiped my hair off my face, and looked across. Thirty open mouths. Total silence. If they'd been playing musical statues, it would have been a dead heat.

Mandy was the first to step forward. "But—but—" she sputtered. "But that's a—how did you—"

I laughed. "Hey, guess what, Mandy? I'm not scared of you—and I don't care what you call me. You can't stop me being who I am. And you don't get to bully me anymore, because I'm leaving. I'm off to a desert island, with a whole bunch of—"

A loud rap on the door stopped me saying any more.

Bob walked over to it in a daze. Mr. Beeston. Right on time. He spoke quietly to Bob. "Of course," Bob said, his voice flat and mechanical. "I'd forgotten. Come on in."

He turned to the class. "Folks, we have a visitor today. He's come to give us a special talk."

Mr. Beeston stood in front of the class, a large bag in his hand. "Now then, children," he said. "Listen carefully. I'm going to teach you about lighthouses and the dangers of the sea."

He opened the bag. "But before we start, let's all have a doughnut. . . ."

I slipped quietly out of the pool as Mr. Beeston held everyone's attention. It was almost as if I'd been forgotten. I would be soon!

"Thank you," I mouthed as I passed behind the class. He nodded solemnly in reply.

I crept away from the pool, changed quickly, and slipped outside. Looking back at the building, I smiled.

"Good-bye, 7C," I whispered. Then I turned and walked away.

We left that night. Mom, Dad, and me, off to a whole new world where who knew what was waiting for us. All I knew for sure was that my life as a mermaid had only just begun.

But remember, it's just between you and me!

ACKNOWLEDGMENTS

Lots of people have helped this book make its way from my computer into your hands. I would especially like to thank:

Mum, for getting rid of all the pounding hearts and lurching stomachs;

Dad, for noticing all sorts of things that everyone else missed;

Peter B., for the title;

Kath, for her eagle-eyed nitpickiness;

Helen, for everything I've learned and gained from working with her at Cornerstones;

Cameron, for lending me books about sea life with great pictures and fantastic facts;

Cath, who hasn't actually had anything to do with the book, but has been a brilliant pal all the time I've been writing it.

With extra special thanks to:

Lee, for an inspirational friendship, and for being so in tune with me and my characters;

Jill, for sharing the journey, and for having endless discussions about mermaids without complaining once;

Catherine, for all her support and guidance, and for finding Emily such a good home;

And Judith and Fiona, for being the perfect editors.

Emily Windsnap
and the
Monster
from the
Deep

For Hannah, Barney, Katie . . .
and Mum

Below the thunders of the upper deep;
    Far far beneath in the abysmal sea,
His ancient, dreamless, uninvaded sleep
    The Kraken sleepeth . . .

from "The Kraken,"
by Alfred, Lord Tennyson

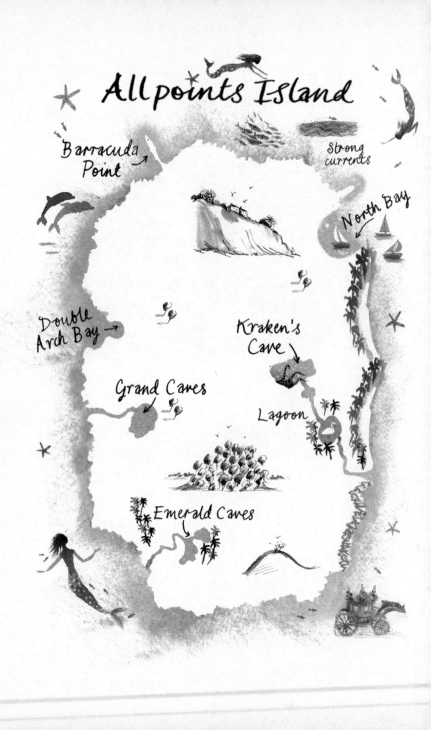

Allpoints Island

Barracuda Point

Strong currents

North Bay

Double Arch Bay

Kraken's Cave

Grand Caves

Lagoon

Emerald Caves

Chapter One

*C*lose your eyes.

Think of the most beautiful place you can imagine.

Are you seeing golden beaches? Gorgeous clear blue sea? Perfect sky? Keep your eyes closed.

Now multiply that by about a hundred, and you're halfway to picturing what my new home is like. The softest, whitest sand, palm trees that reach lazily out from the beaches, tall rocky arches cusping the bays, sea that sparkles like crystals in the sunlight. All thanks to Neptune, the ruler of the ocean.

He sent me here with my mom and dad to start a new life. Somewhere we could live together. Somewhere our secret would be safe.

One of Neptune's guards, Archieval, accompanied us here. He's a merman. He swam beside our little sailboat, *King,* all the way, swishing his long black hair behind him and occasionally ducking under, flicking his tail in the air, silver and sharp, like a dagger.

We edged slowly into a horseshoe-shaped bay filled with shiny turquoise water. Soft foamy waves gently stroked the white sand. A few boats were dotted about in the bay, half-sunken, silently sloping. Some were modern yachts, others great wooden crafts that looked like ancient pirate ships.

A tall rocky arch marked the end of the bay. Through it, the sand and sea continued around a corner. I caught my breath as I stood and stared.

"Shake a tail, someone," Archieval called up. "I could use some help here."

I leaned across to help him pull the boat alongside a wooden jetty as Dad swam around to the back and tied the ropes to a buoy. Mom was still inside with Millie. That's her friend from Brightport. Millie used to read fortunes on the pier. She did a tarot reading for Archieval before we left, and he liked it so much, he invited her to come with us. They had to check with Neptune first, but Archieval is one of Neptune's top guards, so he's pretty much allowed to do as he likes.

Then Millie said she'd have to let the cards decide, so she set the pack out in a star shape and sat looking at it in silence for about ten minutes, nodding slowly.

"Well, it's obvious what I have to do. You'll never catch me ignoring a call from the ten of cups," she said enigmatically before throwing her black cape over her shoulder and going home to pack her things. Millie says everything enigmatically. I've learned to just nod and look as though I know what she's talking about.

Archieval swam around to the side of the boat. "This is it, then," he said. "North Bay, Allpoints Island."

"Why's it called Allpoints Island?" I asked.

"It's right in the center of the Triangle." He stretched out an arm as he spun slowly around in a circle. "Where the three points meet."

The Bermuda Triangle. I shivered. He'd told us about it on the way here, about the boats and planes that had mysteriously disappeared inside it. An ocean liner had been found totally intact but utterly deserted. Twenty tables were set out for

237

dinner. Another ship was found with skeletons on the decks, its sails ripped to shreds all around them. Others had vanished without a trace, often after frantic mayday calls from pilots and fishermen who were never seen again.

I didn't know whether to believe the stories at first, but something had happened out at sea. We'd been sailing along normally, the swells rising and falling, the boat gently making its way through the peaks and troughs. Then it changed. The water went all glassy. The engine cut out; everything died. Even my watch stopped working. It felt as if the sea had frozen, almost as if time itself had frozen.

Then Archieval yanked his long hair into a ponytail with some string and disappeared under the water. A few minutes later, we got moving again, gliding silently across the glassy sea.

"That was it," he called up. "Bermuda Triangle. That's what'll protect you from the outside world now. No one knows how to get through it except for a few chosen merfolk." He threw a rope onto the deck. "Well, a few chosen merfolk and . . . no, I'd better not tell you about that."

"What? Tell me."

Archie beckoned me closer. "I shouldn't really tell you this," he said, "but there's a raging current down there. Not any normal kind of current either, oh no. This one's linked to something that lies deep down in the sea, even below your island."

"What? What is it?"

"What is it? It's the biggest, scariest, most powerful—"

"I hope you're not filling my daughter's head with any more of your lurid tales, Archie!" Dad said, suddenly turning up beside Archie. "She has enough nightmares as it is."

I'd told Dad all about my nightmares on the way here, the ones I used to have in Brightport: swimming around in a fish tank surrounded by my old classmates, all shouting "Freak! Freak!" at me, or being chased by a scientist with a big net.

How many more nightmares was I going to have? Would I get to leave them behind? Would I ever stop feeling like the odd one out?

Archie lowered his voice. "Just be careful," he said. "That glassy plane marks out the Triangle, but it's only like that on the surface. It's a huge well below, leading down to the deepest depths of the ocean. And you don't want to go disappearing down a hole like that."

I rubbed the goose bumps crawling up my arms.

We'd sailed on calmly after that, slipping through water that grew clearer and lighter every moment, melting from deep navy to a soft baby blue. I tried to push Archie's words to the back of my mind.

Gradually, the island came into view. It was quite small, perhaps only a few miles across: a tall cliff at one end, a couple of lower peaks at the other, and a low, flat stretch in between. As we drew closer, I could see that the coastline was made up of long white bays fringed with tall palm trees and clusters of rocks and arches. It looked like a postcard. I'd always thought those pictures must be made up somehow and that when you got there, you'd just find a clump of high-rise apartments next to a building site.

But it was real. And it was my new home.

"Where's your dad?" Mom joined me on the deck, straightening her skirt and bending down to check her reflection in a metal railing.

I pointed ahead. "Helping Archie."

Mom looked slowly around the bay. "I think I've died and gone to heaven," she murmured as she grabbed the railing. "Someone's going to have to pinch me."

"I'll do it!" Dad's head poked out of the water, a glint in his eyes as he wiped his floppy wet hair off his forehead. Mom smiled back at him.

A second later, the side doors crashed open and Millie clambered out. "Tell you something," she said, rubbing her large stomach. "That slippery elm mixture works wonders on seasickness." She covered her mouth as she hiccupped. "Especially washed down with a spot of brandy. Now, where are we?"

She squinted into the sunlight. "That's it!" she said, pointing across at a wooden ship lying on a slant in the bay. It had three tall masts, polished pine railings, and a name printed on the side: *Fortuna.*

"That's what?" I asked.

"Your new home. Archie told me."

I looked at Mom. "What's wrong with *The King of the Sea*?" That's our boat's full name. I've lived on it with Mom all my life.

Millie pinched my cheek as she squeezed past me. "Well, your dad can't live with you on a regular boat, can he now? Don't worry. I'll take care of the place for you."

Dad swam around to the side, staring across at *Fortuna.* "Flipping fins! A little different from where I've spent the last twelve years," he said as he reached up to help Mom off the boat. Dad was in prison before we came here. He's not a criminal or anything. Well, he broke the law, but it was a stupid law. He married a human. That's my mom. He's a merman. Makes it a little difficult when she can't swim and he can't go on land, but they manage somehow. She used to be a great swimmer till she was hypnotized into being afraid of water. Neptune did that, to keep them apart. She's still nervous about it now, but Dad's started teaching her again.

Mom hitched up her skirt and stepped across onto the jetty. It led all the way out to the ship, bouncing and swaying on the water as we made our way along it.

I climbed aboard our new home. It was huge! At least twenty yards long with shiny brown wooden decks and maroon sails wrapped into three neat bundles. It lay perfectly still at a small tilt, lodged in the sand. It looked as if it had been waiting for us.

I stepped into the cabin in the middle of the boat and found myself in a kitchen with steps leading forward and behind. I tried the back way first. It led to a small cabin with a bed, a beanbag chair, and a polished wooden cupboard. Circles of wavy light bounced onto the bed from portholes on either side. Definitely my bedroom!

I ran through to the other side. Mom was twirling around in a big open living room that had a table on one side and a comfy-looking sofa tucked snugly into the other.

"What will we do with all this space?" she gasped. Sunny golden rays beamed into the room from skylights all along the ceiling. Ahead, a door led to another bedroom.

"What about Dad?" I asked. "How's he going to live here?"

Before she had a chance to reply, a large trapdoor in the floor sprung open and he appeared below us. That was when I noticed there were trapdoors everywhere, leading down from each room into another one below. The ship was lodged in the seabed with a whole floor half-submerged, so you could swim around in it underwater.

"You want to see the rest of your new home?" Dad's eyes shone wide and happy.

I inched down through the trapdoor to join him. Almost as soon as I did, my legs started to tingle. Then they went numb. Finally, they disappeared altogether.

My tail had formed. Sparkling and glistening, it flickered into life, sending shimmery green and pink lights around me.

It does that when I go into water. Sometimes I'm a mermaid; sometimes I'm a girl. That's what happens when a woman and a merman have a baby.

I'd only found out recently, when I went swimming at school. Thinking about that first time made me tremble. In fact, the thought of Brightport Junior High made me feel sick even now. I'd started to dread going there. School itself didn't bother me, only some of the people. One in particular: Mandy Rushton. Just thinking about her was enough to make my skin prickle. All those times she'd made my life a misery. Like the time she pushed me into the pool in front of everyone. I almost gave the whole thing away, and would have if the teacher hadn't sent us both to get changed. I can still remember her icy cold tone of voice as she'd hissed at me on the way to the changing room. "I'll get you back for this, fish girl," she'd said. "Just wait."

I lived in fear of the day she'd get me. I'd have nightmares about it nearly every night, then I'd wake up, cold and sweaty, and have to face her all over again in real life.

At least I'd gotten her back in the end when I turned into a mermaid in the pool, right in front of her eyes. It was worth all the bullying just to see the look of stunned silence slapped across her face that day.

No, it wasn't. The only thing that made the bullying worth it was knowing I would never, ever have to see her again.

Bullies like Mandy Rushton were a thing of the past.

"A little bigger than *The King of the Sea,* eh?" Dad said as I lowered myself toward him. He took my hand, and we swam around the lower deck together. The feel of his big fingers closing around mine warmed something inside me and made up for the awkward silence between us. I couldn't think how to fill it.

"Look!" He pulled me through an archway in the center and through purple sea fans that hung like drapes from the ceiling. Fernlike and feathery, they swayed delicately with the movement of the water. Dad squeezed my hand.

A couple of red-and-white fish swam in through an empty porthole, pausing to nibble gently at the side of the boat before gliding between the drapes. One of them swam up to slide along Dad's tail. "Glasseye snappers," I said as he flicked it away. Dad smiled. He'd taught me the names of all sorts of fish on the way here. It was one of the few things we talked about. Where do you start after twelve years?

I swam back to the trapdoor and hoisted myself up. "Mom, it's amazing!" I said as I watched my tail form back into my legs. Mom stared. She obviously hadn't gotten used to it yet. She'd only seen it happen a few times.

Then Dad joined us and Mom turned to sit with her legs dangling over the trapdoor, gazing at him. He reached onto her lap to hold her hands. She didn't seem to notice that the bottom of her skirt was soaking wet. She just grinned stupidly down at him while he grinned stupidly up at her.

I realized I was grinning stupidly at both of them.

Well, most people don't have to wait till they're twelve before they get to see their parents together. I never knew it would make me feel so warm, so complete.

I decided to leave them to it. They wouldn't notice if I went out to explore. They'd hardly noticed anything except each other since we set off to come here! Not that I minded. After all, I'd nearly gotten imprisoned myself, getting them back together. I guessed they wouldn't mind a little time on their own.

"I'm going out for a while," I called. "Just for a look around."

"OK, darling," Mom replied dreamily.

"Be careful," Dad added.

I nearly laughed as I climbed out of the boat. I looked out at the turquoise water and marshmallow sand. Careful? What of? What could possibly hurt me here?

I walked along the beach for a while, watching the sun glint and dance on the water in between the ships. The sand was so white! Back home, or what used to be home, in Brightport, the sand was usually a dirty beige color. This sand was like flour. My feet melted into it as I walked. I could hardly feel the ground. A gentle breeze made the sun's warmth feel like a hair dryer on my body.

Wading into the sea, I couldn't help glancing around to check that I was alone. Just habit. I still hadn't gotten used to the idea that being a mermaid didn't make me a freak here — a secret island where merfolk and humans lived together. The only place of its kind in the world, protected by the magic of the Bermuda Triangle.

There were some people up on the cliff behind me, standing in front of a cluster of white buildings. For a moment, I considered scrambling up the hill to join them. Then I looked out at the water and saw faces — and then tails. Merpeople! I had to meet them! I pushed away a slight feeling of guilt as I turned away from the people — and toward the sea. It wasn't the human folk that interested me. It was the merpeople I wanted to meet!

As my legs formed back into my tail, I wondered if there were any others on the island like me. Half-human, half-merperson. That would be *so* cool! Either way, at least I could live here with my mom and dad without us having to hide what we are.

Shoals of tiny fish escorted me out toward the group, gliding and weaving around me. With thin black bodies and see-through fins, they led me along through the warm water, slowing down every now and then, almost as though they were making sure I could keep up. Wavy lines rippled along the seabed like tire tracks. A troop of silver jacks swam past me in a line, each one silhouetted against the sand below, their shadows doubling their gang's number.

I flipped over onto my back, flicking my tail every now and then to propel myself lazily along, until I remembered I was supposed to be looking for the merpeople.

I stopped and looked around. The island was a speck in the distance, miles away. How long had I been swimming?

The merpeople had moved on. A chill gripped my chest as I realized I was gliding over some dark rocks: hard, gray, jagged boulders with plants lining every crack. Fat gray fish with wide-open mouths and spiky backs glared at me through cold eyes. Long trails of seaweed stretched like giant snakes along the seabed, reaching upward in a clutch of leaves and stems.

As I hovered in the water, I could feel myself being pulled along by a current. It felt like a magnet, drawing me toward it, slowly at first, then getting stronger. I swam hard against it, but it was too strong. It was reeling me in like a fishing line. Blackness swirled ahead of me. Then I remembered. The Triangle.

Everything sped up, like a film on fast forward. Fish zoomed past, weeds and plants lay horizontally, stretched out toward the edge of the Triangle, the well that led to the deepest depths of the ocean.

My chest thumping, my throat closing up, I worked my arms like rotary blades, pounding through the water. My tail flicked rapidly as I fought to get away. I swam frantically. *Keep going, keep going!*

But every time I started to make progress, the current latched on to me again, dragging me back out to sea. We were locked in a battle, a tug of war between me and—and what? The biggest, scariest—what? What hadn't Archie told me? What was down here? I could almost feel it, a kind of vibration or humming. Was I imagining it? Fear surged through me like an electric current, powering my aching arms for one final push.

It was just enough. I was getting away. The current loosened its grip. The sea soon became shallow again, and calm, as though nothing had happened. But I wasn't taking any risks. Catapulting myself through the water, I swam back to our bay and made it to the ship, breathless. I pulled myself out and sat panting on the deck while my tail disappeared and my legs re-formed.

Mom poked her head out of the cabin. "You OK, sweetie?" she asked, handing me a towel.

I nodded, too out of breath to reply. I rubbed myself dry as I followed her back into the kitchen.

"Here y'are," she said, passing me a couple of onions and a knife. "Might as well make yourself useful." Then she looked at me more carefully. "Are you sure you're all right?"

Was I? That was a good question. I opened my mouth to answer her, but stopped when I heard voices coming from below deck.

"Who's that?"

"Oh, visitors, downstairs with your dad. They've been coming all afternoon."

I gently shut the trapdoor. I couldn't face new people yet. I didn't even want Dad to hear what I had to say. I don't know why. Something to do with how happy he was, and the fact that he kept giving me all these smiley, loving looks. Well, he would do that, wouldn't he? He hadn't seen me since I was a baby. And I didn't want him to know his baby wasn't quite so happy right now, or quite so sure about this new dream home of hers. I mean, sure, it was beautiful and everything. But there was something else going on here. I didn't know what it was; just a sense of something lurking, or lying in wait.

My hands shook as I started to peel the onions. "Mom," I said carefully.

"Mm?" she replied through a teaspoon lodged in her mouth. She says it keeps her eyes from watering.

"You know that stuff Archie told us on the way here, about the big well in the ocean?"

"Buh big well im be oshug?" she replied, the spoon waggling about as she spoke.

"What?"

She pulled the spoon out of her mouth. "The big well in the ocean?" she repeated.

"The one that leads to the deepest depths of the ocean," I added as a shudder snaked through my body. "I felt something just now. Pulling me out to sea."

"Emily, you're not to go out there!" she said, grabbing my arms. "You stay close to the island."

The shudder jammed in my throat. "It was really strong, Mom," I said quietly.

"Of course it's really strong! It's protecting the whole area! You know what Archie said. Do you hear me, Emily?"

I nodded, swallowing hard. "Yes, I hear you."

"I'm not going to lose you, Emily. You promise me you'll keep away from there." She stared at me, holding my eyes with hers. I could see fear in them, and I was about to tell her I was fine and not to worry. Then I remembered what she'd already been through with me, how she'd followed me when I went out to sea to find my dad, and how Neptune nearly locked us all in prison. I guess she had the right to worry a little.

"I promise," I said.

She pulled me toward her and hugged me tight. "Good. Right," she said. "You silly thing, you're shaking." She squeezed me tighter. "Come on, it's OK. Let's get these veggies done, and we'll try not to think about big wells and the deepest depths of the ocean, OK?"

"OK." I forced a smile. "I'll try."

We worked in silence after that. I couldn't think of anything to say. All I could think was that it would take more than chopping a few onions to make me forget the fear I'd felt out there, clutching and snapping at me like a shark trying to drag me to the bottom of the sea.

Mermaids? Yeah, right!

You're as bad as my dad.

He thinks they're real, too. Thinks he's seen one. He says it was on his way back from The Fisherman. That's our local bar. Clear as day, he says.

"Well, that goes to show how reliable your vision is after ten beers," my mom says. "You couldn't even tell it was the middle of the *night*!"

"Clear as day," he says again. "It's just an expression, love."

Mom says he'll be seeing more than mermaids if he doesn't start pulling his weight. Then she gets mad at me for leaving my *Girltalk* magazine lying around. That's the only time she seems to notice me nowadays, when she's nagging me about something. And Dad wouldn't know if I disappeared altogether—he's hardly ever around.

It wasn't always like this. Just ever since we heard that the town council is planning to pull down our home. We live on a pier, and they say it's not safe. The problem is, my parents work on the pier, too. So that's job and home gone in one swift swing of a crane. Or blast of dynamite. However they do it.

The place is a dump, anyway. I don't care what happens. Well, OK, maybe I do. But who cares what I think? I wish they did.

So today, Dad charges upstairs at lunchtime. He usually goes to the bar, but he says he's been some-where else.

"Where?" Mom eyes him suspiciously.

"Look," he says. He's got a magazine in his hand. A brochure.

Mom takes it from him. *"Mermaid Tours?"* she says. "Oh, for Lord's sake, Jack, when will you grow up?"

"No, it's not—it's not—" he blusters. "It's just the name of the company, Maureen. It caught my atten-tion, that's all." He grabs the brochure back from Mom and rifles through it as though he's looking for something in particular. "I've been looking for some-thing to take our minds off everything. I thought this might help."

"There!" he says suddenly, opening it up and slamming it onto the table. Mom sits down to read it. I have a look, too. Not that I'm interested or any-thing. I just want to know what the fuss is about, that's all.

"A cruise, Jack?" Mom looks at him in this way she has, with her tongue in her cheek and her eyebrows raised so high they nearly disappear into her hair. "We're on the verge of losing our livelihood, and you want us to spend every last penny we haven't even GOT on some ridiculous vacation!"

Dad takes a deep breath. "Maureen," he says in a rumble. When he speaks again, he says each word on its own, like he's talking staccato. "What. Kind. Of. Fool. Do. You. Take. Me. For. Exactly?"

Mom gets up from the table. "You really don't want me to answer that, Jack."

"Mom, please don't—" I start. But what's the point? She doesn't reply, doesn't even look at me. I might as well not be here.

Hello! I am here, you know. I matter!

"Look!" Dad suddenly shouts. Dad never shouts. We both look. He's pointing at the page. "I'll read it to you, shall I?" And before we have time to answer, he starts reading.

"Enter our EXCLUSIVE contest, and you could win one of our superlative MERMAID TOURS vacations! Every month, one lucky reader will win this FANTASTIC PRIZE. Just complete the following phrase in thirty words or less: 'Mermaid Tours are the best vacations around because . . .'

Remember to tell us which of our fabulous cruise vacations you'd like to go on, and mail the coupon to us. You could be our next lucky winner!"

Dad puts the magazine back on the table.

"Well," Mom says, picking up the magazine. "A contest. Why didn't you just say so?"

I roll my eyes at Dad. He clamps his jaw shut and doesn't say anything.

Mom and Dad are complete fanatics about contests, especially Mom. She thinks she's got a system. It works, too. Our home is littered with teddy bears and toasters and electronic dictionaries she's won from stupid contests in magazines. We had three vacuum cleaners at one point. She even won a weekend getaway once. Not that I know much about that. She and Dad went without me. I had to stay at home with a babysitter while they went off to live it up in New York.

I'll admit it, all right: it was the loneliest weekend of my life. I mean, so the prize was a vacation for two, but couldn't they at least have asked if they could bring their daughter? Would it have hurt so much for the thought to have crossed their minds?

But this. Well, this is for all of us. And I wouldn't mind a cruise vacation. Lying on a lounge chair on an enormous ship gliding through the ocean, hot sun, warm pool, all the food I can eat, nonstop desserts, and no one to stop me from drinking as much soda as I want. I've heard about these vacations. It's all included.

"You know how good you are at these things," Dad says, edging closer to Mom.

"Don't try flattery, Jack," Mom says. "It doesn't suit you."

But I know she'll do it; she can't resist. I catch Dad's eye. He winks, and I half smile back. Well, he's still stupid, believing in mermaids.

Later that day, I see Mom leafing through the brochure. "Look at this one," she says. I glance over her shoulder.

Bermuda and the Caribbean. Experience the magic for yourself. Enjoy all the comfort and enchantment of our Mermaid Tours cruise. Swim with dolphins. Bask in year-round sunshine heaven.

"That's the one, I'd say." She nibbles the side of her mouth. "OK, leave me alone now. I need to think."

She won't show either of us what she's written. Says it'll jinx it. But something changes around the place after she's sent it off. Mom and Dad get along; they even smile at each other occasionally.

We all start talking about what we'll do on our cruise and what it'll be like. All of us, all in it together—it feels great! For a few days. The contest ends in a week.

But then the week's up, and we don't hear anything. Another week passes, and another, and another. Nothing.

We haven't won. Mom's luck's run out after all.

And gradually, the sniping at each other starts again, and the being so wrapped up in themselves that they forget to think about me. Back to normal. And underneath it all is the looming truth that no one's saying out loud, that we're about to lose everything.

Well, why should I expect anything different? It is *my* life we're talking about here.

Oh, I haven't told you my name yet, have I?

It's Mandy. Mandy Rushton.

Chapter Two

I jumped out of bed. Shona was arriving today!

Shona's my best friend. She's a mermaid. Full-time. Not just when she goes in water, like me. Back home — I mean, back in Brightport — I used to sneak out at night to meet up with her. That was before anyone knew about me being a mermaid. Now we could see each other every day!

I couldn't believe it when she said they were coming too. It was Neptune's idea, but I'd never met her parents and didn't know if they'd agree to it. Mind you, looking around me, it was hard to imagine anyone not wanting to come to live here. As long as you didn't go anywhere near the edge of the Triangle. Or think about what might be down there, under the island . . .

Well, I wasn't going to think about that today. I'd stick close to the coast, like Mom said, and everything would be all right. It all looked different this morning anyway. Nothing this beautiful could be dangerous. I'd gotten it all out of proportion yesterday. Like my old teacher used to say, I've got a good imagination.

Dad swam up to the trapdoor in the living room as I was getting some breakfast. "There's someone here for you, little 'un," he said. "And look, I got you something."

He darted away as someone else appeared below me. Someone with long blond hair and a big smile. Shona!

I shoveled a last spoonful into my mouth and jumped down through the trapdoor with a splash. My legs melted away, turning into a tail.

"I couldn't wait to see you," Shona said, swimming toward me to hug me tight.

I hugged her back. "When did you get here?"

"Late last night." She nodded toward the porthole she'd swum through. "Althea brought me over to North Bay. She lives next door to us at Rocksea Cove. Come and meet her."

"Oh. Great," I said. I wasn't going to have

Shona all to myself then? But there was so much to catch up on! Well, I suppose we'd find time soon—and at least I was going to meet another mermaid.

"Here you are." Dad swam back over, smiling broadly as he held something out to me. A doll. It had bright red spots on its cheeks, golden hair, and a frilly pink tail.

"Um. Thanks, Dad."

"You like it?" he asked, anxiously tugging at his ear.

"Sure. I'll play with it later, perhaps."

"I wanted to give you something like this years ago. I've been saving it," he said, his eyes going all misty and dreamy. They seemed to do that a lot. I don't know if he realized I was nearly thirteen. "I mean, I know it's a bit childish, but . . ."

"No, it's fine, Dad. It's great. Thanks."

Once we were outside, I grimaced at Shona, and she laughed. Then I had a pang of guilt. "Hang on," I said. I swam back in to the boat and kissed Dad on the cheek. It isn't his fault I grew up without him. It isn't his fault we haven't worked out how to communicate with each other yet, either. It will come. It has to. I mean, it's great being with him, but we've hardly had a real conversation. It feels as if we don't quite know how to at times.

"What's that for?" he asked, lifting his hand to his cheek.

I shrugged, smiling briefly. "See you later," I said.

Outside the boat, a mergirl with jet black hair tied back in a ribbon was waiting in the water with Shona. The ribbon looked as if it was made out of gold seaweed. Her tail was green, with silver stars painted on the end.

Shona turned to me. "This is Althea. She's going to show us around the island."

"Great," I said with a tight smile as a pang of jealousy hit me. How could I compete with a full-time, real mermaid with stars on her tail and gold seaweed in her hair? I was going to end up without a best friend again.

"We're picking up Marina first," Althea said.

"That's Althea's best friend," Shona added, laughing as she swam ahead with Marina. I think she was trying to put my mind at rest. So why didn't it work?

"Stay close to the coast here," Althea warned as we set off, doubling the fear that was already starting to gnaw at my insides. "There's quite a current around the northern end of the island."

As if I needed to be told that! I couldn't speak. My mouth was so dry it felt like it had sand in it.

Althea pointed to the hill behind us. "That's where a couple of the human families live," she said, pointing up at the white buildings I'd seen the day before. "They take care of gardens for the whole island."

For a moment I wished I'd gone up to meet them yesterday after all. If I had, maybe I'd be looking around at everything with wide innocent eyes like Shona was doing now, instead of waiting for something awful to happen. But then, if I had, Althea and Marina might not be interested in me. They wouldn't want a human hanging around with them. And surely Shona wouldn't either. No, it was the mermaids I wanted to be with. I was one of them now, and that's how it was going to stay.

I linked Shona's arm with mine and smiled at her. Swimming on, I made sure we stayed as close to the shore as possible.

We followed a low line of rocks that jutted into the ocean. "That's Barracuda Point," Althea said.

"Why's it called that?" Shona asked.

"You'll see," she said with a smile. "Wait till we're on the other side."

We rounded the tip and swam on a little farther before Althea stopped. "OK, look now."

We turned and looked back.

"Sharks alive!" Shona gasped. I stared in silence. A low line of rocks twisted out from the shore, stretching out into a long thin body. At the tip, it narrowed into a sharp point, dented and creased along the middle, like a jawline filled with sharp teeth. Jagged rocks stood along the top like fins. Dark and menacing, it looked as though it could easily come to life with a snarling twist of its body. A cold shiver darted up my spine, prickling into my neck.

"It's supposed to protect the island," Althea said.

"What from?"

"Everything. There's all sorts of bogey-mers lurking, you know."

"Really?" I asked, shivering. "Like what?"

Althea laughed. "It's just kids' stories. Monsters and stuff." Then she stopped smiling. "But there's something to them, I think. I've never been able to quite put my fin on it, but I've always had a sense of something . . . something below the surface."

"Me too! Have you ever been pulled out to sea?" I blurted out before I could stop myself.

"What?"

"By — by the current," I faltered.

"We avoid certain spots. We learn very quickly about that."

"And what happens if you don't?" I asked, holding my breath while I waited for her to answer.

Althea lowered her voice. "The bogey-mer will get you!" she said. Then she looked at my face and burst out laughing. "Come on, I'm only joking. It's kids' tales, like I said." Then she turned suddenly, shaking her hair so it splashed onto the water, spreading golden droplets in an arc around her. "Come on. Let's go and get Marina."

She moved on. As we swam, Shona gave me an occasional sideways look. I smiled at her and tried to act casual, but my body felt stiff and clumsy as I pushed myself through the sea. I couldn't shake the feeling that I just wasn't as good at all this as they were. It didn't come as naturally. I mean, up until a few months ago, I'd never even been in water! My cheeks flushed as I prayed Shona would never tell anyone that.

The water soon became warm and shallow and colorless as we skirted the island. No currents, nothing weird. Althea was right. We just had to avoid certain spots and everything would be fine. I began to relax. We came to a wide bay. As we swam into it, the water turned cool and deep. Twisted rock formations stood along the edges.

"Double Arch Bay," Althea said.

Ahead of us, two giant arches were cut deep into the rocky shore. Althea ducked under to swim through one of them. Shona went next. Then I flicked myself down and slipped through.

We swam across a small reef. Neat clusters of plants and coral were dotted about, making it like a well-tended park. An elderly merman with shiny blue eyes and a thin gray tail swam across them, snipping at weeds with a knife made from razor shells.

"Hi, Theo," Althea said.

He nodded at us. "Morning, girls."

"Theo's the gardener," Althea explained as he swam off to tie some wilting pink plants into a bundle with seaweed.

There were archways everywhere. Some were tiny gaps in the rocks that I'd have missed if Althea hadn't pointed them out, others were wide jagged holes big enough for a whale to get through.

Eventually, we came to a shimmery purple rock with a neat round hole in the middle. "This is where Marina lives," Althea said. She tapped a pink fish hovering at the entrance, a gold bell dangling from its tail. Immediately, it wriggled its body and a delicate sound chimed.

A mermaid swam toward us from inside. She had curly red hair and a long gold tail with a shiny crescent moon painted on the end. "You must be Shona and Emily!" she said, her freckled face creasing into a smile. "Come in while I get my things." She grabbed Althea's hand and they went on ahead, along a narrow pathway lined with rough walls. It soon widened out into a wide living space divided up by trails of fern and kelp. An older mermaid bustled past us. She had red hair like Marina's, only hers was longer and frizzy. Her tail was bright yellow and tapered into soft white tassels at the end.

"Don't be out all day, Marina," she said. "It's jellied eel soufflé tonight, and we're eating early. I've got my synchro swim class at seven." Then she smiled at Shona and me. "Hello, girls," she added. "Welcome to Allpoints Island."

Shona and I smiled back before following the others into a small space with a soft seaweed bed and drapes all around it. A huge pink sponge was squashed into one corner, a crystal mirror in another.

"My room," Marina said.

I sat on the sponge. It squelched and bubbled under me. Shona laughed. "It's swishy!"

Swishy—that's Shona's word for *everything* she likes. "Squishy, more like," I said as I tried to get up.

Althea swam toward the entrance. "Come on," she said. "There's loads to show you."

Marina grabbed a patchwork bag made of leaves and reeds and followed Althea, with Shona close behind. I fumbled my way out of the sponge and caught up with them as they slithered through the arches and back out into the bay. We swam along stretches of rocky coastline, interspersed with coves of all shapes and sizes: some wide and sandy, others tiny winding channels you could almost miss.

Everywhere we looked, spots of sunlight bounced on the water, white foamy waves washed gently over rocks, and palm trees reached gently out from marshmallow sand. High on the island, some people called down to us from a woody hill. In the sea, merfolk smiled and greeted us as we passed them. A couple of young mer-children riding piggyback on a dolphin waved and shouted to us. We waved back. A group of mermen diving for food nodded at us on their way out to sea. A mermaid with long flowing hair streaming down her back smiled as she was pulled along by a swordfish on a leash.

It was all so different—and yet so familiar. I belonged here. The fear that had gripped me since yesterday floated further away with every new sight.

Swimming on, we approached a half-hidden

cave in the rocky shoreline. "There are loads of caves on the island, but we only use a couple of them," Marina said. "School's in one of them. The other's only for really major events, like when Neptune comes. That's the Grand Caves. We can show you the other one, though, Emerald Caves. You want to see your school?"

Did I? Just the thought of school washed the smile off my face. But surely this couldn't be anything like Brightport Junior High. No one was going to make fun of me here or delight in making my life a misery. And it *was* a mermaid school! A mix of emotions and questions swirled around inside me as I followed Althea into the cave. It wouldn't happen again, would it? It couldn't; I'd make sure of it. I'd do everything I could to show the mermaids I was just like them.

We inched along a narrow tunnel. As it twisted and turned, it grew darker and darker. Soon we were swimming in pitch-blackness.

"Feel your way along the walls," Marina called from somewhere ahead of me. I ran my fingers along the craggy layered sides as I edged down the tunnel.

Just as my eyes were getting used to the dark, the tunnel opened out and grew lighter. We came to a fork.

"Down here." Marina pointed along a tunnel that shimmered with green light.

It led up into a deep pool inside the cave. Above us, the ceiling stretched high and jagged. Stalactites hung all around us: enormous pillars reaching almost to the water, tiny spindles spiking down like darts. Rocks glimmered and shone purple and blue and red. Next to the pool, smooth boulders were dotted about on the gravelly ground like an abandoned game of giants' marbles.

A long scroll hung from the ceiling, pictures of underwater life drawn all over it, a pile of different-colored reeds underneath.

A young mermaid was cleaning some hairbrushes lined up on a rocky ledge that jutted across the water. She smiled at us as we gazed around.

"Swishy!" Shona said, swimming over to the hairbrushes. "You have Beauty and Deportment?"

Beauty and Deportment. Shona had told me all about that. I'd be studying it with her soon. And Diving and Dance, and all the other mermaid subjects. No more long division!

"Of course," Marina smiled. "It's my favorite subject."

"Mine, too," Shona breathed.

Althea looked at me. "I prefer Shipwreck Studies."

I tried to think of something to say, to join in the conversation. But it was all so new and alien to me. They'd all been studying these subjects for years. What if I was no good at them?

"Althea likes going out on Geography Reef Trips," Marina said with a laugh. "Anything to get out of doing her tides tables."

"It's beautiful," Shona whispered as we took it all in. "Much better than my old school."

"And about a million light-years away from mine," I added, trying not to think too hard about Brightport Junior High.

"There are two classes," Althea explained. "This one's for the older kids. There's another one for the babies."

"Two classes?" Shona asked. "Is that all?"

"There's only about thirty families here alto-gether," Marina said. "Mostly mer-families and a few human ones."

"Do they mix?" I asked. I realized I was holding my breath while I waited for the reply.

"Yes, of course," Althea said as she started swimming back out of the cave. "But they're kind of separate, too." She blushed. "If you get what I mean." She glanced quickly at my tail. I got what she meant. I was the only one. Still the odd one out.

The old fears resurfaced, hitting me like a

punch in my stomach. I couldn't keep them away any longer. I'd *never* find a place where I could fit in.

"But everyone gets along really well," Marina said quickly, swimming across to touch my arm. "And we're all really pleased you've joined us. The island's organizing a party for you next week, once you've settled in."

"We haven't had any new families here for ages," Althea added. "Come on, let's show you the rest of the island."

They were organizing a party, just for us? Maybe I was wrong. Maybe things would work out, after all.

We continued around the coast, Althea and Marina pointing out sights all along the way: a hole in the ground that spouted orange flames in the summer, little channels leading to a maze of caves and caverns where some of the merfolk ran craft stalls. I made a mental note to tell Dad about that. At least it could be something for us to talk about. He'd learned to make jewelry while he was in prison. Maybe he could get one of the stalls.

Swimming up the jagged east side of the island, we came to a channel leading into the rock.

"Now this is something you must see," Althea said.

We set off in single file along the channel. The sides became steeper and higher as we swam; the water grew deeper and colder, and so dark it was almost black. A soft wind whistled through the chasm. Then nothing. No movement, no sound, the sun beating silently down. I'd never experienced such stillness. It felt as though it was inside me, as though it was part of me. For a moment, there was nothing except me and the stillness, silently winding through my body like a snake. Was it a pleasant feeling? I couldn't even tell.

I shivered and shook myself. The others had swum ahead—again. I tried not to show them how tired it was making me to keep up. And I decided not to mention the weird snakelike feeling either. Somehow I didn't think it would help me come across as normal.

As we wound our way along the channel, Althea and Marina kept pointing things out in our path: a fossil on the canyon wall, hairline cracks in the rocks making tiny channels that split off from the main one.

"Look." Althea pointed ahead, to where the

channel seemed to come to an end. I couldn't see anything at first, just a lot of overgrown bushes and reeds lining the walls. Then I noticed what she was pointing at. A gap in the rock, through the reeds. There were pieces of driftwood attached to either side of the gap, covered in plants and algae.

We parted the reeds as though they were curtains and peered through the gap in the rock. On the other side, a shimmering blue lagoon sparkled with diamond glints. The water lay virtually still; green ferns hung down across gaping holes in the rock; a group of flamingos gathered at the edge, standing motionless on spindly legs, their long pink necks stretched straight and high. Two pelicans flew past, their wings reaching wide as they skimmed the water's still surface.

It was like paradise. How you've always imagined paradise would look.

"Swishy!" breathed Shona.

I stared so hard my eyes watered.

Marina looked nervous. "Come on. We need to get back."

"But we just got here," I said.

"We shouldn't be here at all."

"We're not really supposed to," Althea said, swimming closer and lowering her voice. "But *you* don't know that. You could go in and find out what it's like. I've always wanted to know."

I stared at the lagoon.

"I'm not sure," Shona said. "I mean, if we're not allowed . . ."

"None of the kids is brave enough. We've been told not to go in there so many times," Althea said. "But you haven't. You've only been here five minutes! Who's going to tell you off?"

"She's right," I said.

Althea smiled at me. "Exactly," she said.

This could be just what I needed! My chance to make sure Althea and Marina would definitely accept me. If I did this, they'd have to see me as one of them. That was it, I'd decided. I was going to do it. I wasn't going to be whispered about and made fun of again. And I *wasn't* going to be the odd one out. This was my chance to make sure of it.

Besides, it looked *so* tempting in there. I could almost feel it inviting me in, beckoning me in, almost pulling me. What was it? Was I imagining that, too?

Shona edged away from the reeds, her tail fluttering nervously. "Let's think about it," she said.

We dropped the reeds and drew back, but I couldn't get the image out of my mind. The stillness of the water, the ferns hanging down like delicate chains. And more than that, the chance to seal my place as one of the mermaids. I had to do it—but I wasn't brave enough to do it on my own. I would have to persuade Shona.

We set off in silence. All around us, nature bustled. Tiny brown lizards raced across rocks. Crabs scuttled under large stones, sneaking into the safety of their hidden homes. Above us, white birds with long sharp tails pecked at the cliff, disappearing into invisible holes in the rock. Eventually, the channel's walls widened once more and the sun warmed our necks as we arrived back at the open ocean.

When the others left us, Shona came to North Bay with me. I grabbed her before we went into the boat. "We've got to go back," I said.

"Oh, Emily, I don't know," Shona said. "I mean, we've only just gotten here."

"That's the whole point!" I said. "Like Althea said, we're new, we don't know our way around, it would be *easy* for us to get lost. Think how impressed they'll be. Please!"

Shona half smiled. "It did look amazing," she murmured. "And I suppose we haven't really had long enough to properly understand the rules yet."

"Not long enough at all," I said, my tail flicking with excitement, and something more than that. A need, almost a hunger. "We're just having a look around our new home. We're curious, we're a little vague about directions, and—whoops— we've gone the wrong way. No one will be upset with us."

I'm the first one to the door when the mail arrives. I flip through the pile: just more bills for Mom and Dad to argue about.

But there's something else. A letter in a shimmery pink envelope. I turn it over. *Mermaid Tours!*

"Mom! Dad!"

They're at the door in seconds.

"Oh, my God!" Mom says, snatching the letter from me. "Who's going to open it?" Her hands are shaking.

"You do it, love," Dad says. "You entered the contest." He holds my hands. I'm shaking, too.

"It's probably just some junk mail or something," Mom says, tearing at the envelope. "Let's not get excited."

She reads aloud. "'Thank you for entering our contest. We are delighted to inform you that you have won our—' Jack!" Mom drops the letter and stares at Dad.

I pick the letter up and read on. "'. . . delighted to inform you that you have won our Bermuda-and-the-Caribbean cruise vacation. You and your family will spend two weeks aboard one of our luxury ships and experience all the delights of a Mermaid Tours vacation. Many congratulations and have a good trip!'"

For a second, there's silence. Then Mom grabs me and screams. She pulls me into a tight squeeze. She's jumping up and down. "We won! We won!" she yells. "We're going on vacation! Oh, my God, we won, we won!"

I jump up and down with her till I can hardly breathe. She's holding me too tight. I pull away. Mom grabs Dad around the neck and kisses him. Kisses him! I don't think she's done that for about five years.

It worked. She won us a vacation! Maybe they'll start getting along again and everything will be all right. For a couple of weeks, at least.

Wonder if anyone will notice I'm gone. Julia might. She's kind of my best friend, not that she acts like it. She never really wanted to be my best friend. She always preferred that Emily Windsnap. I was just someone to fall back on when Emily wasn't around. Julia was really upset that day when Emily didn't show up. What am I supposed to do? Turn my back on her? Well, Emily wasn't there and I was. So Julia and I are best friends now. Fair's fair.

I wonder what happened to Emily and her mom. It feels kind of weird without them. Not that I miss her or anything. No way. Just that, well, it's kind of quiet around here without her. Sometimes I find myself looking out to sea, wondering if they'll ever come back. Stupid, huh? I'm not saying I want them to, don't get me wrong. Just, I don't know, maybe it could have been different. I mean, if she hadn't gotten me into trouble last year when she told on me for cheating in the arcade, then I wouldn't have had to hate her. I wasn't even cheating; I was trying to help her. Trying to be nice. Taught me not to bother trying *that* again in a hurry. It never works. Better just to keep your mouth shut and not get your hopes up.

Anyway, we're out of here. We're going on a cruise!

Chapter Three

We swam side by side to begin with. Below us, occasional shoals of parrotfish and bright red snappers swept across the sandy bed. When the channel narrowed, I swam ahead, slinking along the silent passageway. The ground soon became uncluttered: clear golden sand beneath us, the sun shining down, almost directly above our heads. Two silhouetted mermaid figures gliding along below the surface, our shadows came and went, appearing briefly before suddenly growing distorted with the splash of a tail breaking the water's still surface.

We came to the curtain of reeds draped down the channel's walls and the algae-coated wooden plaques. That's when the feeling started inside me. I didn't know what it was. A quivery kind of sensation jiggling around in my stomach. Nervous. Waiting for something—and a feeling that there was something waiting for me, too. Trying not to let Shona see my quivering hands, I parted the curtain and looked through the hole in the wall. The water sparkled and fanned out into a wide lagoon. Ferns hung down over cracks and gaps in the walls. A white tropical bird flew into a hole behind me, its long tail disappearing into the rock. Nothing else moved. Shona stared.

I turned to her. "Ready?" My voice shook.

She broke her gaze to look at me. "Let's just get this over with."

I glanced around to check that no one had followed us, then I squeezed through the gap and swam into the lagoon. The sun burned down, heating my neck and dancing on the water. Its light rippled below us in wavy lines across the sea floor.

As we slid across the stillness, the water grew colder and murkier. When the lagoon narrowed back into a channel, I couldn't see my reflection swimming along below me anymore. The walls lining our trail had lost their hardness. They were like chalk. I stopped and scraped my finger down the side. I made myself focus on the walls, almost flicking a switch to turn off the nagging wordless worry in my mind. Rock crumbled in my hand. The channel walls stretched upward, cold and gray and deserted.

"Emily!" Shona was pointing at something ahead. An engraving on the wall: a perfect circle with a fountain spiraling out from the center. It looked like a pinwheel, full of energy, almost as tall as us. I had this weird feeling I knew the picture, recognized it. Had I seen it in a book? Dreamed about it? What *was* it?

"Look at *this*!" Shona had swum ahead while I stared at the engraving.

I joined her in front of some ferns loosely covering a hole in the rock. The hole disappeared below the surface. We dived down. Under the water, it was just big enough to swim into.

"Cool!" I grinned at her. A secret tunnel reaching into the rock! "Shona, we *have* to see what's in there."

She frowned.

"Althea and Marina will be *so* impressed. No one else has dared to do it." I hoped that would be enough to make her want to do it. I wasn't going to tell her it was so much more than that for me, that I was doing this to prove I was a real mermaid—not just to them, but to her, too. Before she had a chance to argue, I'd slithered into the slimy, echoey darkness. Eventually I heard her follow behind.

The winding tunnel led us deeper and deeper into dead rock: tight, cold, and claustrophobic, but gradually widening and growing brighter as we swam. Bit by bit, a growing circle of light opened up ahead of us.

We swam toward it, finally coming out into a dome-shaped space in the middle of the cave. A high ceiling rippled faintly with the water's reflection.

"I don't understand," Shona said, looking around. "What's that light?"

I shook my head as we swam all around the rocky edges. It seemed to be coming from under the water.

"Come on." I dived down. "That's our answer!" I gasped. The floor of the cave was absolutely littered with crystals and stones and gold, all shining so brightly I almost had to shield my eyes. I'd never seen jewels like these. Dazzling pink rocks with sharp white edges lay on the ground in a circle, joined together by a thin line of gold. In their center, a bright blue stone shaped like a rocket pointed up to the surface of the water.

"What in the ocean . . . ?" Shona swam around and around the display, her mouth open, her eyes huge, shining with the reflection of the blue stone.

I looked around. There was more. Once we started looking, it seemed that stones and crystals covered the entire floor of the cave, packed and tucked into gaps in the rock all around us.

"Emily, I think we need to get back." A fat green angelfish hovered between us, its startled eyes staring into ours before it spun around and disappeared into a rocky crevice. "We've seen it now. We're not supposed to be here."

I stopped gazing around. Shona was right. "OK," I said. "Let's go back." We'd found the answer to Althea's and Marina's questions. The lagoon hid a cave filled with jewels. But why? It didn't make sense.

Shona turned immediately and started making her way back toward the tunnel. But then I noticed something on the cave's wall: a picture exactly like the engraving we'd seen earlier, only even bigger. It looked like a mosaic. I knew that shape — I was sure of it. And even though it didn't make any sense, I had this overwhelming feeling that it knew me too! As we got closer, I could see it was made out of jewels: a huge golden one in the center, oval shaped and about half as tall as me, with multicolored strands spinning outward from it. I put my hand out to touch it. It wobbled.

"Shona!"

"Come on." She kept swimming.

I pushed at the jewel. It was lodged in the rock, but only loosely. We could probably get it out. I *had* to try. There was a secret in here—I was sure of it. Something was drawing me on and I couldn't resist it.

"Shona!" I called again. "Just look at this."

She stopped swimming and turned.

"It's loose!" I pulled at it, edging my fingertips underneath to lever it up. "Help me."

She swam reluctantly back to me. "I thought we were—sharks alive!"

"You thought we were sharks?"

Shona stared at the mosaic. "What is it?"

"Help me get it out."

"You're pulling my tail, aren't you? We can't go around vandalizing the place!"

"We're not vandalizing anything. We'll put it back. Let's just see what's behind it." An image of Althea's and Marina's faces flickered across my mind, their eyes wide and impressed with my bravery. All the other mermaids crowding around me, wanting to be my friends, accepting me as one of them, not the odd one out, not the freak. This cave was going to change my life; I just knew it.

Shona sighed heavily, then reluctantly dug her fingers under the jewel, and we gradually levered it little by little out of its hole. A moment later, we were holding it between us. We lowered it to the ground and it plopped onto the seabed with a soft *thunk,* scattering a shower of sand in a swirl around us.

"Now what?" Shona stared down at it.

I swam up to the hole it had left behind and poked my head into it. Another tunnel. I grabbed Shona's arm, pointing into the blackness. "We *have* to go down there."

"We don't *have* to go anywhere!" Shona snapped.

"*Please!* Aren't you dying to know what's in there? Can't you feel it?" This wasn't even about Althea and Marina anymore. It was more like a thirst, or a magnet pulling me.

A magnet? My throat closed up as I remembered. . . . But it couldn't lead to the Triangle. We were in the middle of the island.

Shona peered into the tunnel. Her eyes sparkled against the reflection of the crystals. I could see the dilemma in them. "We just have a quick look, see what's there, and then we go home," she said eventually.

"Deal!"

We edged our way carefully into the hole,

slithering along in the silent dark. Me first, Shona following closely behind. The tunnel grew colder as we made our way deeper into the rock. The edges became craggy and sharp.

And then, without warning, it suddenly stopped. A dead end.

"Now what?" I called to Shona.

"We go back. We've looked. There's nothing here. And I'm not exactly surprised, or disappointed. Come on."

How could it suddenly end like that? I was *sure* it was leading somewhere. I felt around on the rock in front of me. It was different from the walls. Smoother. I inched my hands around it. Then I realized why it was different.

"Shona! It's a boulder!"

"What?"

"There's something blocking the tunnel. Look, it's different from the walls. Feel it."

Shona squeezed forward to touch the boulder.

I felt my way around its edges. "There's a crack all around it." It was almost the same shape as the crystal at the other end. "Maybe it'll come loose."

Shona looked at me.

"Let's just try."

"How do I let you talk me into all these things?" she said with another sigh.

"Because you can feel it, too? Because there's something down here that's making you tingle with excitement? Because the last time we went exploring, we ended up finding my dad? Because being my friend means you get to live on a beautiful desert island? Because—"

"OK, enough." Shona half frowned, half smiled. "Don't get your tail in a tizzy. Let's just get on with it."

Because I couldn't turn back now if I wanted to, even if I don't know why. I didn't say that part out loud, though.

It didn't just slip out like the jewel at the other end. We pushed and pushed, but nothing happened. Or nearly nothing. The boulder moved slightly, rocking backward and forward as though it was on a hinge, but we couldn't shift it.

"It's useless," Shona gasped. "We'll never get it out."

"We need to use the rocking. Get a momentum going. Look, it's swaying. If we both push it from above, it might topple. Wait till I say. On the count of three. You ready?"

Shona nodded without looking at me.

"One." I felt around for a good hold on the rock.

"Two." I stretched out my tail, getting ready to flick it as hard as I could.

"Three!"

We swished and pushed, grunting and heaving.

"Now, let go!" The rock swayed away from us, and then back. "And again." Another shove against the rock, another slight movement. Again and again, we heaved and pushed until, finally, it started to loosen.

Then Shona stopped pushing. "I've had enough. I'm exhausted."

"But we're nearly there!"

"I want to go back," she said. "I don't want to do this."

"What's the problem?"

"The *problem* is that we don't know what's on the other *side*!"

"Exactly! But there is something, isn't there? I can almost feel it vibrating in my body."

"Me too. And I don't like it, Em. It doesn't feel good. I don't want to know what it is, and I want to go before this place collapses in on us."

"It's just a boulder. It's not going to collapse!"

But Shona turned to go back.

"Just one more push."

"You do it if you like. I'm going."

"Fine!" I went back to the boulder. It was teetering on the edge of the hole now. I could probably push it on my own. I didn't even know why I was doing it anymore. I just knew there was something here. I could feel it. Low vibrations hummed rhythmically through the cave, and inside me, growing stronger. What *were* they?

Fueled by frustration, I spun my tail as fast as I could, pushed all my weight against the rock, and heaved.

Very slowly, it teetered, swaying with the rhythm of the water before eventually toppling: a huge, smooth, oval rock slipping down and away from us, almost in slow motion. Water swirled all around. The boulder was still traveling—rolling, hurtling down through the water.

It felt like when you roll a snowball down a hill and it grows bigger and bigger. Something was building up on the other side of the tunnel, below us, below the island, deep inside the rock. Nerve endings jangled and jammed like simmering explosions under my skin.

"I told you, I told you!" Shona screamed. "It's caving in! We're going to be trapped!"

"It's OK. Look." I tried to keep my nerve. Everything was still intact in the tunnel. It was just on the other side that the water was foaming and swirling everywhere. And there was something else: a presence. The vibrations had turned into a low rumbling, way down below. Something was down there. Something that didn't feel quite so exciting anymore. What was it? Images swirled around my mind: the mosaic, the spiral, whirling, spreading out, writhing.

"What's *happening*?" Shona screamed.

"It's just—it's the rock falling to the bottom of the caves," I said, much more confidently than I felt. "It's all right. Just stay calm. It'll stop in a minute."

The rock kept plummeting and crashing, getting fainter and fainter. Sand and rock particles swirled around, a few of them spinning softly through the hole into the cave.

And then it stopped. No more crashing. No swirling rocks or sand, no hurtling anywhere. Complete silence.

Total silence. Kind of eerie silence.

I smiled nervously at Shona. "See," I said. "Told you it'd all be OK."

And then we heard it. The rumbling. Not a flutter of excitement in our stomachs, or a thrilling vibration that we might have imagined. This was very,

very real. And it was growing. Soon, a roaring noise sliced through the caves, growling louder and louder, rumbling toward us. I couldn't move. I looked at Shona. Her lips were moving—but I couldn't hear a thing. The rumble turned into a high-pitched whine, shrieking and screaming through the hole into the tunnel. I slammed my hands over my ears.

The next thing I knew, Shona had grabbed one of my hands. She pulled it away from my head. "We have to get OUT OF HERE!" she was yelling in my ear. "QUICK!"

I'd forgotten how to move. My tail, my arms, everything had turned completely stiff.

"Come *on*!" Shona yanked my arm, pulling me with her. My body jackknifed into action and we hammered through the tunnel as an explosion erupted in the water behind us.

I turned around to see the end of the tunnel crumble and dissolve. Rocks fell and bounced in the water, scattering sand and bubbles everywhere, clouds bunching and spilling across the seabed like lava.

Something was reaching out from the tunnel, feeling around. Oh, God! What *was* it? A huge tube, slimy and dark green, almost as thick as the tunnel itself. One side was rubbery and shiny, then it flipped and twisted over and its underside was gray and covered in black spots. They looked like giant warts. In between them, great thick suckers grabbed onto the wall like the suction cups on the soap holder Mom keeps in the shower, only about fifty times bigger—and a hundred times uglier.

That was it! That was what I saw in my mind only moments ago—and now it was here, for real, in front of me!

The tube flapped and flicked about, maniacally batting and thwacking against the sides, reaching out farther and farther toward us. An icy stake of terror pinned me to the spot.

The siren noise shrieked into the cave again as the tube thing moved around in the tunnel, feeling its way along. Getting closer!

Someone was screaming and screaming.

Shona shook me. "Emily, you have to pull yourself together!" she yelled. The screaming stopped. It had been me. She pulled me through the water. "Just swim for your life!"

We threw ourselves along the tunnel, working our arms like windmills in a tornado. I took brief glances behind us as we swam. The tube lashed out, extending toward us like a giant worm, ripping at the tunnel walls and doubling my panic.

Propelling myself faster than I had ever swum in my life, I flung my body through the passage until I finally made it to the open space. The rock was collapsing around us as we swam.

The thing was reaching out of the tunnel toward us! No! Its end was tapered and blood red, and covered with brown hairy strands swirling around as it felt its way through the tunnel. It slid farther and farther out as we dashed across the cave to the next tunnel, the one that would get us out of here.

CRASH! THWACK! Slamming against the roof of the cave, the walls, the ground, the monster worm was destroying the cave, little by little. We were almost within its reach. *Swim! Swim! Faster!*

As we heaved ourselves into the next tunnel, I glanced behind me again. The giant worm wasn't on its own. There were at least three others, maybe more, all searching and feeling around the cave walls, crashing through the water, reaching out toward us. Slimy, scaly tentacles. What *was* it? A giant octopus?

A scream burned silently in my throat. Shona had virtually disappeared. She was ahead of me, but the water was murky with swirling pieces of rock and debris. *One more corner, one more corner,*

I repeated to myself again and again as I plowed down the long narrow tunnel.

I threw myself at the end of the tunnel. Nearly out! I was panting and gasping, my energy slipping away. And then a tentacle spun out, coiling itself down the tunnel. It touched me! *Arrggghhh!* Rubbery slime grazed my arm. My speed instantly tripled.

A moment later, I was out. Out of the tunnel! Back outside in the channel between the cliffs. Sunlight.

Shona was there, panting and heaving.

"It touched me! It touched me!" I screeched.

"Keep moving," she said.

But I looked back. And this time I saw something I hadn't noticed before.

"Shona!"

"I told you, keep—"

"Look." I pointed at the wall. How had I not seen it before? Carved into the wall. A trident. Neptune's trident! The huge pitchfork he carries everywhere with him. Instantly, an image flashed into my mind: the last time I'd seen Neptune. Standing in front of him in his courtroom, his booming voice issuing orders that no one would ever dare to disobey, the trident held out—the instrument that could create an island or a storm with a single movement.

"Keep moving," Shona said again. But her face had turned white.

We swam on, scattering shoals of tiny yellow fish as we pounded through the creek. Back into the lagoon, and out through the hole on the other side. Turning to close the curtain of reeds, I noticed the wooden plaques again. They were covered in algae, but there was something underneath. I rubbed at the algae, brushed reeds away—and I could see it. Another trident. We'd been trespassing in Neptune's own territory!

What had we done?

Shona was ahead of me. I caught up to her without speaking. Swimming in silence, I could hardly believe any of this had really happened. Everything was totally still and quiet. No movement at all. We stopped, listened.

"It didn't follow us," I said lamely. "We're safe. It's OK."

Shona looked at me. There was something in her expression that I'd never seen before. A hardness in her eyes. "You think, Emily?" she said. "You really think so?"

Then she turned and swam on. She didn't say another word all the way back.

My whole reason for coming to the lagoon, to secure Shona's friendship and my place on the island—all my hopes, and I'd done completely the opposite. I had no words either.

Well, I don't know about you, but this is not MY idea of a luxury cruise!

Swimming pool? I don't *think* so. Nonstop food and drink? Uh, hello? Enormous ship? Yeah, right!

We've been conned. Our vacation of a lifetime, full of "magic" and "enchantment," turns out to be two weeks on an old wreck of a sailing boat with me, Mom, Dad, and some old guy to drive us. Fabulous.

There's absolutely zilch to do. We've been out at sea for—well, I think it might be two days, but it's hard to tell since there's nothing to distinguish one deadly boring second from the next. I'll never forgive my parents for this. Especially Dad. Why did he have to see that stupid magazine?

And guess who's left to entertain herself all day while her parents go back to being totally wrapped up in themselves?

He's the only one who's enjoying himself. Mom's spent all her time inside so far, cooking or sleeping and occasionally turning green and rushing over to the side to be sick. Why I thought it might be different I don't know. When will I learn that nothing nice *ever* happens to me?

I wish one day it would. Just once.

Even the captain looks like death warmed over most of the time. Just stands at the wheel looking out at the sea. Not that there's anything else to look at. He hardly talks to any of us. He must be at least fifty, so it's not as if I want to talk to him. But he could make a little effort.

Dad doesn't seem to realize that the rest of us are having the most awful vacation in the world. I wish he'd pay some attention to Mom, but he's too busy running around with a fishing net, getting all excited about the stupidest things. Like now, for example. I'm lying on the deck reading a magazine—well, trying to read. It's not exactly easy while you're careening up and down and having to watch out for water splashing all over the place. Dad's on the deck next to me, leaning over the edge with a pair of binoculars. He's wearing bright yellow shorts, and his back is bright red to complement them.

Then he leaps up. "Mandy, love. Come and see. Quickly!"

I put my magazine down. Maybe he's spotted the cruise that we're really supposed to be on. Perhaps this was just a joke and we're on our way to start our real vacation on a real ship! I look out to sea. "There's nothing there, Dad."

"Wait. He'll do it again soon."

Turns out he's seen a turtle. A turtle! Well, excuse me, but BIG DEAL!

I decide to go inside. It might be even duller in there, but at least Mom won't try to convince me that I'm having the time of my life.

Only something stops me. I squeeze past the captain, and I'm about to open the cabin door when I catch a glimpse of something. Not just a stupid turtle. A . . . well . . . a kind of nothingness. Just ahead of us, it's all dark. The sea looks black and shiny, and the sky above it is suddenly filled with heavy clouds. Great. That's all we need now, a thunderstorm.

I look at the captain. He's taken off his cap. He rubs his eyes.

"What is it?" I join him at the wheel.

"Look!" He's pointing to a load of dials. They've got numbers on them, but they're changing too fast to make any sense.

"What do they mean?"

He bends down to study the dials more closely. "They should stay pretty much constant," he says. "Might just be a loose connection."

"What about that?" I nod toward the compass. The pointer's spinning around like mad.

The captain wipes his cap across his forehead. Beads of sweat bubble down his face. "I don't know what's going on," he says, his voice quivering. "It happened once before. It's—we need to get away from here!"

The boat's heading toward the darkness. And I don't know why I haven't thought of this before now, but I suddenly remember a comprehension test we did in English, about the Bermuda Triangle. It was called "The Ocean's Graveyard," and it was about all these ships that sailed into the Bermuda Triangle never to return.

The Bermuda Triangle. Is that where we are?

I glance across at Dad on the back deck. He's still staring through his binoculars.

"Dad."

"Hang on, I think there might be another one in a sec."

"Dad!"

He puts his binoculars down. "What?"

I point ahead, at the darkness. We're getting closer and closer. It's as though we're being pulled along, toward where the water's lying motionless and black.

Dad turns around. "Mother of . . . what's that?"

We gaze in paralyzed silence as the boat slowly begins to pick up speed, gliding toward the glassy blackness.

I don't notice Mom coming out from below deck, but at some point I'm aware that she's there, too. We're slipping over to one side as we careen through the water.

"We're going to drown," Mom says suddenly. Almost calmly.

"Not if I can help it!" The captain grabs at the wheel, flinging it around as hard as he can. But it hardly makes any difference. His cheeks are purple. "Hold on!" he yells.

We're edging closer toward the silent black water. It's pulling us sideways, drawing us in like a magnet. We're slipping farther and farther to the side. Bits of spray spatter the deck. The boat starts to rock.

Mom's fallen onto her knees. The captain's lurching at the wheel. I'm gripping the mast. I reach out to Mom. "Get hold of my hand!" Spray lashes against my face as the boat leans farther and farther over to the side. Mom reaches out, our fingertips almost touching before she slips back across the deck.

"Maureen!" Dad lets go of the rail to reach out for Mom. He's holding her in one arm, gripping the rail with his other hand. He's got his arm around her—at last. I didn't want it to happen like this.

The captain is shouting something at us. He's spinning the wheel one way, then another. It's not making the slightest bit of difference. I can't hear what he's saying. I think I'm shouting, too. I don't even know what *I'm* saying. Seawater is everywhere. We're spinning sideways toward the strange glassiness, mast first, the bottom of the ship almost out of the water.

All is darkness, water, shouting, screaming. We're going to die! Out here in the middle of nowhere, on our own. A stupid, stupid death. I close my eyes and wait for the boat to veer into the blackness.

And it does.

Or it starts to.

We're teetering on our side when the boat suddenly jiggles and shakes. It's leveling out. What's happening? It slips and rocks a bit, there's water all over the deck and I'm soaking, but we're straightening out. We're not going to die! We're safe! Everything's going to be—

But then I see Dad's face, gray and heavy, as though he's suddenly aged thirty years. He's staring at something behind me.

"Don't tell me you've seen another turtle," I say shakily.

Then the boat lurches again and I fall to the floor. That's when I see it, rising out of the water. *What is it?*

First, huge tusks, curving upward like giant bayonets. Below them, a long, long, olive-green lumpy snout. It's taller than the ship's mast. It almost blocks out the sun. Horror seeps into my body. Huge white eyes bulging and popping out like great big fat full moons on either side, lumps all over the snout. Oh, GOD!

Enormous tentacles slap the water, extending outward and up, khaki-green greasy things with suckers all the way down, waving around, splashing, making a whirlpool. We're spinning into it.

I'm trying to scream, but all I can manage is a kind of dry clicking sound. We're being sucked into something, into the whirlpool, a mass of tentacles rising all around us.

And then Mom's screaming. I think maybe I am, too. One of the tentacles reaches right up into the air, then hurls itself down toward the boat and grips the mast.

I'm screaming for Mom; the boat's on its side. Where's Dad?

Water everywhere, a crashing sound, and then—

Chapter Four

S hona didn't talk to me all week—that first week in our new home. It was supposed to be a fresh start, a dream come true. Instead it was the worst week of my life. Think Brightport Junior High's worst moments and multiply by a hundred. I was still the odd one out, still the one who didn't fit in, who no one wanted to know. Was it always going to be like this for me?

Shona started hanging around with Marina and Althea. Maybe she thought anyone was better than me. Maybe she was right. After all, I was the idiot who had finally gotten to live with both of my parents and been given a new life on an island full of merpeople and glistening turquoise sea and white sandy beaches, and what did I do? I couldn't bear to think about it.

And yet I couldn't think of anything else. I even forgot to be scared of starting school. I drifted through it, like everything else, in a daze. I couldn't even get excited when I learned to dive with the grace of a dolphin and brush my hair like a real mermaid and sing the wordless songs of the sirens. None of it mattered. Everything was ruined because of what I'd done, and marred by a constant fear of the consequences. What was going to happen? Had it already started? The weather had changed a little since we went in the cave. Nothing all that dramatic. It had just been really windy, sudden sharp gusts making the sea all choppy. Probably just coincidence, but people had been commenting on it.

Millie and Archie came over one night. Millie stared at me all the way through dinner. "Are you all right?" she asked as she helped herself to a huge scoop of ice cream.

Mom turned to look at me, cupping my chin in her hand. "Are you, sweetie?" she asked softly. "You have been quiet."

"I'm fine!" I snapped. "Why shouldn't I be?"

"Your aura's looking gray and patchy," Millie said. "Usually means you're fighting demons in your mind."

Dad burst out laughing. "Don't think my little 'un would stand a chance against demons," he said with a smile. Millie glared at him.

I got up to clear some plates. Anything to get away. But just then, the boat rocked violently as a wave thrashed against the side, knocking half the dishes from the table and tipping me back into my seat.

Archie and Dad darted outside to see what had happened while I helped Mom and Millie pick up the broken dishes.

"Freak wave," Archie said, pulling his hair behind his head as they swam back up to the trap-door to join us again. "Seem to have been a few of those lately. Wonder what that's about. I'll have to report back to Neptune about this."

"Neptune? Why?" I asked.

"It's my job to keep him informed of everything. That a problem?" He seemed to look at me suspiciously as he spoke. I must have imagined it. A freak wave couldn't have anything to do with me—could it?

On Friday morning, I bumped into Shona on the way to school. She'd avoided me all week but could hardly pretend she hadn't seen me when I was right beside her in the water. For a brief second, I wondered if she wanted to make friends again, but the look on her face said otherwise. Her expression was like mine when I'm faced with a plate of mushy peas, or a spider near my bed.

"Have you told anyone?" she asked, pulling me into a tiny cavern that led off from the main tunnel toward Emerald Cave.

"No! I don't know what to say. What are we going to do?"

"*WE?*" She stared at me. "*I* didn't even want to go up that stupid creek in the first place! *I* didn't want to go in the cave. *I* didn't want to knock the wall down. *I* am not going to do *anything!*"

A tear burned the corner of my eye. I'd never seen Shona like this. "Well, what am *I* going to do, then?"

"I don't think we should say anything," she said more softly. "We just forget it, OK?"

"Forget it?"

"Pretend it didn't happen. Whatever it was, it must have gone back where it came from. It didn't follow us. So we say nothing. Please?"

"But what if—"

"Em, think about it. We've only just gotten

here. Do you want everyone to hate us before we've even had the chance to make any friends?"

"Of course not. But—"

"But nothing. We leave it. Please, Emily."

I nodded. "OK." A drop of water plopped down from the ceiling into the pool between us. "You're still my best friend, aren't you?" I asked as we set off along the tunnel.

Shona didn't meet my eyes. "Let's just act normal, OK?"

A couple of merboys were coming along the tunnel. Shona smiled at them as they caught up with us, and then swam ahead with them. I trailed behind, pretending to get something out of my bag. I didn't want anyone to think I was all on my own with no friends. Which is exactly what I was.

We hadn't gotten much farther when I noticed that the water around me was swaying and swirling. It was building up, spinning around. I tried to move forward but got thwacked against the side. The monster! Was it here?

The caves were shaking. A thin stalactite fell and crashed down from the ceiling, missing me by inches. I jerked backward through the water, scraping my back on the rock. Within seconds, merpeople were rushing from the caves.

"Quick—out!" a merboy shouted as he raced past me.

I didn't need telling twice. We pelted out through the tunnels, back to open water. Outside, others were already gathered. Someone was swimming in between them, talking to groups of people, telling them to move on. Then he turned and I saw his face. Archie!

What was going on?

I swam over to him. He hardly looked up. "Just follow the others," he said gravely. "We'll meet in the Grand Caves."

The Grand Caves? The ones Marina had told us about? But weren't they only for really special events?

I followed the others in a daze, my mind swirling with images of what I'd seen—and fears of the destruction and horror that might be ahead; thoughts churning like the sea.

I gasped as I entered the Grand Caves. Impossible shapes hung all around us: upside-down forests, frozen bunches of arrows waiting to fall as one, long paper-thin flaps that looked like dinosaur wings. Drips from the ceiling bounced off majestic boulders and into the pool, ringing out like church bells.

Ahead of me, a stone platform jutted over the water. On one side, thick, marblelike columns reached down from the ceiling into the depths of the water, frilly edges folding around them like icing on a cake. On the other, the wall stretched up like a cliff side, stalagmites lining its surface, clumped together in chunky groups. Lanterns glowed among them, spreading shimmering lights across the pool as they shook. The walls were still trembling. Surely it wasn't safe to be inside if there was an earthquake?

I looked around for someone I knew. Shona had disappeared. *Probably with Althea and Marina,* I thought miserably.

In front of me, a long wooden walkway divided the clear azure pool. A few people were carefully picking their way along it. I looked away, feeling guilty as I did so. The last thing I needed now was for Shona and the other mermaids to see me as one of the humans. They'd *never* want to be my friend then.

But then I spotted Mom! She was here, too, edging across the walkway with Millie.

"Mom!" I couldn't stop myself from shouting out. She looked up and waved briefly before grabbing the rails as the caves shook again. She pointed up to the stone benches that stretched high up on the cave's sides. I wondered if I should get out of the pool and join her. A glance at the mermaids. No. I was staying in the water. Then another mighty crash thundered through the caves, throwing me under, leaving me with no choice anyway.

Gasping, I gave myself up to the water. It wasn't as bad underwater: it was a little like a Jacuzzi. It might almost have been enjoyable if it wasn't for the fact that I didn't have a clue what was going on, my best friend wasn't speaking to me, and the island seemed to be crumbling around us.

As I resurfaced, I spotted Shona with Althea and Marina. I knew it! A shot of anger speared through me. It wasn't fair! I hadn't exactly gone to that lagoon on my own. She'd done wrong just as much as I had. Nearly. I mean, it wasn't as if I'd forced her to go. And it was their suggestion in the first place! She looked up and caught my eye, just for a second. I nearly smiled. Then Althea said something to her and she turned away. She didn't look back. Traitor.

This was worse than Brightport Junior High! At least then, I could sneak out at night to meet Shona. Now I'd lost her, and it seemed as if all three of them had turned against me. It was so unfair! I'd be better off going back to Brightport, I thought, my heart heavy, my eyes stinging with tears.

I didn't have long to dwell on it. All thoughts were catapulted out of my mind by an explosion of rocks as the caves shook even more violently. A column that looked like marble fell into the water with a mighty splash. Forests of stalagmites shuddered and trembled. I looked up to see Mom gripping the bench. Millie was holding her arm and looking serene. As serene as anyone can look when they're sitting on a bench that seems to be doubling as a seaside rodeo horse.

Where was Dad? I scanned the pools. And then I saw him. Terror on his face, he was hurtling across the pool.

"Emily!" he cried into my hair as he pulled me toward him.

I grabbed onto him while the caves crashed and crumbled all around us. It was growing louder. It sounded like thunder, cracking right over our heads, coming from everywhere.

And then something happened. Something almost familiar. I almost knew it was going to happen, almost remembered it from somewhere else.

The shaking stopped.

Just like that.

The sudden stillness was almost as much of a

shock as the violent movement that had come before it, throwing people across the floor, dunking merfolk under the water. I gripped Dad so hard it must have hurt him. He held me close.

"Look!" Someone was calling out. I turned to see where everyone was looking. The caves were splitting! A crack opened up, starting from the base, shaking and creaking as it crumbled open. The whole thing would fall in on us. We'd be buried alive! Oh, God. The monster—the monster! It was here! I fought back waves of terror.

But I soon realized that nothing else was moving. Just one section of the caves was splitting open, almost like a hidden door. Almost as though it was being opened by someone. Or something.

Or Neptune.

The caves had split wide and high enough to let in a thick shaft of sunlight. I had to cover my eyes.

When I opened them, I saw him, riding into the caves, shrouded by dusty sunbeams. First the dolphins, then the chariot, gold and grand, carrying Neptune into the caves.

I should have known I'd be found out! His voice burst into my memory so clearly I could almost hear it. The memory so sharp: standing in front of him in his courtroom listening to him tell us we'd be spared prison on the condition

we'd come to this island. "If you break this condition, you will be punished most severely," he'd
added in that booming voice of his. Had I broken
it? What would he do to me?

The dolphins pulled Neptune into the center
of the caves before swimming back into the corners, surrounding us like bodyguards. Archie swam
beside the chariot.

Pausing to wait for silence, Neptune rose in
his seat, lifting his trident in the air. As he waved
it above his head, the cave closed again, sealing us
together to face his wrath. I knew what *that* was
like. Knowing I was to face it again was almost
enough to make me give up hope altogether.

Neptune looked around the caves. "Do you
KNOW why I am here?" he asked, his voice deep
and grave. His sentence echoed over and over,
*KNOW why I am here, KNOW why I, KNOW,
know . . .*

No one dared to answer. No one knew.
Almost no one. He was here for me—I was sure
of it. I tried to calm my thumping chest before
Dad heard it.

"I shall ask another question," he said, his voice
ringing around the caves. "Do you know why
YOU are here?"

He looked around, narrowing his eyes. I willed

myself to shrink into nothingness. Luckily his gaze passed me by.

More silence. Neptune clicked his fingers. At once, a line of sea horses appeared at the side of the caves. They gathered into a perfect formation and swam toward him. Then, hooking his golden gown in their tails, they raised it up behind him. Neptune sat down and nodded curtly, his diamond-studded tail fanning out in front of him. The sea horses instantly darted away.

"I will tell you," Neptune said. "You are here because of ME! Because of MY generosity. This island hasn't always been the happy little paradise you have here today. This was once a place of grave importance."

He banged his trident on a rock. "Archieval!"

Archie swam forward. Then, bowing low, he kissed Neptune's tail. "Your Majesty," he said solemnly. I'd never seen Archie look like this. He had a gold sash running along his tail; his hair was tied back in a neat ponytail and seemed to shine with splashes of deep green against the pool's reflection.

"Tell these folk their history," Neptune said coldly. "It's about time they were reminded." Then he sat back in his chariot, waving his trident at Archie to beckon him forward.

The caves became silent as we waited for Archie to speak.

He cleared his throat. "Many years ago," he began, "life here was very different. The Bermuda Triangle was an important stronghold. Together with a most trusty servant of Neptune's, our bravest sirens worked well here, in the rich waters around Allpoints Island." Archie paused. His tail flicked nervously. His cheeks had reddened a touch. "This is where ships were brought down. They were relieved of their riches, which were returned to the rightful owner of all that passes on the oceans."

Ships were brought down? That wasn't what he'd told us on the way here. He'd just said that they'd disappeared, not that they were brought down on purpose! Right here! Was our new home one of those ships? Maybe someone had died in my bedroom!

My mind swirled with grim and gruesome images: bodies under my bed, killed by the "trusty servant." Did he mean the monster? This place wasn't paradise at all. It was more like a setting for a horror film. I could hardly concentrate as Neptune started talking again. "Thank you, Archieval. And then what happened?"

Archie glanced back at Neptune before clearing

his throat again. "The, er, the trusty servant I told you about. One day, he—"

"TELL THEM WHEN!" Neptune exploded.

"Almost a hundred years ago—"

"EXACTLY! NOT a hundred! Ninety-two years ago! Do you hear me? Ninety-two. That is my POINT!" As he shouted, a wave washed through the pool. I held on to Dad to steady myself.

Neptune sat back down in his chariot, his face purple with rage. He clicked his fingers and a dolphin rushed forward. Turning onto its back, it flapped its tail in front of Neptune's face like a fan. After a while, Neptune cooled down and he waved the dolphin away. He motioned to Archie once again. "Continue."

"Ninety-two years ago, this trusty servant went to sleep."

Dad pulled away from me. "You're talking in riddles, Archie."

What was he doing? Had he forgotten how powerful Neptune was? Or that it was only thanks to him that we were here? Or how easy it would be for Neptune to send him back to *prison*? He let go of me and swam toward Archie. "Tell us what this is about. Who is the trusty servant that you keep mentioning? If you're telling us a story, tell us the whole thing."

Archie glanced at Neptune, who shrugged disdainfully.

"All right," Archie said. "I'll tell you." He took a deep breath. "I'm talking about the kraken."

The cave filled with sound: people whispering, talking, gasping. Merpeople turning to each other with questions on their faces and fear in their eyes.

A mergirl from my class was in front of me in the water. "What's the kraken?" I asked in a whisper. I think in my heart I already knew.

"It's a huge, fierce monster," she whispered back. "It's just a myth, though. It's not real." She turned back to face Archie. "Or at least that's what we've always thought."

My body shook. My tail was spinning so vigorously the water was frothing around me.

A mermaid I didn't recognize held up her hand. She had deep wrinkles in her face and piercing blue eyes. "Archieval, if this is true, why didn't our parents tell us about it? My great-grandparents would have been alive while it was around. Surely they would have passed this on."

Archie glanced once more at Neptune for approval. A brief nod in reply.

"The merfolk who lived here at that time were the kraken's keepers. The kraken works for a hundred years, then sleeps for another hundred. The last time it went to sleep, one small ship somehow managed to find its way through the Triangle's border. With no kraken to bring it down, the ship ended up here." Archie looked at the people sitting along the stone benches. "Those folk were your ancestors," he said.

"But we don't know anything about this," one of the women called down. I recognized her from one of the ships in our bay. "Surely someone would have told us!"

"Once the people had landed on the island, it turned out that many of the merfolk were happy for them to stay. In a short time, friendships were formed. Apart from a very small number of the kraken keepers who were assigned to special duties elsewhere, most of the merfolk decided to stay here, as did most of the humans."

"You haven't answered my question!" the woman shouted.

"Memory drug," Archie said simply. "They volunteered. That was their choice."

"All of them?" the woman insisted. "The merfolk, too?"

"We can use it on anyone," Archie replied. "And it will wipe out almost everything. What remains — well, you have all heard half-tales, stories you never quite knew what to make of, myths passed on and distorted with every telling."

Archie's words were slowly filtering into my brain. I didn't want to understand, didn't dare to follow his thinking to its logical conclusion. But the memory drug, well, I knew all about that. It was what my mom had been given for twelve years, so she wouldn't remember that she was married to a merman. Fed to her in so-called treats from her so-called friend Mr. Beeston, the so-called lighthouse keeper! He'd always given me the creeps. He used to drop by to visit Mom all the time, for coffee and doughnuts. He never said a lot, but he just had this really odd manner. He'd look at me sideways, and his eyes were different colors and his teeth were crooked. Well, he just made me feel uncomfortable. And then, when it turned out he'd been spying on us my entire life, it all made sense.

I'd half forgiven him in the end, when he helped me get back at Mandy Rushton. He used the memory drug on my class so no one would remember me turning into a mermaid. But he wasn't to be trusted—and neither was anyone else who went around doling out that drug!

"As you all know, Neptune is a just and kind ruler," Archie continued with a slight cough. "He allowed them to live together here on the island.

No one needed to know about the kraken. Not yet. And so, you are here today. Allpoints Island has existed in this way for ninety-two years."

A mermaid with glitter in her hair and a pink tail that flicked and splashed on the water raised her hand. "But why are you telling us this?" she asked in a timid voice. "Why now? And who are you, anyway? We hardly know you."

Neptune rose from his chariot, motioning Archie to move out of his way. "Archieval works for me," he said. "And he has told you your history. Now let me tell you something about your present."

He sucked in his cheeks, clenching his teeth. "Someone," he said, almost in a whisper, "*someone* has dared to challenge my power." He took a breath, lifting his trident in the air. Then, in a voice that shook the caves as much as his arrival had, he bellowed, "Someone woke the kraken before its time!"

Darting backward and forward in the pool, agitated and angry, he spoke quickly. "Eight more years. That's how long it had. That's how long it NEEDED. That's when I would have been here for it. But no! Someone couldn't wait that long. SOMEONE had to wake it early. Do you KNOW what happens when my kraken has not had the sleep it needs?"

The caves responded with silence. No one was going to attempt to answer Neptune in this kind of mood. Not that he was known for having any other kind of mood.

"I'll tell you. It wakes in a rage. Too much of a rage for even NEPTUNE to calm it. My truly loyal servant—someone has robbed me of it!"

"What will it do?" someone asked.

"The first signs are relatively small. It will lash around in its lair, creating freak waves. This is what it does while it is still in its cave. As far as we know, it still IS in there. But it will find its way to open seas sooner or later, and when it does, it will set out on the only path it knows." Neptune paused as he slowly surveyed the caves. "Destruction."

My tail was shaking again. "It's OK, little 'un," Dad whispered, pulling me close. "I'll look after you." He knew nothing. Nothing.

"That is why I am the ONLY one who should wake the kraken. The one who wakes it is the ONLY one who—" Neptune stopped abruptly. He smoothed back his hair and straightened his beard.

"Well. Let me just tell you this. Without my direction, it can destroy anything in its wake. Perhaps this whole island will crumble from its rage."

The end of the island? All because of me?

I tried to swallow and found I couldn't. I had to fix this!

"Oh yes," Neptune continued. "And you should know this: it can bring ships toward it. Apart from a few of my loyal aides, the kraken is the only creature who knows how to pierce the magic of the Bermuda Triangle. Once the kraken leaves its cave, you are no longer safe. Discovery cannot be far away. When this happens, the days of Allpoints Island are numbered."

Neptune sucked in his breath again. "I have not yet decided what I shall do about you all. In the meantime, I want to know WHO DID THIS! I WILL find out! It is IMPERATIVE that he or she come to me!"

He stared around the caves in the silence. An occasional drop of water plopped softly into the water. No! I couldn't. I *couldn't*! I *wasn't* going to get Mom and Dad thrown off the island. I wasn't going back to that awful jail. I had to think of something.

"WELL?" he bellowed.

Then someone coughed gently. There was a bustling sound up on the stone benches. Someone was getting up. Millie! What on earth was she doing?

She flung her black cape over her shoulder

and stepped toward a barrier at the edge of the pool.

"Your Majesty," she said firmly. "I'm not one to interfere, but I may be able to help you."

Neptune almost smiled. He looked as though he was smiling, anyway. It might just as easily have been anger twisting his face into a contorted frown. He pulled on his beard. "*Help* me?" he repeated.

"I can see things," Millie explained. "I don't like to boast, but I *have* been told I have something of a gift. I just need your star sign."

"My STAR SIGN?" Neptune yelled.

"Yes, you know, your horoscope, your—"

"I know what you mean! It's PISCES, of course!"

"Thank you," Millie said through tight lips. "That anger won't do your karma any good at all," she added in a stage whisper. Then she closed her eyes and folded her hands over her chest. "I believe I can tell you exactly what has happened," she said. "I just need some quiet."

Neptune looked as though he was about to burst, but he didn't speak. Nor did anyone else. Could she really see what had happened? Millie's cosmic ways didn't often come to much, but she did have an accurate moment now and then. What if this was one of them?

"I see riches of some sort," Millie murmured. "What is it? Gold? Let me focus."

Gold! She was describing the cave! No! Trust Millie to have one of her flukes and get it right when I desperately needed her to come out with her usual wacky nonsense. I'd heard enough. I had to get out before she told them everything. Maybe her vision had me in it!

I glanced up and tried to catch Mom's eye. She was watching Millie with a look of admiration on her face. How would she look at me when she found out what I'd done? I couldn't bear to imagine it.

I edged quietly away from Dad toward the darkness at the back of the pool. I could hear Millie's voice warbling across the water. She sounded as if she was humming. Everyone was watching her. This was my only chance.

"I'm sorry," I whispered into the darkness, and slipped quietly away.

I swam frantically through the dark tunnels, not even thinking about where they were leading me. I pounded past underwater stalagmites faintly lit up with soft, glowing crystals, around twists and turns and crevasses, almost gasping for the sight of the sky. I had to get out of the caves. Had to think.

Eventually, I came out into the open water. The light shocked me. Two little blueheads hovered at the cave's mouth, pecking at the rock as though giving it little kisses.

A noise behind me. Splashing. Someone was following me!

I dived down into a thin cave under the rocks, stumbling upon a group of fat hogfish who looked up at me with black eyes before scattering away to find another den.

I watched the cave's entrance. It was Dad!

I swam out from under the rock. "What are you doing here?"

"Emily!" He swam over toward me. "Why have you run away?"

I retreated farther under the rocks. "I've let you down. You, Mom, everyone. We'll get thrown off the island and it's all my fault. I'm so sorry."

Dad squeezed into the crevasse with me, scattering clouds of sand as he slithered along the rock. "No one's going to throw you off the island, little 'un. Why would they do that?"

"You don't know!" I wailed. "You don't know what I've done." A tear snaked down my cheek, mingling with the water. All this time! All those years without him, and now that I'd found him,

I'd done something so stupid, so awful, he'd hate me forever. I'd ruined everything.

"What? What have you done?"

I bit hard on my lip, squeezing my eyes shut.

"Whatever it is, you can tell me. We'll figure out what to do together."

My face was wet with tears. "It was me!" I blurted out. "*I* woke the kraken!"

"You *what*? But how—"

"I went exploring! I knew I shouldn't have, but I did. It was in a cave. I'm so stupid! I found it. I woke it up, Dad. I've ruined everything. I'll never be able to show my face on the island again. You've only just got out of prison and now—oh, Dad, I'm sorry."

Dad stroked my face. "Look. I don't quite understand, but it'll be OK. We'll fix this. I'll look after you."

I pushed his hand away. "Dad, it *won't* be OK. Don't lie to me. I'm not a *baby*!"

He stared at me, his face red as though I'd hit him. As I held his gaze, he nodded slowly, as though he was watching me grow up in front of his eyes, catching up with who I really was, instead of who he remembered me being. "You're right," he said eventually. "Of course you're not." He turned to swim away.

"Wait." I grabbed his arm. "I'm sorry."

"You know what you are?" he asked, his voice as tight as his mouth.

I shook my head, holding back fresh tears.

"You're my daughter, that's what you are. You're a Windsnap. And you know what that means?" Before I had a chance to answer, he added, "It means we're going to straighten this out."

"I'm not going back to the meeting. I can't. Please."

"Who said anything about going back there?"

"What, then?"

Dad stopped swimming and searched my face. "We're going to the cave. Show me where it happened."

"The *kraken's* cave?"

"Why not? You heard what Neptune said. It's probably still in there. Maybe we can straighten this mess out, somehow. Seal it back up so it's safe again or something."

"Dad, it was really frightening. It was the most terrifying thing ever!"

"Worse than going back to face Neptune? You stood up to him in his own court, remember."

I dropped my head. "I know. That was pretty frightening, too."

"Exactly. And you did that, so you can handle this as well."

"I suppose."

"Come on." He held out his hand. "Let's see what we can do."

Letting out a breath it felt as if I'd been holding in for a week, I took his hand and we swam on.

"It's that way," I said as we came to the lagoon. It looked different. The water was murky and muddier than I remembered. Sand-colored flat-fish skimmed over the seabed, moving beneath us like shifting ground.

My throat closed up. We'd reached the carving on the wall. The trident. How on earth could we have missed it last time? Maybe if we'd seen it, none of this would have happened.

It was pointless thinking like that.

We came to the pinwheel, except this time when I looked at it, I realized I knew exactly what it was. The long shoots spiraling out from the round body in the center . . .

"That's it," I said, my voice rippling like a breaking wave. "I don't want to go any farther."

He stopped swimming. "We need to do this, little 'un — I mean, Emily."

"Dad, you know, it's OK if you want to call me —"

"No." He put a finger over my lips. In charge. Strong. "You're not a baby. You're a scale off the old tail, and I couldn't be more proud of you. And we're going to get to the bottom of this, find out what we can, right?"

"But it's out of bounds. This was how the whole trouble started."

"And this is how it'll end, too," he said. "You don't think we found ourselves at this place by the pair of us doing what we were told, do you?"

I didn't say anything.

He reached out for my hand. "Come on. I'll go ahead, but you need to tell me where I'm going. I'll look after you."

Eventually, I took his hand and we swam in silence.

Everything looked familiar, until we came to an enormous gash in the rock. Maybe the size of a house.

"In there." I held out a shaky arm. "Except it was a tiny hole last time!"

Dad swallowed. "OK, then. You ready?"

"I'll never be ready to go back in there." A solitary fish flashed past me: soft green on one side, bright blue on the other, its see-through fins stretched back as it swam away from the cave. Sensible fish.

"Come on. You'll be OK. I'm right beside you." He squeezed my hand and we edged inside, slipping back through the rock.

But it was completely different. So different that I started to wonder if we were in the wrong place. There were no thin winding channels, just huge gaping chasms all the way. We swam through them all.

And then we came to the gold. We *were* in the right place. Jewels and crystals lay scattered across the seabed. As we swam lower, the surroundings felt less familiar. Colder. And there was something else. Something very different. The deeper we got, the more we saw of them.

Bones.

Just a few at first, that could perhaps have passed for driftwood. Then more: clumps of them, piled up like the remains of a huge banquet. Long thin bones, twisty fat ones — and then a skull, lying on the sea floor. A dark fish slipped through an eye socket. I clapped a hand across my mouth.

"Dad!" I gripped his hand so hard I felt his knuckles crack.

"Don't look at them," he said, his voice wobbling. "Just stay close to me."

We swam into every bit of the cave. Every inch.

"What do you see?" Dad asked as we paused in the center of the biggest chasm.

I looked around. "Nothing."

"Exactly." He turned to face me, suddenly not in charge anymore. Not strong. Just scared. "It's gone, Emily. The kraken—it's on the loose."

How long have we been here? A couple of days? Who knows? All I know is we're stranded on a deserted scrap of an island, the boat's broken, and I'm hungry.

And scared.

Nuts! How long can a person live on nuts? And water from an iffy-looking stream. Dad figures he'll catch us some fish. And he thinks we could fix the boat if we all "shaped up a little." He's acting as if he's on some kind of Boy Scout trip, as if this is all part of the adventure. I know he's putting it on, though. It's too manic. I can see the truth in his eyes. He's just as scared as I am.

Mom's hardly spoken. It's best that way. If we talked more, we might end up talking about what happened. About how we could have died. About the . . .

Anyway.

It's hardly even an island. I can vaguely see something that might be a real island, out at sea.

Far too far to swim. Just our luck to get stranded on this tiny speck of land instead. Two hundred paces from one side to the other. I counted yesterday. Or the day before, I don't remember. Some time when I was collecting twigs so that Dad could build us a so-called shelter. Not that I'm likely to get any sleep. It lends itself to a touch of insomnia, getting stranded on an island the size of a pair of underpants, with nothing to eat, no way of getting home, and no one to talk to except your parents.

Not even the captain.

That's another thing we don't talk about. I try not to think about that, either. What happened to him? Could he be—

My hands start to shake uncontrollably. My legs feel as if they'll give way any second now. Like I said, best not to think about that.

There's a splashing noise behind me.

"Mandy! Where's your mom?" It's Dad, coming out of the water with one of the nets from the boat. He's wearing purple shorts down to his knees and he's waddling onto shore in his flippers. He's been off looking for fish. That's all he's done since we've been here. That and mess around banging and hammering on the boat. It's washed up on the tiny beach, half-filled with water and littered with shells and stones and broken bottles. Yeah, sure, Dad. It's going to be so easy to fix.

The net's empty, as usual.

Dad pulls his mask and snorkel off. He's grinning. What on earth can he find to smile about? Doesn't he realize we're stranded and we're all going to die? Maybe he got knocked on the head when the boat went under.

He's shaking himself dry. "Come with me. I've got something important to tell you both."

I follow him back to the pathetic bundle of twigs that seems to have become our home. Mom's sitting on the ground leaning against a palm tree. She's not doing anything, just staring into space. Her hair's sticking out everywhere, as though she's had an electric shock. Her face is white, her eyes unfocused. She looks like a madwoman.

"Maureen, Mandy—our problems are over!" Dad announces.

I can't help it; I burst out laughing. I mean, look around you, Dad—wake up and smell the coffee. Oh, sorry, I forgot. THERE ISN'T ANY COFFEE BECAUSE WE'RE MAROONED ON A STRIP OF LAND YOU COULD MISS IF YOU BLINKED, WITH NOTHING BUT NUTS, INSECTS, AND A SMASHED-UP BOAT FOR COMPANY!

"Just hear me out," Dad says. "You're not going to believe me, but I swear, every word is true." There's a tic beating against his red cheek. "I *swear*," he repeats.

Mom sighs. "Just tell us. What ridiculous idea have you come up with now?"

"It's not an idea, Mo. Well, not exactly. It's something I've seen."

Mom raises her head a fraction. "What have you seen, then?"

Dad puffs out his chest and looks from one of us to the other. "Mermaids." I watch the lump in his throat bob up and down. "I've seen mermaids."

"Oh, for heaven's sake, Jack!" Mom pulls herself up and shakes out her skirt. "When are you going to act like a proper man and fix this mess, rather than indulging your stupid fantasies?"

She starts to walk off, wiping sand off the backs of her legs. Dad grabs her arm. "It is not a fantasy, Maureen!" he says furiously. "I swear on every breath I've ever taken, there are mermaids! Not here, farther out. I've seen them swimming, under the water. They've got tails—long, glistening, shiny tails!"

Their eyes are locked. It's as if they're acting out some surreal sketch and the teacher has just said "OK, freeze, everybody!"

But there's something about what he's said; something just out of reach . . .

"Don't you understand what this means?" Dad says. His neck's bright red and bulging. He's gripping Mom's arm.

Mom stares at him. "No, Jack. I'm afraid I don't

know what it means at all. That you're cracking up, perhaps? Well—don't worry, I'm sure I won't be far behind you." She pulls out of his grip.

"Mo, I'm *not* cracking up!" he shouts. "You've got to believe me! We could save our home, the amusement arcade—the whole pier!" He turns to me, his eyes wild and intense. "Mandy, you believe me, don't you?"

"I—" Of course I don't believe him. Of *course* I don't! But there's something. Something. What is it?

Mom's shaking her head. "You'll forgive me if I don't quite follow your logic."

Dad holds up his net. "We capture one! Take it back to Brightport. We can have it on show, charge admission and everything. We'll take care of it, of course. Give it a good life. People will travel from all over the country to see it! From all over the world, maybe! We'll be heroes in the town; we'll pay for the pier to be renovated. Don't you see? This could solve all our problems!"

Mom sucks in her cheeks. "Jack," she says, "you haven't managed to catch so much as a *goldfish* since we got here! Even if I were to believe that you have seen a mermaid—which, frankly, I don't—how in heaven do you propose to catch the thing?"

Dad pulls at his net. "I haven't got the whole plan figured out yet, have I? I've only just *seen* them. A group of them. Swimming in the deep

339

water. One of them had gold stars shining in her tail. There was a merman too, with long black hair and a shiny silver tail. A merman! For God's sake, Maureen!" He grips her arm again. "I'm telling the truth! You'll see I am."

Mom pulls away and turns to me. "Come on, Mandy. Help me get some dinner. I've had enough of your father and his daydreams for one afternoon."

I follow Mom as we pick our way through undergrowth, scavenging for food like vagrants. As usual, we don't talk. But this time, it's because of the thoughts going around in my head, thoughts I'm not sure I dare share with Mom. There's definitely something familiar about what Dad said. Something niggling away in the back of my mind. I can't put my finger on it.

Maybe it's something I've seen on TV. A film about mermaids or something. I've got this picture in my mind. Someone swimming. She's got a tail and she's spinning around, smiling, grinning—at me! She's in a pool. It's not from TV. I'm sure it isn't. It feels real. It feels like a memory.

I grab a couple of nuts and shove them hard into my pocket. Mermaids! As if! I force myself to laugh.

We'd better get away from here before we *all* crack up.

Chapter Five

"Dad."

He didn't reply. Just kept on staring out to sea. We'd spent half the day swimming around the coast, trying to keep out of sight, and trying to figure out what to do next. We stopped to rest at a large rocky bay on the east side of the island, just a little farther down from our bay.

I swam over to join him next to a huge boulder at the edge of the bay. "Dad," I said again.

"I'm thinking," he said without turning around. "Just give me a minute."

I counted to ten. "What are we going to do?"

He shook his head. "I don't know, Em. I just don't know."

I looked out to sea with him. The water lapped gently into the cove behind us. Daylight was starting to fade.

I stared out at the horizon. So much ocean, stretching for miles and miles and miles—forever, it seemed. Nothing but water. And the monster. Somewhere. A cold shiver rattled through my body. The water lay still, but how long till it would seethe with the kraken's rage? The stillness was almost worse— knowing it was out there, waiting.

Something flickered on the horizon. A brief flash of light. I jerked upright and peered so hard my eyes watered. There it was again.

"Dad!"

"Emily, will you leave me alone! I've told you, give me five minutes. I need to think."

I shook his arm. "Look!" I pointed out to the horizon.

Dad followed the line of my finger. "Mothering mussels," he breathed, squinting into the distance. His words came out like a whistle. "What's that doing there?"

"What is it?"

"Look—red, then green." Dad turned to me. "It's a ship, Emily."

A ship had gotten in! The kraken had already pierced the Triangle's border.

"It's not coming any closer, is it?" I asked with a gulp. What if it was? One way or another, that would spell disaster. Either the kraken would destroy the ship — or the ship would discover us. Either way, it was completely unthinkable.

"Doesn't look like it. Doesn't mean it won't, though." Dad pushed off from the rock and started to swim away. "Come on."

"Where are we going?"

"We'll have to say something."

"Say something?" My words jammed up my throat. I swallowed hard. "Who to?"

"I don't know. Archie, I guess." Dad took hold of my hand. "Emily, there's a ship coming toward the island. The others need to know that the kraken's gotten out."

"No! Dad, they'll want to know everything. They'll make you tell them it was all my fault."

"Em, love, the monster could attack that ship. Or the ship could discover us here. That'll be the end of us all. You heard what Neptune said. We can't stay here if the secret gets out. Can't you just see it? Hordes of tourists swarming the place? They'll turn us into a zoo or something." He turned to swim away.

A zoo. My old fears of discovery resurfaced in a wave of anguish. That was one of the nightmares I used to have in Brightport. What had I *done*?

"There must be something we can do," I said, swimming hard to keep up.

"This is the only thing." Dad's voice was firm.

He didn't speak again. The water soon grew warmer as we reached the shallow sand, rippling like tire tracks across the sea floor.

Dad wouldn't look at me. "You go along home. Mom'll be worried."

"What about you?"

"I'm going to see if I can find Archie."

I didn't move.

"It'll be all right," he said with a tight smile. Then he turned and swam toward the end of the bay, taking my last shreds of hope with him.

Mom threw her arms around me the second I arrived back at *Fortuna*. "Emily! I've been worried sick. Where've you been?"

"With Dad. I felt claustrophobic in the caves and we — we went exploring." My cheeks burned. I hate lying to Mom.

"Mary P., you really should listen to me. I told you she was safe," Millie said, pouring some herbal tea from a pot and settling down on the big sofa.

"Millie saw a ship," Mom said.

"She *saw* it?" I burst out.

Mom looked at me quizzically. "When she did Neptune's reading. She had a vision of a ship. What ship did you think I meant?"

"Oh. No. Nothing. Yes, that's what I thought you meant," I blustered. *Great move, Emily. Just give the game away to* everyone. "I thought you'd said something about gold." I tried to keep my voice even.

"Yes, well, you can't be expected to get everything right, all the time," Millie replied, sniffing as she picked up a magazine.

"So what did Neptune say about the vision?" I asked, holding my breath.

Millie flipped the pages. "Not everyone appreciates my gift."

"He told her he'd throw her off the island if she wasted any more of his time with her hocus-pocus," said Mom, smiling.

How could she smile? I could hardly *speak*. I had to get away from here. "I'm going to my room," I said. Before they had a chance to argue, I'd gone through to the back of the ship and closed my door behind me. Shaking, I sat down on my bed and looked around. Like all the others, the room had a trapdoor that led to the floor below, to the sea. I'd hardly used it yet. The one in the living room was open all the time and it was bigger.

I crept over to the trapdoor next to my bed and opened it. Maybe . . .

"Emily." Mom was at my door.

I jumped away from the trapdoor. "I was just looking at the fish," I said quickly.

"Are you all right?" Mom stepped into the room and came over to me. She lifted a strand of hair off my face, stroking it behind my ear. "If there's anything you want to talk about . . ."

"There isn't," I said, trying to make myself smile. I imagine I looked like a scared rabbit with a twitch. A while ago, I could talk to Mom about anything, and didn't know how to relate to Dad at all. Funny how things had changed. If *funny* was the right word. Which it wasn't.

"I'm fine, honestly," I said. "Just a little tired." I stretched my mouth into a yawn. "Look, see. I think I'll have a nap."

Mom stared at me quizzically for a moment before shrugging. "Well, we'll be next door if you need anything." She kissed my forehead and left.

I waited five minutes. She didn't come back. OK, this was it. I knew what I was going to do.

I had to get to the ship, make it change its course or something—just stop it from causing disaster to everyone on board, and probably all of us on the island too. I didn't have a clue how I was going to do it; I just knew I had to try.

I eased myself through the hole. Then, dangling over the side, I lowered myself down as gently as I could and let go. I dropped with a splash. Had they heard? I held my breath and waited. Nothing.

I waited a little longer, to make sure my tail had fully formed. When the tingling and numbness had completely gone, I ducked under, swam through the big open porthole, and headed toward the ship.

It was almost like the old days: swimming out to sea under a sky gradually filling up with stars. A striped butterfly fish raced along beside me before slipping away into the darkness and disappearing under a rock. Shoals of silver bar jacks hovered nearby, shining like pins in the darkness. Purple fans waved with the current, caressing me as I sailed over them.

It was nothing like the old days.

In the old days, I was swimming out to meet my best friend; now I didn't even know if I still *had* one. Shona would have been by my side on an adventure like this. My chest hurt as I pushed myself to swim harder, swim away from

347

the painful thoughts. The water grew colder and darker. I picked my way out toward the ship, praying there was no current around this side of the island.

After a while, I stopped to scan the horizon. Two dim lights, facing me. It was a long way out, but definitely inside the Triangle. I couldn't even see the island anymore. Just blackness, except— what was that? Something flashed through the water. A boat? I held my breath while I watched. Nothing. It must have just been the moon's reflection.

I swam on toward the ship. I had to stop it from finding us, get it away from the island. I had to buy some time.

Eventually, I was close enough to study it: a cruise liner with three levels of portholes and balconies, all lit up with lamps. The sides rose steeply out of the water.

I swam all around it, looking for a way in. There was a rope ladder hanging down at the back. I tried to make a grab for it but missed by inches. I heaved and jumped up in the water. No good—it was just out of reach.

I swam around again, looking for something else. And right at the front, I found it. The anchor!

Gripping the chains, I pulled myself out of

the water. My tail dangled and flapped in the sea. Panting and gritting my teeth, I managed to inch my way up. Eventually, I'd done it. I clung onto the chain like a koala, my body clear of the water. Within moments, I got that tingly sensation I knew so well. My legs had come back.

I hooked my feet into the loops, then slowly and carefully climbed up to the ship's deck.

Hauling myself over the metal rail, I landed heavily on the deck. A quick look around. No one. Just me and the darkness and a row of deck chairs. I dried myself on a towel someone had left on one of them and pulled on the shorts I'd brought with me. Then I went to look for some signs of life.

It didn't take long.

Halfway down the side of the ship, I found some stairs and a door that led inside. There were sounds, somewhere near. I followed the noise, almost sniffing my way toward it. Music. Laughter.

Soon I came out of the narrow corridor into an open space with a few people dotted around. I tried to saunter in casually, as though I belonged there, even though I knew I'd be spotted in a second.

But I wasn't. Some kids were playing in a tiny

arcade on one side; on the other, a couple of men were drinking at a small bar. A man and woman behind the bar laughed together. No one even looked up.

A flight of stairs led up toward where the real noise was coming from. *OK, you can do it.* I took a deep breath, twirled my hair a few times, nibbled on my thumbnails—and went upstairs.

It wasn't till I saw all the food that I realized I was starving! I'd hardly eaten all day.

I grabbed a paper plate and joined the line behind a girl who looked about my age. Maybe she'd know something.

"It's great, this vacation, isn't it?" I said as we shuffled along the food table, shoving tiny sausages and crackers and chips onto our plates.

"Mm," the girl replied through a pizza slice.

"Wonder how long before we shove off," I said casually.

She swallowed her bite of pizza. "My mom says we're not even supposed to be here. She thinks we've gone off course. Doesn't matter though, if we see it."

See it?

"Yeah, that's what I thought," I said, trying to stay calm. I popped a mini sausage into my mouth. "So has anyone seen it yet?"

The girl put her plate down. "Don't you know?"

"Oh, I, um — I forget. Remind me?"

"That's why we're here! Mom says more than half the passengers canceled at the last minute. That's how we got our places. I bet Carefree Cruises is totally fed up with that captain!"

What was she going on about?

"Yeah, I bet," I said seriously. "What did he do again?" I asked, quickly turning away to grab another handful of chips.

"How can you not know? He saw Triggy, of course! First sighting in absolutely YEARS!"

A chip got stuck halfway down my throat. "Triggy?" I asked, swallowing hard.

"Don't tell me you haven't heard of Triggy."

I tried a lighthearted shrug and a frown.

"Triggy! The Triangle Monster! I've always believed in it. Mom said it was just a silly fairy tale, but now she's not so sure. I hope we see it, don't you?"

I couldn't reply. I couldn't do anything. I tried. I opened my mouth, even moved my lips a

351

little, I think. But nothing came out. *Triggy?* It sounded like a cartoon character. She had no idea! I thought of the slimy tentacles racing down the tunnel toward me, the suckers all along it, grabbing at the walls, the way it extended out, the hairy tapered end touching me.

The bones.

Now these people were hunting it down. Which either meant it wouldn't be long before they found us — or they'd be its next victims.

"I—I've got to go now," I said eventually. I staggered away from the food table.

"See you in the morning," she called before going back to the table.

"Yeah." *Whatever.*

I stumbled back down the stairs. At the bottom, I took a turn that I thought led back to the corridor I'd come down earlier. But I emerged into another open space. I was about to turn back when I noticed a shop just ahead of me. It was closed now, but there was a poster in the window. I went over to take a closer look.

It was the front page of a newspaper: the *Newlando Times.*

BRAVE CAPTAIN TELLS OF HORROR AT SEA the headline screamed across the top of the page. I read on.

The old myth of Triggy the Triangle Monster rose up again today when Captain Jimmy Olsthwaite was rescued from stormy seas by a local fisherman.

Captain Olsthwaite lost his boat when it was attacked by what he described as "a monster beyond imagining. The size of a dinosaur! And a dozen tentacles that wrapped around the boat."

His story has horrified and delighted tourists in equal measure.

Katie Hartnett was among those setting sail today with Carefree Cruises. "It's so exciting," she told the *Newlando Times.* "My parents used to tell me stories about the Triangle Monster when I was little— but we never thought it might exist for real!"

Others have canceled in droves. Retiree Harold Winters was among them. "We wanted a peaceful trip, not the fright of our lives," he said.

The captain's sighting has not been confirmed. The coast guard is warning that it could be a case of delirium brought on by his traumatic capsize and rescue.

Three others were believed to be on

board the boat with the captain. Neither
they nor the boat have yet been recovered.

The boat was owned by a company called
Mermaid Tours.

I stumbled away from the shop. I was in one of
those nightmares where you're stuck somewhere,
trying every exit, but there's no way out and
every step takes you deeper into the horror. It had
happened already. The monster had attacked a ship,
all because of me. My head swirled with nausea
and panic.

I found myself out on the deck again. I leaned
over the railing, and my stomach heaved. My
mouth tasted like iron. I looked down at the sea,
deep navy in the darkness. Little bright flecks
sparkled white as the water lapped and splashed
against the ship. There was another boat down
there. I could just make out its shape. A small yacht.
It looked as if it was coming toward us. Maybe
they were checking to see if their lifeboats were
working or something. Well, they'd be needing
them soon, unless I could come up with a miracle.

I had to do something! I couldn't just stand
here staring at the sea.

Then it came to me.

I ran up steps, down ladders, along corridors,

banged on doors, called through open windows: "TRIGGY! THE MONSTER!"

People emerged from their rooms. Dressing gowns were pulled around bare bellies and boxer shorts; women came out of their cabins in silk nighties, kids in twisted-up pajamas.

"Triggy!" I shouted at everyone I saw. "The monster! I've seen it!"

"Where?" Open-mouthed gasps.

"Over there!" I pointed—away from the island. I pointed and pointed. "Tell everyone. Tell the crew!" I ran on as everyone I spoke to gathered along one side of the boat: all gazing out to sea, desperate for a sighting of something I wished with all my heart I would never see again.

I had to find the captain.

I ran on, down more corridors—until I barged slap-bang into someone.

"Hey, what's all this?" It was a woman in a uniform. She grabbed hold of my elbows, holding me at arms' length.

"I need to find the captain," I gasped. "I've seen the monster!"

The woman frowned. "Yes, dear. I'm sure you have. Now, come on, why don't you—"

"I have!" I burst out. "I can prove it. It's— it's—" I gulped. The memory of it took the breath out of me for a second. I started again. "It's enormous, and it's got tentacles."

"We've all seen the papers, sweetheart," the woman said, smiling. "Now, if you want an excuse to visit the captain, you can just say so. He's always happy for you kids to have a quick look around the cabin."

Bingo! "OK!"

The woman gently shook her head as she pointed toward some stairs. "It's up there. Turn right at the top, straight on to the end, and it's through the door ahead of you. But knock first. He doesn't take kindly to being barged in on."

"Thanks!" I took the stairs three at a time.

I bashed on the door. *Come on, come on!*

No one answered. *Come* on*! No time for politeness. I tried the door. It swung open.

"I need to talk to the captain," I said breathlessly as I burst into the room.

Two men were sitting in front of a load of dials drinking coffee. One of them swiveled around. "Now, hang on. What's the—"

"Are you the captain?"

"I certainly am," he said, "and you can't just—"

"I've seen the sea monster!"

The captain leaned forward in his seat. "The sea monster?"

I nodded.

His face relaxed into a slight smile. "Now, listen, you want me to tell you something about this sea monster?" he asked. I swallowed, and nodded again.

He lowered his voice. "It doesn't exist."

I held his eyes. "It does! I've seen it."

The captain leaned back in his seat. "OK, let's have it, then. Big thing with tentacles, was it?"

"Yes! That's exactly what it was!"

"Right." He was smiling, laughing at me. I had to convince him.

"It's—it's enormous!"

"Mm-hm. Anything else?" the captain asked in a bored voice.

"The tentacles—they're tapered at the end."

He turned back to his tea. I racked my brain. *What else—what else?*

"And hairy! And they've got huge great suckers all along them!" I blurted.

The captain put his cup down. "They what?" he asked, his face suddenly hard, and focused on mine.

"And they're—they're green, and gray underneath, and warty . . ." My voice trailed away as I remembered the sight of it. My teeth chattered.

The captain turned to the other man. "That's exactly what my friend at the coast guard said."

"Sir, the newspaper report—"

The captain shook his head. "Those things weren't in there. Come on, man. Face the facts. You saw the dials. You know we've been stuck here, spinning on the spot like a child's top."

"Yes, but you said yourself that if we made a mammoth effort, we could get out of it."

"Exactly, and we need to do that now. There's something going on and it's time we faced up to it."

He moved his chair closer to mine and leaned toward me. "OK, then," he said. "You'd better tell me exactly where you saw the sea monster. . . ."

I'd done it! The ship had changed direction and we were heading directly away from the island.

I sneaked along the empty deck. Every single person on the ship must have been crowded on the other side, peering into the darkness for a sight of something they thought would make their vacation. I thought of its flailing tentacles, the floor littered with bones, and I shivered. If only they knew. I hoped for their sake that they never would.

I had to get back to the island. Maybe I could confess, after all. If I told Neptune what I'd done here, how I'd stopped a whole cruise ship full of people from discovering us, he might even forgive me.

I checked around one final time to make sure no one could see me. Then I slipped back into the water.

Moments later, the familiar warm feeling spread through my legs as they turned back into my tail. It shone bright in the moonlight.

Fish around me seemed to be dancing. I could make out their shapes in the darkness. They must have been happy for me. Maybe it was a sign. Everything was going to be all right. I swam along, lost in my hopes that I could somehow make up for everything that had happened over the last couple of weeks. Perhaps Shona and I would be best friends again and the island would be safe. The kraken might even go away and our lives in our new home could really start.

"EMILY!"

I started and looked back, twisting around in the water. Two people were leaning out over a balcony on the cruise ship, waving frantically. Why weren't they on the other side with everyone else? I edged back toward the boat.

That's when I saw who it was. Mom! Thin and wiry with wild hair, waving her arms. Someone was with her. Larger than life in a black cape. Millie! What the heck were —

"Emily!" Mom screamed again.

I swam closer to the ship, but it was picking up speed. I could hardly keep up.

"Watch the propellers!" Mom screeched. "Don't come too close!"

Millie had sunk into a deck chair next to her, her head in her hands. A small yacht was moored on a buoy, near where the ship had been only moments ago. The one I'd seen coming toward us. I recognized it now: it was our old boat! They'd followed me!

"Mom! What are you doing there?"

"We came to find you, but you'd just jumped off! It was Millie's idea. The vision, the boat. She'd seen you on it."

"What? You never told me that."

Millie got up and stumbled across to clutch onto the railing. "I kept it to myself," she wailed. "I thought it would have sounded crazy. I've heard what people say about me." She leaned out over the railing. "I'm sorry, Emily. I was too busy worrying about my reputation."

"We didn't think they'd get going again tonight." Mom called.

Oh no. My fault again. I'd made things worse *again*. The ship was only on the move because of me. And now it was moving faster and faster away—and taking my mom with it!

"Mom!" I tried to keep up. She was shouting something, but I couldn't hear her anymore. I could hardly even see her as the ship picked up speed.

"MOM!" I yelled again, uselessly, into the darkness.

As the ship slipped away, I let the current carry me along. No energy left. I drifted away from the ship, from the island, from everything that mattered. Tears streamed down my face as I howled in the darkness.

And then—

Noise.

Clattering—shuffling. What was happening? I mopped my cheeks with my palms.

I'd got caught in—what? Seaweed? I flapped and scratched at it. *Please, not the monster.* I looked around me.

A net! I was trapped in a net! A man was holding it, pulling at a piece of rope, dragging me through the water, propelling himself along with flippers.

Flapping my tail, I tried to push myself away, but he was too strong. I struggled and fought, biting at the net, pulling at it with my fingers, cutting my hands, scraping myself all over. It was like wire. There was no way I could get through it. I scratched and screamed as he drew me through the sea.

Soon the water grew warmer and shallower. We were at a tiny island: a little sandy bay with a few palm trees, a small boat moored to a pole, and a makeshift lantern propped on the beach. The man tied my net to the pole.

He pushed his mask and snorkel onto the top of his head. I couldn't make out his face properly in the shadowy light. "I'm not going to hurt you," he said, panting from swimming so hard. "Trust me."

I didn't say anything.

"Do—you—speak—English?" he asked in a very loud voice. I ignored him.

"Stay here," he said, as though I had a choice. He disappeared up the beach as I scraped and scratched at the net, trying to get out. Moments later, he was back with someone.

"Dad, you are completely obsessed," a girl's voice was saying. "It's the middle of the night!" The voice sounded familiar. But it couldn't be.

"I said, didn't I?" the man replied as they came closer. "I told you—I TOLD you! *Now* do you believe me?" He pointed in my direction. The other person waded toward me and peered at me in the darkness. As she came closer, I could just make out her face from the lantern's light.

It was—

It was—

I gasped and jerked backward against the net, my mouth stupidly open. It couldn't be! How—?

It was someone I knew. Someone I knew well. Someone I'd thought I would never *ever* have to see again.

Dad's caught a fish at last.

Hallelujah.

He's screaming and yelling at me to come and see it. You'd think no one had ever caught a fish in the sea before.

But it's not a fish. He's got someone with him.

"I told you! I told you!" he's yelling. "I said I'd catch a mermaid, didn't I? Do you believe me now?"

I get closer, and I notice a tail. No! It can't be!

He has! He's actually caught a mermaid!

It turns around. I see its face, its mousy hair, skinny little arms. It *can't* be! It's impossible! But it is. It is. I grab the lamp and bring it closer as I stare at her.

It's Emily Windsnap!

And then I remember. I remember everything! The pool, the swimming lessons. She came to us once before she left, showing off as usual. She had a tail! She swam in front of us all, swirling it around. Grinning at me as if to say she'd won. It wasn't enough for her that everyone thought she was *so* wonderful. Julia, the swimming instructor—they all liked her more than they liked me, all thought she was better than me. She had to rub it in, didn't she? Had to prove they were right. As if I didn't already know it.

How could I have forgotten?

There was something afterward—they gave us doughnuts. That was when it all faded. The doughnuts! Had they drugged us or something? And what the heck is she doing *here*?

Our eyes meet. She's as shocked as I am.

"Mandy!" she says.

I pull myself together quickly. "Oh, hi, Emily," I say, nice and calm. I sniff and turn to Dad. "Why are you bothering with *her*, Dad?"

Dad pulls off his mask and snorkel. "What are you talking about, Mandy? It's a mermaid!"

"Dad, have you actually looked at her face?"

He gawks at me for a second before turning to Emily and then back to me. I can almost see the realization crawling into his mind. He points at Emily. "But that's, that looks like—"

"Yeah, Dad," I say, trying to sound bored, or at least as if I've got a *clue* what's going on here, "it's Emily Windsnap."

"But how . . . but she's a . . ." His voice trails away. He looks at her again, then at me. "Don't be

365

stupid, Mandy," he says suddenly. "Of course it's not Emily Windsnap. It just looks a little like her. This is a mermaid!"

Mom joins us on the beach. "What's the fuss, Jack?"

Dad runs toward her, ignoring me, and ignoring reality, it seems. "No time now, Maureen," he says. "We need to get ready. Where's all our stuff?"

"What stuff?"

"Everything. Everything we need. Get it in the boat. We're off as soon as it's light."

"Off?" I follow Dad out of the water. "What d'you mean 'off'? Where are we going?"

Dad stops and turns back to me. "We're going home, Mandy. With our mermaid. We're going to save the pier. Just like I said."

He runs over toward the boat.

"But it's broken!" I say, following after him. "We capsized, remember?"

"I've been working day and night on this boat," he calls back. "I think she's ready to sail again. Pack your things, and then get some more sleep. First light of dawn and we're off."

"Mom?"

Her eyes are vacant. She looks as if she's already given up hope. "I haven't got a clue what's going on," she says. "What's that he's got in the net?"

I leave her to find out for herself as I follow Dad

to the boat. Maybe we can sort everything out. Maybe he's right. It's worth a try, I suppose. Anything's better than rotting on this stupid island for the rest of our lives. Even if it does mean sailing home with *fish girl*.

The boat seems to be just about holding up. It would be better if Dad had the slightest idea how to sail it. We're buffeting about all over the place. He keeps staring at the navigation dials and then yelling things at Mom, like "Get over onto starboard!" and "We need to tack! Watch the boom! Hard alee!"

She yells things back, but her words are washed away by the wind and by the seawater spraying us on the back deck. Just as well. Judging by her expression, it's probably best if neither of us can hear what she's actually saying.

Anyway, I'm busy with Emily. I've got to keep an eye on the net, make sure it doesn't come loose. Can't have her escaping.

"Comfy down there, are you?" I call down to her. She's being pulled along like a water-skier. "Enjoying your little trip?"

"What are you going to do with me?" she whimpers. She's scared. I swallow my guilt. Why shouldn't she suffer? Why shouldn't she understand how *I* feel most of the time? Would it hurt for someone to understand?

"Oh, didn't Dad tell you? We're taking you back to Brightport," I say.

The boat swerves and surges, so I don't hear her reply. Just a kind of yelp from inside the net.

"Yeah, we're going to put you on display," I continue when she bobs above the surface again, her hair plastered across her face with seawater. I smile down at her. "Hey, maybe all your old school friends will come and visit. That'd be nice for you, wouldn't it? We were thinking maybe five dollars a visit. What d'you think?"

"What about my mom? She's stranded on a ship! I've got to find her! And my dad? Let me at least get a message to him!"

I want to. Part of me wants to shout and cry and ask why it has to be like this. But I can't. Show her my weakness and she can hurt me even more. Forget it.

"Yeah, right," I say.

"Mandy, I need you!" Dad's calling.

"Back soon," I call down to fish girl. "Don't go anywhere now. Oh, sorry, I forgot. You can't!"

I stand up to see what Dad wants. But I don't need to ask. The boat has leveled out; all is calm. But just ahead of us is something I'd almost forgotten about.

The darkness, spreading like an oil slick in the pale morning light, pulling us in.

368

"Dad, what are we going to do?"

He shakes his head. "I haven't got a clue, dear. We've got to get across it, somehow."

Mom's inching along the side deck to join us. "Jack, are you crazy? Have you forgotten what happened last time? The last two weeks foraging for food like beggars after nearly drowning? And that *poor* captain. *Have* you?"

"What choice do we have, Maureen?"

"We can think about our choices as soon as you've gotten us away from here. But I, for one, am not going to gamble with my life when the odds look like that!" She points to the sheet of water, glistening like glass ahead of us.

"Well, *I,* for one, am not going to live on nuts and berries for the rest of my life!" Dad yells. "And I'm not going to go back and watch my home and my livelihood demolished either."

"So you'll kill us all then, will you?" Mom screams.

"Mom! Dad!" I try to get between them, but the boat suddenly lurches and I slip across the deck. We're starting to tilt. We're being drawn toward it again. "Please—please don't fight."

Neither of them is listening. They'd rather scream at each other than try to work out what to do.

"DAD!" I yell, clutching the railing as the boat dips farther. I nearly fall over the side. Emily is down below in her stupid net. We're going to capsize again. I'm going to drown out here, all because of *her*. I can't believe it!

The boat lurches again.

"I can help." A voice from down below.

"What?"

"I'll help you."

I grab the railing as the boat leans over. Spray hits us on all sides as we skid through the water, soaking me. She looks up at me pitifully, her big brown eyes round and shiny. I can't bear it. I turn away. I bet she's only putting it on anyway. "And why would you do that?" I ask.

"I don't want you to die," she says.

"I'm supposed to believe that, am I?"

"I've got enough on my conscience," she calls up. "I don't need that as well. You can keep me in the net. Just let the rope out. I'll pull you away."

I glance over at Mom and Dad. They're not screaming at each other anymore. Mom's trying to make her way over to me. She's not even holding on to anything.

"Mom! Stay where you are!"

"Let the rope out!" Emily yells. "Do you want to be killed?"

I glance at the rope. It's looped around and around over a hook. "Don't try to do anything clever, all right?"

"Just do it!" she shouts. "It'll be too late in a second."

I lurch over to the back of the boat. One last glance at the water ahead of us, then I unhook the rope. "I'm warning you!" I shout as I throw it into the water.

The coil lands with a splash. Then nothing. Where's she gone? She's disappeared! I scan the surface of the water. Where is she? She must be in there somewhere.

I'm staring so hard at the water it looks like it's changing color, getting darker. It *is* changing color! There's a shape in there! A huge gray outline of something—something very, very big. Something we saw before and like idiots pretended to ourselves we hadn't.

Without warning, it bursts through the surface. A piercing, screaming siren sound screeches into the sky as an olive-green tentacle rises up, way up above us, then sheers downward to wrap itself over the top of the boat like an arch.

No!

"Mandy!" Emily's yelling. Where is she? Did she know it was here? Did she somehow make this happen? I know it's a crazy thought—but maybe, I mean, she had the rope. She was in the water; she hates me. She could have done it. Just as I was start-ing to trust her—that'll teach me.

The monster lifts the boat right out of the water, high up into the air. I can see the underside of its tentacle. It looks like a giant worm, extending and retracting, slithery and lumpy. Gasping and retching, I fall against the railing, clutching on for my life.

With an almighty crash, it drops us back down onto the water, and the surface explodes.

We're such fools! How could we let it happen *again*? *She's* done this to us. She's made it happen. She tricked us somehow.

The thing has tentacles all over us, sliming over the boat, roaming, searching for things to grab and latch on to. I'm slipping across the deck, water everywhere. It sucks the boat down, throws it around, tosses us one way and then another.

Any second now, we'll all be in the water. Should I pray?

As if praying would help.

The only thing giving me courage as the boat is thrown over, as I clutch the railings, hold my breath, and grab the lifebelt, is one single thought:

I'll get you for this, fish girl. I will SO get you for this.

Chapter Six

*T*otal stillness. Utter darkness.

What had happened? Where was I?

I rubbed my eyes, tried to move. I was still inside the net, trapped under a rock. Out of the darkness, a shape was coming toward me. It looked like a submarine, gliding along the very bottom of the sea, black on top, white underneath, large fins flapping below. As it came closer, it opened its jaw. Serrated lines of teeth, above and below: the sharpest bread knives.

A killer whale!

I grabbed the net, rubbing it hard on the edge of the rock, sawing and scraping frantically. My fingers bleeding and raw, I yanked and tugged at the net. *Come on, come on! Break!*

The string started to fray and tear. I was nearly out.

But then the water was swirling all around me, whisking up and around, faster and faster, like a whirlpool.

It was back.

The sea filled with giant tentacles, writhing and grasping and sucking. I crouched tight under the rock and prayed it wouldn't see me.

THWACK! The tentacles crashed against a rock, only a few feet away from me. It split and crumbled instantly. My tail flapped wildly; my teeth rattled so hard my jaw hurt.

CRASH! The tentacles came down again, scattering a spiraling shoal of barracuda before searching for their next target.

And then they found it. The whale! Jaws wide open, the whale thrashed, snapping its teeth at the monster. I crouched under my rock as the kraken moved closer, and for the first time, I saw its face. I clapped a hand over my mouth, swallowing back a scream.

Horned and full of snarling lumps, with huge white eyes on either side of its head, it opened its mouth to reveal teeth like shining daggers. Briefly opened wide, its teeth came crashing together, snapping shut, again and again, pulling and tearing at the whale. On and on it went, flinging the whale from one side to the other as tentacles and horns and teeth grabbed and tore at its skin.

Eventually, the thrashing slowed. The whirlpool stopped. The sea began to change color, blood seeping into the cracks around me. *Go away, go away,* I said silently, over and over, until, miraculously, the water became calm again, almost as though it had heard me.

In the darkness, I cried.

Mom.

I kept seeing her, reaching out to me from the ship, wild and screaming as she was taken farther and farther away. The image bit into me like wire. I curled into a ball and tried to push it away.

I had to find Mandy and her parents. There was no way of knowing where I was or how to get back. I knew it might be madness to search for them but, much as I hated to admit it, they were my only hope now.

I tore at the net till I'd made a hole big enough to squeeze through. Edging out of my hiding place, I forced myself not to think about what I'd just witnessed, although my twitching body made it hard to forget. I scanned the water. Nothing. It had gone.

Swimming away from the rocks, I searched desperately for something familiar. I soon came to a deep sandy stretch, rocks on either side. Around them, weeds floated and swayed, surrounding me like a thick curtain. I swam along the sandy channel until it came to a rocky reef, full of holes and ridges and gray peaks like castles and hills.

I fought the rising panic in my chest. This wasn't familiar at all. I was completely lost. A large, sullen gray fish drifted silently ahead of me, hovering like a hawk. Bright blue eyes bore down on me as I passed it.

"Who's that?"

A voice! A male voice.

"Come no farther!" The voice called out again. I stopped swimming.

"Who are you?" My words bubbled away from me.

Silence. Then, "You'll do as I say. I am armed. Do you understand?"

Armed?

"I—yes, I understand." Understand? Of course I didn't! I didn't understand any of this.

Out of the shadows, a thin, lanky figure swam toward me. A young merman, maybe in his twenties. He pulled some fishing line out from a packet on his back. "Hold your arms out."

"Who are you? Why should I—"

"Do as I say!" he bellowed, reaching for something at his side that looked like a knife. I thrust my arms out in front of me and watched while he tied my wrists together. "This way."

With that, he turned and swam, pulling me along behind him. All thoughts of my mom and the kraken and Mandy were dragged away by this—my second capture in one day. I let myself be pulled along. What choice did I have? No strength left to fight, this time.

The reef stretched and curved, a lunar landscape dotted with ornamental gardens. Deep brown plants lined rocky chasms. Round boulder-like chunks of coral clung to every surface; thick green spongy tubes waved and pointed threateningly as we passed over them. I glanced at the merman as we swam. He had a thin gray tail with silver rings pierced along one side. Wild blond hair waved over his shoulders; a chain made of bones hung around his neck.

We came to a cave with green and blue weeds hanging down from the top of its mouth in a curtain. Crystals were embedded in the rock all around the entrance.

"In here." He pushed me forward.

"Where are we?"

"You'll see."

Inside, the cave ballooned out into an enormous dome. Crystals, jewels, and gold lined the route. Mosaics filled with gems of every color swirled along the seabed: a round body, swirling arms . . .

"Where are we?" I gasped. "Who are you?"

"You'll find out soon enough," he replied. We'd reached a building. It looked like a castle, or a ruin of a castle. Half-collapsed turrets were filled with diamonds; crumbling walls held pale jewels in clusters around their base. A giant archway for a door, a marble pillar on either side. As we came closer, I could see something embossed onto each pillar. A golden sea horse.

I knew this archway! I'd seen it before, or another one very much like it, when I was taken to Neptune's courtroom. "This is one of Neptune's palaces, isn't it?" I asked, shuddering as I realized we were swimming over a mosaic shaped like a mass of tentacles.

The merman didn't reply.

Through the arch, a chandelier hung from a high ceiling, jangling with the water's rocking. That confirmed my fear. Neptune had found me.

We ducked low to swim through a smaller

arch, adorned, like the others, with elaborate jewels. A wooden door lay ahead. The merman paused to neaten his hair. Then he turned a shiny brass handle and nudged me inside.

We were in a small room. A stone desk embedded with shells took up half the space. Conches and oyster shells lay scattered on its surface. Next to it, an old merman turned as we came into the room. He had a scraggly beard and dark eyes that stared at me, holding me still.

"What's this you've found, Kyle?" the merman asked in a deep grumble. As he spoke, he stroked something lying very, very still by his side. It looked like a giant snake. Greeny yellow with purple teddy bear eyes, its gills slowly opening and closing as its mouth did the same, it swayed its head gently around to face me. A moray eel!

I opened and closed my mouth too, rigid with fear. Nothing came out.

"She was trespassing, sir," Kyle answered briskly.

"Untie her. She won't try leaving here in a hurry, if she has any sense." The old merman smiled at his pet. It leered back, stretching up almost as tall as him.

Kyle clenched his sharp jaw into a scowl as he pulled at the fishing line. I rubbed my wrists. "Tell us how you got here," he demanded.

"I don't know!" I said, tearing my eyes away from the eel. "I don't even know where I am. I had an accident, got lost, and you found me." Then, trying to control the quiver in my voice, I added, "Can I go home?"

"Home?" The old merman leaned toward me. The eel rolled its neck down into a spiral and closed its eyes. "And where would that be?"

I looked away from him. "Allpoints Island."

The two of them exchanged a look. What was it? Shock?

"Allpoints Island?" Kyle blurted out. "So you know about—"

"Kyle!" the old merman snapped. "I'll handle this."

"Of course. Sorry." Kyle drew back, bowing slightly.

Pausing briefly to pat the moray, the old merman swam toward me. "Now then," he said in a voice as slimy as the eel, "I don't believe we've been introduced. I'm Nathiel. And you are . . . ?"

"Why should I tell you who I am?" I said, my heart bashing against my chest. "Why won't you let me go? What are you going to do with me?"

Nathiel laughed and turned away. "Questions, questions. Where shall we start, Kyle?"

Kyle shuffled his tail, pulling on his necklace. "Um . . ."

Nathiel waved him away. "Very well, little girl. I'll tell you who we are. Seeing as you've been kind enough to drop in. We are your biggest fear . . . or your greatest protectors. Depending on how you view your situation at this moment."

"You're not my biggest fear," I said, my heart thumping. "My biggest fear is much worse than you!"

"Oh yes?" Nathiel swam back toward me, no trace of kindness or favor on his face. He twitched his head and the eel rose up, uncoiling itself to slither along behind him. I flinched as it stretched almost up to my face.

"Do you know how powerful we are?" Nathiel asked in a quiet, biting voice. I shook my head quickly, without taking my eyes off the eel. "We are Neptune's chosen ones, his elite force, the only ones he trusts with his most prized possession." Nathiel edged an inch closer to me, his cold eyes shining into mine. "We, little visitor, are the kraken keepers."

A million questions jammed into my mind. "The kraken keepers? But if you're—but it's—"

Nathiel laughed, a throaty sound that echoed around the room. The eel slowly stretched up. It was about three times taller than me. *Please don't open your mouth, please don't open your mouth,* I prayed silently as its jaw twitched.

With another click of Nathiel's fingers, the eel slithered to the back of the room, folding itself once more into a perfect coil.

"Now," Nathiel said, "that's my side of the introductions. I think it's time we heard a little more about you. You see, we know quite a bit about Allpoints Island, don't we, Kyle?"

Kyle swam forward. Copying Nathiel's sneer, he replied, "Neptune tells us everything."

"That's right. So, for example, he tells us about merfolk who break his laws." Nathiel swam farther forward. "Merfolk who go meddling in places they shouldn't," he added, edging closer still, his nostrils flaring. "Merfolk who WAKE his beloved KRAKEN!" he shouted.

"But, I — how did you know?" I cried. My body was shaking. Water frothed around my tail. I tried to make it lie still.

Kyle stared at Nathiel. "Yes. How did you?"

"I *didn't* know!" Nathiel replied. "Swam right into it, didn't she? Come on, Kyle. What do you get if you add the kraken on the loose, an island full of merfolk who know nothing about it, and a scared merchild clearly running away from trouble? It's a simple case of mathematics."

"So we've found her?" Kyle said.

"We've done good work." Nathiel patted Kyle's

arm. "Neptune will be very pleased with us. Very pleased indeed."

"Neptune? You're going to tell him?" My voice quivered.

"Of course! That is the whole point. Don't you realize the danger we are all in, you foolish girl?"

"But Neptune! He'll be furious with me."

"You think we give a fin about that?" Kyle snapped. "We need you. All of us. There's more than just yourself to consider."

"What do you mean? What use am I to you?"

Nathiel shook his head. "Kyle, I've had enough of this whining. I think it's time we got the boss in."

"The boss? Neptune? He's coming here?" I squeaked.

"Not Neptune, no. One of his most trusted aides." Nathiel picked up a conch. Turning away from me, he spoke softly into it. I couldn't hear what he said. I quickly scanned the room, looking for an escape. My eyes met the eel's. *Try it,* they seemed to say. I shivered back against the wall.

"He'll be along very shortly." Nathiel put the conch down and tidied some shells on his desk.

A moment later, the door opened. I squeezed my eyes shut in terror. Someone was swimming toward me. I bit my lip as hard as I could, forcing tears away.

"Well, what have we here, then?" a voice said. A creepy voice.

A very familiar voice.

My eyes snapped open to see a crooked smile, an odd pair of eyes: one green, one blue. A scruffy-looking merman who wasn't all he seemed. Here he was again, all the way from Brightport.

It couldn't be! The so-called lighthouse keeper. Mom's so-called friend who was anything but that in reality.

"Hello, Emily," said Mr. Beeston.

He turned to the others. "Good work, both of you," he said, snapping something around my wrists. Handcuffs made from lobster's legs! They bit and scratched at me.

Then he pushed me toward the door. "I'll take over now," he said before turning back to give me another of his lopsided smiles. "It's time we were reacquainted."

How could they let this happen? Twice! I can't *believe* my parents! My dad. It's all his fault. I can't believe I agreed to this nightmare vacation in the first place.

We're hanging on to our useless, broken boat, lying across it, gripping onto ropes. Only problem is, it's upside down! How long before it sinks and we *totally* end our vacation in style? I grab the rope tighter as the swells carry us up and down. My stomach seesaws with them.

Are we through that, that whatever it was, that great big sheet of glass in the middle of the ocean?

And the other thing.

I refuse to think about it. It didn't happen. Mom and Dad haven't mentioned it. I must have imagined it. Delirious, that's what I am. It was probably just the waves. Or a vision, because I'd seen it before. Yes. That's it. Definitely. A mirage.

There's nothing to worry about. I'm just cracking up.

"Maureen, Mandy—look!" Dad lets go of the rope with one hand and points out to sea.

It's a ship. Coming toward us!

"Wave! Both of you! Splash your feet!" Dad yells. For the first time in our lives, Mom and I do what he says without arguing.

The ship's coming closer and closer. Have they seen us? They *must* have! There's nothing except us moving for miles all around. We're kicking and yelling, every atom of hope screaming out of us.

"I can't splash anymore, Dad. My legs are killing me." I stop kicking for a moment while I catch my breath. The ship's stopped moving. They haven't seen us, after all. That's it. There's nothing we can do now. The realization slams into my mind like a block of ice: we're going to die.

But then I notice something attached to the ship. "Look!"

They're lowering a lifeboat into the water! It's coming to get us.

We've been saved!

Chapter Seven

*M*r. Beeston unhooked the lobster claws from my wrists and pulled out a couple of jelly-like cushions. He motioned for me to sit down on one of them while settling himself on the other. I'd hardly ever seen him as a merman. He was half-human and half-merperson like me, the only other one I'd met. He looked just as creepy either way, with his crooked teeth and his crooked smile and the odd-colored eyes that stared at you from the corners.

We were in a bubble-shaped room. It felt like the inside of a huge round shell. No windows, just one small hole divided by thick metal bars. Tiny chinks of light threw pencil-thin beams across the darkness. A black damselfish with fluorescent purple spots and a bright yellow tail weaved between the rays.

I tried to stay calm. My mind wouldn't stop racing, though. What were they going to do with me? Would anyone find me? Dad? Shona? Were they looking for me? And what about Mom and Millie? My heart ached at the thought of them on that ship. They'd be miles away by now.

"What are you doing here?" I asked in a daze. Among the millions of questions racing around in my head, it was the only one I could seem to form into words.

"Surprised to see me?" he asked, his voice slipping across the room like slime.

"Of course I'm surprised to see you! Who's taking care of the lighthouse in Brightport?"

"The lighthouse?" Mr. Beeston laughed. "Emily, why would I be taking care of a lighthouse?"

"It's what you do!"

"The lighthouse was a cover. You know that."

"Oh, yes. Of course," I said numbly. I'd found out before we left Brightport that Mr. Beeston was one of Neptune's agents and that he'd been spying on us to make sure we never found out about Dad. Well, it didn't work, did it? I found my dad. I'd beaten Mr. Beeston once. Maybe I could do it again. "But that still doesn't explain—"

"I was promoted," Mr. Beeston said, a crooked grin twitching at the side of his mouth. "For my bravery and good work."

"*Good work?*" I spluttered. "Is that what you call turning me and Mom over to Neptune? You were supposed to be our friend. We could have been thrown in prison, like my dad." I squeezed my eyes shut and pressed my fingernails tightly into my palms. I wasn't going to cry. He wasn't having that satisfaction.

Mr. Beeston flicked his tail nervously. "I— well, Emily, I did my duty. And look, I was needed here. They're working on rebuilding this palace, and there's a lot to do, monitoring activity in the area and keeping a gill open for any kraken-related incidents." He narrowed his eyes at me accusingly.

"So what are you going to do with me?"

"Do with you? It's not about what I want to do with you. It's about what you need to do for us."

"What d'you mean?"

Mr. Beeston shuffled forward in his cushion. I shuffled backward in mine. He tightened his lips. "I am still an agent of Neptune's, you know," he said sharply. "One of the highest ranking of all, now. And if I tell you that you are going to do something, you will do it. You don't question my authority."

I folded my arms, anxiously flicking my tail while I waited for him to continue.

"We are all in grave danger. The kraken is on the loose. It has to be calmed and brought back to Neptune."

"But what's that got to do with me?"

He held my eyes for a long time before replying.

"You, Emily, are the only one who can do it."

Someone was banging on the outside of the shell. Mr. Beeston opened the porthole-shaped door we'd come through. Kyle surged into the room on a sudden wave. It flung me against the wall.

"Sir," he said breathlessly. "I've had a sighting. It's coming closer. The sea—it's getting rough."

"Thank you, Kyle. Good work," Mr. Beeston said.

"It's heading toward the palace!" Kyle panted. "I think it's going to get us all. We might have to make our escape."

"Make our escape? Are you off your fins, boy?" Mr. Beeston barked. "Have you been given the wrong job? You have one purpose and one purpose only. You have a wonderful opportunity to return to the old days and restore the power of the kraken. Do you hear me?"

"Yes, sir." Kyle reddened. "I'm sorry."

"Now, don't let it out of your sight. I'm dealing with it. Have some faith."

Kyle retreated, leaving a swirling cloud of silt behind him.

"Are you going to explain any of this to me?" I asked as Mr. Beeston swam back into the room. A tiny silver fish swam toward him, slithering across his stomach. He batted it away.

"The kraken is Neptune's pet," Mr. Beeston began.

"I know that."

"And it sleeps for a hundred years. Without its full sleep, it wakes in a murderous rage."

"I know that too."

"Stop interrupting me, child! I shall tell you the story my way or not at all."

I slammed my mouth shut.

"All but Neptune are forbidden to approach the kraken during its sleep. Neptune is the only one who should wake it. And only at the specified time. You see, when it wakes, the only person it will listen to is the one who wakes it, the one it sees first on opening its eyes. This should always be Neptune. But this time, it was you."

"You mean . . . ?"

"Yes, Emily. The kraken will obey you and only you."

I realized I wasn't saying anything. My mouth moved. Opened. Closed. Nothing. The kraken would obey me and only me? I slumped back against the wall, my mind empty, my limbs numb. A thin ray of sunlight threw a diagonal line across the room like a dusty laser beam, lighting up barnacles that lined the walls. The beam shimmered and broke, rocked by the constant water movement.

"What do you want me to do?" I asked eventually.

"We need to move quickly. Neptune's power over the kraken is fiercely protected. It wasn't expected that anyone else would ever wake it. *Most* merfolk obey his rules." He paused to scowl briefly at me. "First, you have to go to the edge of the Triangle, where its magic is strongest."

"The edge of the Triangle?" I gasped. "You mean the current that leads to the deepest depths of the ocean?"

"Nonsense!" Mr. Beeston snapped. "It doesn't do that. That's what we tell folks to keep them out of the way."

"So where does it go, then?"

"It leads into the realm of the kraken."

"The realm of the kraken?" My voice cracked. Somehow, that didn't sound much more inviting than the deepest depths of the ocean.

"The place where you can communicate with it. You must go to the edge of the Triangle and come face to face with it."

"Face to face?" I burst out. "With the kraken?" I couldn't face the monster again. Please no! An image squirmed into my mind: those horrific tentacles, searching, batting and thrashing, smashing into the tunnel. My eyes began to sting with tears. I didn't care anymore if Mr. Beeston saw me cry. I couldn't hold it back.

He spoke softly. "It's the only way."

"What happens then?" I asked, swallowing hard. "When we're at the Triangle's edge?"

"It will come to you. It will listen to you."

"And I can save the day?"

"What? Yes, yes, of course you can save the day."

"And it'll do what I tell it?"

"As I told you, it will listen only to you. Its power lies in your hands."

I suddenly realized what Mr. Beeston was telling me. I could end all of this. I could bring the kraken into my power. It would listen to me. I could calm it down and everything would be all right. I just had to face it one more time.

"OK," I said. "I'll do it."

Mr. Beeston smiled his crooked smile. "I knew you would."

He turned to leave. "There's just one last thing," he said, pausing at the door. "You *were* on your own when you woke the kraken, weren't you?"

"I—why do you want to know that?" I blustered.

Mr. Beeston darted back toward me. Coming so close that I could see the jagged points of his crooked yellow teeth, he leaned into my face. "If someone else was with you when the kraken woke, we need them too."

"Why?" I asked in a tiny voice.

"Emily, if there was someone else there, it means the kraken will not obey you on your own. Whoever it saw on waking, that is who it will obey—whether that is one person or twenty. We need them all or the plan will fail."

"I . . ."

I couldn't do it. I couldn't! Not after everything. I wasn't going to drag Shona into this. They'd have to think of something else. "There was no one," I said eventually, my cheeks on fire.

Mr. Beeston grabbed my arm, jerking my body like an electric shock. "You're lying! You *have* to tell me. There was someone with you—I know it. Who was it?"

"I can't tell you!" I cried. Tears slipped down my cheeks. "I can't do it! You can't make me."

"Oh, I think you'll find we can," he hissed.

I gulped. "What if I refuse?"

Mr. Beeston twitched slightly. "Then the kraken won't stop until it has destroyed everything in its sight. These waves we're seeing—you know they're just the start of it."

I thought back to what I'd seen: the kraken smashing up Mandy's boat, what it did to the reef, the rocks . . . the whale. But could I really make Shona face it again? Could I betray her like that? It would finish off our friendship forever.

"I—I'll think about it," I stammered.

He swam over to the door. "Don't think for too long, Emily," he said quietly. "Time is an option we don't have."

Now, this is more like it! This is what our vacation was supposed to be like all along. Luxury cruise liner, lounge chairs, swimming pool, free drinks. We're even getting special attention from the crew because of our trauma.

Yeah, it's all great.

Except. Well, except Mom and Dad haven't spoken a word to each other since we were saved. The atmosphere's so cold when they're around, you'd think we were on a cruise to Antarctica. They're so busy ignoring each other, neither of them has even asked how I am. I sometimes wonder if they'd even notice if I disappeared. I'm tempted to try it—but I'm too much of a coward. What if it only confirmed my worst fears—that no one cares about me?

And then there's Emily. Apart from wondering what she's doing here anyway, and not to mention the fact that she happens to be a *mermaid,* I just can't believe I let her put one over me, yet again. OK, and I'm worried about her, too, all right? Just because she hates me doesn't mean I want her dead.

We set sail again soon. They've been trying to get away from here, but there's something wrong with the ship. It keeps going off course for some reason. They're trying to figure it out, and once they do and we're away from here, I'll *never* get a chance to repay her. She'll always have won.

For once, Dad had actually come up with a brilliant plan, and we let it slip away. If only I could find her. Kill two birds with one stone. Get fish girl back AND save our home. Now *that* would be satisfying!

Maybe I could. Who says it's too late?

I'm wandering around the back of the ship trying to think of something when I hear voices. Three people are standing near the lifeboats. One of them's waving her arms in the air, shouting at someone in a Carefree Cruises uniform.

"But why on earth can't you just let it down?" she's yelling. "I know you used one of them to let a family come aboard. We have to get off the ship! I have to find my daughter!"

"Madam, they were in trouble. We couldn't leave them to drown," the Carefree Cruises person replies. "And you won't tell me anything about your daughter's whereabouts. You won't even give me your name. You can hardly expect me to break ship's regulations just because you and your friend here feel like taking a ride in a lifeboat."

The other one looks up. That's when I see who it is. A big woman in a black cape. It's Mystic Millie, the crazy lady who used to read palms on the pier in Brightport! What the—

"A child is in trouble," she says. "That's all you need to know. We've seen things. *I* have seen things. And if you don't mind my saying so, I am rather known for the accuracy of my visions. Isn't that right, Mary Penelope?"

The other woman turns her head as she nods. I duck behind a plastic box full of diving equipment before she can spot me. But I've seen her face. It's Mrs. Windsnap! What are they doing here?

They're moving away. I can't hear the rest of the conversation. But then a thought occurs to me. They want to get off the ship to find Emily. That means she must be nearby.

I could get her! She's probably really near us. Maybe I could get one of those lifeboats myself and find her. Someone's got to do something—and it doesn't look as though Mom and Dad are going to bother. Too busy ignoring each other.

It's not as if they'll even miss me. No one would miss me. And if I get lost at sea, well, they'll be sorry then, won't they.

Before I can talk myself out of it, I'm grabbing everything I'll need—snorkel, mask—and clambering down a ladder that reaches the lifeboats. I *know* it's crazy; I know it is. But what are my options? Stay here being Mandy-no-friends or actually do something with my life? And if I get her, maybe Dad can have his dream after all and save our home. He might even remember who helped him do it. But what about her mom? I'd have to get around her. Well, I'll think of something. I'll have to.

I'm lost in thought—so lost, in fact, that I'm not looking at what I'm doing. Standing on the edge of the lifeboat, fiddling and yanking at ropes and belts, trying to figure out how you release the boats. It's ridiculous. I'd never manage it. The whole plan is ridiculous. Mrs. Windsnap's not going to stand by and watch while I snatch her daughter—if I could even find her. I don't know what I was thinking. I must be losing it.

I'm about to clamber back up to the deck. But as I'm reaching out to grab the ladder, something slips: my hand—I miss the ladder. Then my foot—the ladder's too slippery—I'm falling! No! I lurch out to get hold of the ladder, but it's too late. I miss again, bashing my hand against the ladder and banging my leg as I fall.

With an enormous splash, I land in the sea! HELP!

No one can hear me. The cold jams my brain as the ship speeds away. Oh, God—help!

Then Emily's face comes into my mind and with it a new thought: she's my only hope of getting out of this mess. The only person who might possibly, possibly help me. I need to find her.

I can see all the way to the bottom of the sea. It's incredible: so clear, so blue. Tiny speckled fish, spongy purple and green plants, trees almost. It's a whole other world down here.

There's something else down here, too.

But I'm not thinking about that. I refuse. I can't afford to think about anything—least of all how I got myself into this ridiculous mess.

How can the ship just leave without me? Leave me totally alone? I've *got* to find Emily. She must be around here somewhere. She can't have gotten far— she was in a net. I swim on.

And on.

And on.

The rocky coral is just below me, all furry, as though it's covered in dust and fluff. Pink, gooey, jelly-like clumps clutch at the rocks. A dull gray fish glides toward me. Then suddenly it flaps bright purple fins. It looks like an airplane with fancy painted wings.

Where am I?

I'm exhausted. There's no sign of her anywhere. I tread water while I adjust my mask and look around. The ship's miles away.

There's a plank of wood floating nearby. I've just got enough energy to reach it. It looks like a piece of our boat! My teeth chatter as I cling to it and try to figure out what the heck I'm going to do next.

The water's really dark here, and murky. I dip under to look around, but I can hardly see anything. The jelly stuff seems to be reaching higher, trying to grab me. And there are too many sea urchins.

And then I see something stringy, floating up toward the surface. I paddle over to examine it. It's a piece of net; I'm sure it's hers.

She got away, then.

There's something else. Something very big. Black on top, white underneath, a giant fin on its back. It's coming toward me!

I want to scream. I know I want to scream—but I can't. I can't get anything out of my throat. I couldn't even if I wasn't underwater, in the middle of the sea, miles from anywhere. It's the monster! I knew it! I should have trusted my instincts. I'm an idiot. And now I'm a dead idiot.

Maybe I can get away before it eats me.

But it's not moving.

Yes, it is. But not toward me. It's kind of floating, gliding slowly upward. And it's not the monster.

It's a killer whale. And it's dead.

As it floats past me, I watch with morbid fascination. There's a chunk missing from its side. My body starts to shake.

My legs don't seem to be working anymore. *Please just get me back to the ship! Please get me away from here. I'll do anything. I'll be nice to Mom and Dad; I'll even forgive Emily for everything. Just get me back to the ship alive!* Please!

Something grabs my legs. That's it. I'm dead.

I don't even struggle. I can't. My body feels as useless as the half-eaten whale. I close my eyes and wait for—

"Who are you?"

What? I open my eyes. A man's face has appeared in front of me in the water. Young, almost a boy. He's gripping my arms. Where did he come from?

I open my mouth and swallow about a gallon of water. He waits while I splutter half to death and put my snorkel back on.

"Come with me," he says.

Still holding my elbow with one hand, he pulls me along in the water. I catch a glance under the water as we swim—and that's when I see. He's not a man. He's a merman! He's got a long tail with silver rings all the way down.

We're heading toward something that looks like an island. As we get closer, I realize it's just a collection of rocks and caves. We swim among the rocks.

"Nathiel," the merman calls. Still holding on to me, he yanks me downward. I quickly adjust my snorkel so I can still breathe.

Below us, a rabbit warren of rocks and tunnels and caves spreads out as far as I can see. It's like a city, packed with too many buildings crammed together as closely as possible.

An old guy with a scraggly beard appears from inside a large crevice. Another merman! We come back up to the surface together.

"Another one?" he says.

"Another what?" I burst out. "Have you got Emily?"

The young merman looks at the older one. "Emily?" he says. "Sharks alive, Nathiel—d'you think this is the one?"

The older merman turns to me. "You're Emily's friend?" he asks.

"I—" What has Emily got to do with this?

"You were looking for her!" he shouts, shaking me.

"Yes!" I burst out. "Yes, I'm looking for Emily. Is she here?"

"Kyle, tell the boss right away," the old merman orders. "Take her to the Lantern Cave first. It's the only safe place above water."

Kyle turns to swim away with me.

"No!"

They both swivel their heads to stare at me.

"Please," I say. A tear streaks down my cheek. I don't care. Anyone would cry in these circumstances. Anyway, I'm not crying. It's the sun. It's shining right into my eyes. "Please let me go home."

"Where's home?" Kyle asks.

Good question. Home. You know, the place that's about to get pulled down, where I live with two people who can't stand the sight of each other.

"I need to get back to my parents. Please." I blub like a baby. Have I really been reduced to this? Begging to be with my parents!

Nathiel says, "And where are they?"

"I don't know."

He turns to Kyle. "Just get her to the Lantern Cave for now. We can always—"

"They're on a ship," I say.

Nathiel snaps back to face me. "What?"

"They're on a ship, over there somewhere." I point back in the direction I think I came from. I sob. I can't help it. "Please let me get back to it."

The pair of them look at each other.

"A ship." Kyle's eyes are shining. "This is it!

First the kraken, now a ship for it. We can get back to work, back to the old days. We need to move fast."

What's he talking about? "Are you going to let me go?" I ask.

Nathiel turns to me, grips my shoulders. "You want to go back to your ship?" he asks.

I nod.

"And you can show us where it is?"

"I—I think so."

Nathiel lets me go. "Handed to us on a plate," he says, smiling at Kyle. "Good work. We're going to be rich."

Kyle's cheeks flush. He doesn't speak again, just takes me toward a cave. I squeeze through the tiny entrance. It opens out when we get inside. It's dark, and creepy. I can just about make out strange shapes hanging down from the roof. Tiny chinks of light coming through holes way above me, huge boulders with brown gooey stuff that looks like caramel icing dribbled over them.

He closes a barred metal door and locks it from the outside. I grab the bars. "Wait!"

"We'll take care of you," he says, his face cold and expressionless. "Don't worry."

Don't worry, I say to myself as he swims away from me. I climb out of the water onto a rocky ledge, my body shaking and cold. Sure. Absolutely. Why would I worry? I mean, I've only been locked in a dark cave by myself, with nothing but weird clumps of rocks hanging from the ceiling like enormous crooked fingers pointing at me.

I turn away from the pointing fingers. I've got to get out of here. I just need a plan. I'll think of something.

I shiver as the darkness closes around me.

Chapter Eight

I swam around my cell for the hundredth time.
"Let me out!" I yelled, scratching my hands
down the rocky walls. My voice echoed around
me. Finally, I slumped in the corner.

The next thing I knew, the door was rattling. I
leaped up as Mr. Beeston came in carrying a net
basket filled with shellfish and seaweed. He placed
it on a rocky ledge beside me. Water crashed around
me as I reached for it, throwing me against the
sides.

"See that?" he snarled as I grabbed the ledge to
stop myself from being thrown back against the
wall. "That's virtually constant now. And it'll keep
getting worse, until you've done what you need
to do."

I didn't reply.

"Eat your breakfast," he said, nudging a finger at the basket. "You need to be strong."

"I don't have to do what you say." The edges of my eyes stung.

"Really? Well, you won't be interested in our new visitor, then. Kyle tells me he's found some-one who might make you feel differently."

"A visitor?"

"A friend."

I quickly rubbed my eyes. "You've got her here? But how did you know —"

"Eat up quickly," he growled in a voice that made my skin itch. "It's time for a reunion."

We swam up toward the surface, Mr. Beeston's hand gripping my wrist so tightly it burned. The water grew lighter and warmer as we made our way along tunnels and out into clear water. He pulled me down under a clump of rocks, scatter-ing a group of striped triggerfish. A metal gate filled a gap between the rocks.

"Up there," he said.

My heart thudded. I was really going to see Shona! But what if she wouldn't speak to me after everything that had happened? She'd probably hate me even more now, for dragging her into it again. I had to explain. "Can I see her on my own?" I asked.

"What for?"

"It's personal."

"Ah, friendship, so sweet," Mr. Beeston snarled, his throat gurgling into a laugh. He gripped my arm, his broken nails scratching my skin. "You can have five minutes," he said. Then he fiddled with a lock, and the gate bounced open. I swam through it, along a narrow crack. "And don't try anything smart," he called through the bars.

"I won't."

I swam all the way up to the surface. I was inside a cave, in a tiny pool. Gray pillars lined the edges, their reflections somber in the greeny blue water. A tiny shaft of sun lit up the stalactites hanging from the ceiling like frozen strands of spaghetti. Where was she?

I swam between the pillars, where the pool opened out. Slimy brown rocks lay all around. Thick clusters like bunches of candles protruded upward from the water, black, as though they'd been singed.

"Shona?" I called.

And then I saw her. Sitting on one of the rocks, her back to me.

But it wasn't Shona.

Her hair was short and black. She turned around. For a moment, she looked shocked. Then she forced her angular face into a twisted smile.

"Hi there, fish girl," she said. There was a smug look on her face, but I was pretty sure her voice wobbled a little. "Long time no see."

"Mandy!"

"Having fun?" she asked with a smile.

"Having *fun*? You think being captured and locked in an underwater tunnel is *likely* to be my idea of fun?"

"Oh, sorry. I didn't realize." Mandy examined her nails.

"Didn't realize what?"

"That they didn't like you as much as me. Should have guessed, though. I mean, people never do, do they?"

"What are you talking about?" I gasped.

"Oh, aren't they looking after you nicely? Haven't they promised to take you home?" She glanced at my face. "Oops. Obviously not. Sorry. I always seem to say really hurtful things, *totally* by accident! Don't worry. You can't help it if people don't like you, can you?"

"Yeah, right, Mandy. I don't think so," I said, clenching my hands into tight fists.

"Whatever." Mandy picked up a stone and

threw it into the water. I watched the ripples grow wider and more faint. Then she stepped back up the rock and twirled around the pillars, prancing around the place as though she owned it.

"Why would they like you?"

She stopped prancing and glared at me, eyes wide open and innocent. "What's not to like?"

"Where do you want me to start?" I spluttered.

Mandy frowned. "Anyway, they're stupid," she said quickly. Then she turned to look at me. "Hey, that's a point. *They're* stupid and so are you. Isn't that funny? You'd think you'd get along better, having something in common like that. Anyway, I don't care. They're taking me back to the boat soon."

"Your boat? You didn't sink?"

"Not that old washed-out lump of tin." She laughed. "No, our new boat. Oh, did I forget to mention that we got saved by a luxury cruise liner? Funny enough, they want to treat us like royalty, too! A shame, isn't it?"

"A cruise liner?" My voice suddenly shook. "What cruise liner?"

"The one that we should have been on in the first place. The vacation we were *destined* to have. But not to worry. It's all OK now. They're taking me back later today."

"Taking you back? But why?"

Mandy bit her lip before turning away. "Told you. They like me."

"Mandy, you can't trust these—"

A sound of metal on metal clanked below me. Mr. Beeston appeared. "Five minutes is up."

"Why are you taking her to the ship?" I demanded.

"Think we want to be poor forever?" he asked, adding, "Anyway, we're going together."

"Why? What do you mean about being poor? What aren't you telling me?"

"You know all you need to know," he said. "Let's go."

"That's not her!" I yelled, pointing at Mandy. "*She's* not my friend!"

Mr. Beeston glanced across at Mandy as she turned around. Seeing her face for the first time, he suddenly faltered. "But that's—but you're—"

"*You!*" Mandy spluttered, looking up to notice him for the first time too. "Mr. Beeston. From Brightport! Does someone want to tell me what's going—"

Just then, a huge wave rushed into the cave, filling it almost to the ceiling. Mandy lost her footing and slipped into the water beside me. I grabbed her.

"Get your hands off me, fish girl," she spat. "I can look after myself!"

"No, you can't. You don't know what you're involved in!" I shouted.

Mr. Beeston had disappeared under the water. A moment later, he resurfaced, fighting his way back up against the tide. I turned to face him. "I'm not doing anything for you till you tell me exactly what's going on."

"Want to bet?" he replied. Mandy opened her mouth to speak, but a wave washed her words away. She spluttered and swam for the edge of the pool. Mr. Beeston lunged toward me, grabbing my arm. I tried to struggle, but he tightened his grip, his fingers scorching into my flesh as he pulled me back toward the grille at the bottom of the cave.

Mandy was shouting something as Mr. Beeston pushed me out, fighting against the raging water. I couldn't hear her words anymore.

"What are you doing with me?" I cried as a wall of white water rushed toward us, flinging me against a wall. "What's going on? Tell me!"

"Don't you understand?" he shouted. "We're *all* in danger here. Look at this. We can't live like this. You're the only one who can fix it." We'd reached my cell. He yanked on my arm, pushing me inside. "And you *will*!"

Without another word, he turned and left. I heard the bolt slam across the door.

* * *

I slumped back against the wall and closed my
eyes. How had it come to this? All I'd wanted
to do was fit in. How had I managed to cause
such devastation? I looked around my dark cell.
Shadows came and went on the walls as the hours
passed and daylight faded, along with my hopes.

"Emily?"

Who was that? It sounded like . . .

"Emily!"

Dad? I swam to the door. *"Dad!"* I screamed.

The door burst open. It was! It was him. He
wrapped me in his arms.

"How did you find me?" I asked, pressing
into his chest.

"I—"

"Wait!" I pulled away from the door as I heard
a noise outside. "There's someone out there," I
whispered. "How did you get past them?"

Dad took hold of my hands. "Emily," he said
in a tight voice. He wouldn't meet my eyes.

"What? What is it?"

"They know I'm here."

"They know? But how—"

"Archie," Dad said simply. "I had to tell, Em.
You knew that." He looked briefly at my face and
turned away again. He let go of my hands and

swam around the cell. "Mr. Beeston came soon after," he continued. He ran a hand through his hair, pulling at it as he struggled to speak. Eventually, he looked up at me. "He told me you hadn't been on your own."

Suddenly it clicked. I felt as though he'd punched me. "So that's why you're here," I said. "You just want me to tell you who I was with."

Dad looked down. "We have no choice, Em."

My throat ached. He hadn't tracked me down, after all. He only came because he had to. Well, I didn't blame him. Why would he want me back after what I'd done?

Dad swam back toward me. "Emily, I *begged* Archie to let me come. He wanted to do it himself."

I didn't say anything. I couldn't. Lifting my chin, Dad spoke almost roughly. "Remember when you found me at the prison?"

I nodded, gulping a tear away.

"That was the happiest day of my whole life," he said. "Did you know that? And you know what was the worst?"

I shook my head.

"The day I thought I'd lost you again."

I held his eyes for a moment before falling back against him. "Oh, Dad. It's been so awful!" I cried. "They want me to face the kraken again."

415

"I know, little 'un, I know." He held me tight while I sobbed. "I'll be there."

"But you won't! I've got to do it on my own."

"Not on your own, Emily," he said, his voice stern. "You weren't on your own." He spoke slowly and deliberately. "You have to tell. You don't know what it's been like at the island. Typhoons, giant waves. One side's totally devastated. All the trees knocked flat. Ships have come off their moorings, and it's only going to get worse."

"It was Shona," I said eventually. I squeezed him tighter. Closing my eyes, I prayed I hadn't just killed off any last chance of her ever making up with me. I couldn't bear to lose her forever; I just couldn't bear it.

Dad swallowed hard. "There's something else I've got to tell you." He held me away from him and picked up both of my hands. "It's your mom and Millie. They went out looking for you, and we can't find them. There's folk out searching and I'm sure it won't be—"

"Dad! I know where they are."

He jerked backward. "What?"

"I've seen them." I told him about everything: the ship, Mandy, Mr. Beeston.

Dad listened with wild eyes. "Emily, there's no time to waste," he gasped when I'd finished.

"We've got to do this. I'll send a message to Archie."

"Don't leave me!" I gripped his arm. I couldn't be left alone again now. I couldn't lose Dad again. Please no!

"I'm not going anywhere," he said firmly. "I'll be by your side the whole time."

"Do I really have to do this?" I asked, my voice quivering.

Dad held me close as he spoke into my hair. "I'm sorry, Emily. It's the only way."

That creepy Mr. Beeston's pulling me along through the water on a kind of raft. I *never* liked him, back at Brightport. He's even worse now. He keeps shouting things to me. "Where's the ship?" he bellows.

"I—I think it's—"

"WHERE'S THE SHIP!" he repeats, about ten times louder.

"It must have moved," I call back to him. "It was somewhere over there." I point vaguely ahead of us.

"You know nothing, child," he says. "I don't know why we even brought you. No matter, we'll find it soon. It's probably already there."

"Already where?" Emily calls. She's here too, with another merman. I think it's her dad. They keep smiling at each other. Lucky them. My chest aches as I wonder if I'll ever get to smile at my dad again.

"The edge of the Triangle. Same place we're heading."

"You have to *tell* me!" Emily's screaming. "*Why* do you need the ship?"

"We're just getting our bearings," Mr. Beeston says.

Emily turns to the other merman. "He's not telling us everything," she whimpers. "I *know* he's not. Why would they be taking Mandy home? It doesn't make sense."

"Shh, just let's get there. We want your mom back. This is our best chance," he replies in a quiet voice, glancing nervously at Mr. Beeston. What are they up to? "It'll be OK," he says, holding Emily's hand. "I'm here to take care of you."

We swim on. I keep having visions of seeing Mom and Dad again. *Please get me to the boat. I promise I'll change. I won't be horrible anymore.*

The water breaks in sharp waves all around us. It's getting really rough as we plow through enormous peaks and crash down into huge troughs. I'm grabbing the side of my raft, totally soaked.

And then I see it.

In the distance. On the horizon. I think it might be portholes, glinting in the sunlight. Yes, it is! A whole row of them! It's the ship!

"That's it!" I shout. "Over there!" I point to the right.

We speed toward the cruise ship. I'm going to see Mom and Dad again! I'm going to be safe!

As we get closer, I can see its shape more clearly. And then it goes out of sight. There's something in the water, in front of the ship. It's like an island; a sickly khaki-green island with hills and bumps. And it's moving. Long arms reaching up, propelling it forward, blotting out the sun. I grip hard onto the raft as my stomach turns over.

The monster's going to get the ship.

I realize I'm screaming.

"Mandy, I can stop this!" Emily yells to me. "They've told me I can calm it."

"Why should I believe you?" I shout back. "You think you're so special, don't you? Think you can do everything better than anyone else!" Tears are streaming down my face. Mom, Dad. They're so near and I'll never see them again.

"Listen to me!"

"No! I *won't* listen to you. If I hadn't been trying to find you, none of this would have happened! It's all your fault! Every single thing that's gone wrong here is YOUR FAULT!"

Emily doesn't speak again. Her face looks like it's been slammed between two walls. I force myself not to look, not to care.

Why should I care? No one cares about *me.*

I'm going to die out here, and absolutely no one cares.

J gulped as we swam, trying to swallow, trying to breathe. Trying not to think about what I had to do.

Could I really calm the kraken's rage? Did I have any choice?

We were getting nearer to the ship — and so was the kraken. The thought of Mom on the ship was all I needed to spur me on. I *had* to do it.

"Look!" Dad pointed at two shapes in the water. Archie and Shona!

Archie swam up to Mr. Beeston, pulling Shona along with him. "We've got her," he said simply.

Mr. Beeston nodded curtly. "Just in time."

Shona! Excitement bubbled inside me — but quickly turned to ice when I saw her face. She wouldn't meet my eyes. Well, I didn't blame her. After everything I'd put her through, now she had to come face to face with the kraken again, and it was thanks to me — again. I fought back tears.

Archie looked across at me. "I'm glad you're safe," he said, trying to smile.

"Safe? What makes you think I'm safe?"

"Come on. We don't have any time to lose." He started swimming again, Shona joining Mandy and me as we trailed along behind the others. Dad swam up ahead with Archie.

"I'm not surprised you're not speaking to me," I said, building up the courage to speak to her as we sliced through the water. *Please don't ignore me, please!*

Shona looked at me through heavy eyes. "What d'you mean?" she asked. "I thought you wouldn't be talking to me! I was so horrible to you. I've been a coward and a terrible friend. I wouldn't be surprised if you never want to speak to me again."

I grabbed her hand as we swam. "Shona, you weren't a terrible friend! If anyone was a terrible friend, it was *me.* I dragged you somewhere you didn't want to go."

Shona squeezed my hand. "I should never have let you take the blame. I'm so sorry," she said. Then more quietly, she added, "And so are Althea and Marina."

"Althea and Marina? Your new best friends, you mean?"

Shona laughed. "My what? Why would I want them when I've got the best best friend in the world?"

I held my breath. "You mean . . . ?"

"Yes!" She grinned. "I mean you! I mean a best friend who's crazy and impossible and mad-dening and strong and brave." She held my eyes. "And unique," she added.

My cheeks burned. "You do?" I gulped.

Shona nodded. "I was just too stubborn and stupid to realize it for a while. And you know, Althea and Marina want to be friends with you too," she added. "They feel awful about taking us to the lagoon. They think it's all their fault. They wanted me to tell you they're going to make it up to you at the welcome party, when we get back."

The welcome party. Were they still really going to hold a welcome party for us? Would I really ever be truly welcome there?

"Well, excuse me for not joining in the happy moment," Mandy burst in, "but does either of you realize we're all about to *die* out here? Shouldn't we be trying to get *out* of this mess?"

"Mandy's right," I said, suddenly realizing Mandy and Shona had never met. Somehow, this didn't feel like the best time for introductions. "We need to think about what we're doing."

Ahead of us, the kraken had dipped underwater, an occasional tentacle lashing out across the surface. The sea bubbled with expectation.

Shona turned to me. "What *are* we doing?"

That was a very good question.

We were there. The edge of the Triangle; the realm of the kraken. It was no longer a glassy plane over the ocean. An endless chasm stretched across the sea, giant waterfalls tearing down into the blackness below.

The ocean raged as the kraken surfaced in front of the chasm. Huge tentacles surged out of the sea, thick and lumpy, spraying water all around as they crashed onto the surface again and again.

I froze.

I couldn't do it.

Someone was shouting at me. I think it was Archie. It could have been Mr. Beeston, or even my dad. It didn't matter. I couldn't change this, I couldn't face the kraken. I closed my eyes.

"The ship." Mandy was pulling at my arm. "The ship," she said over and over again. "It's going to sink the ship! *Do* something!"

The monster was looming over the ship as it edged toward the chasm. Tentacles reached high into the air. One swipe and it would all be over. "MOM!" I screamed into the wildness, my eyes blurred from tears and seawater.

Archie grabbed my arm. "Face it!" he screamed. "Both of you!"

"*Then* what?" Shona cried.

"Just do it! Face it together and be silent. Wait till it turns this way. I'll tell you what to do then. Quick!"

Shona turned to me.

"Come on," I said. "It'll be OK."

I grabbed her hand and we turned to face the kraken together, waiting in silence for the awful moment when it would turn that long, hard, horrible face toward us.

And then it did.

Nothing else moved. The sea swells stopped. The crashing waves leading down into blackness, the chasm—everything was still, held in a freeze frame. The kraken stood like a terrifying statue, motionless like iron, a giant tentacle poised over the ship, its bulging, weeping eyes locked with ours.

"It's working," Dad whispered into the still-ness. "It's working!"

In the distance, a chariot was gliding over the water, pulled by dolphins. Neptune was on his way.

Archie glanced across at the chariot. "You have to do it now!" he urged. "Bring the kraken here, calm it down. Now!"

"What do we do?"

"Think."

"Think?"

"In your minds, try to communicate with it."

"*Communicate* with it?"

"Try to hold it in your power, bring it out of its rage so it can return to Neptune. You have to move fast."

"OK." I pulled at my hair, twirling it around as I flicked my tail. I glanced at Shona. She nod-ded quickly. OK. I just have to calm the kraken's rage. Think thoughts.

OK.

Calm down, nice kraken. I forced the words into my mind, my face squirming up with disgust and horror. A tentacle twitched, lashing out into thin air.

"You have to really feel it," Archie said. "It's no use pretending. It'll know."

Neptune was coming closer. I had to do some-thing before he got here, prove that I wasn't completely and utterly useless, that I hadn't ruined absolutely everything. Shona's eyes were closed, her face calm and focused. OK, I could do this.

Please, I thought. *Please don't destroy anything. There's no need. Take it calmly, listen to us, trust us, it's all OK. No one's going to hurt you.*

Random thoughts raced through my head, anything I could think of that might have some effect.

And it did — it started to. The kraken's tentacles were softening, flopping back down onto the water, one by one. The swell of the sea had started shifting slowly, rising and falling steadily, the huge choppy waves with their sharp crests smoothing into deep swells. The chasm closed over, lying shiny and smooth like an oil slick.

"Good!" Mr. Beeston called. "Keep doing it!"

Don't be angry. Everything will be all right. Just be calm, calm, calm.

Beside me, I could almost feel Shona's thoughts, the same as mine, weaving in between my own words. The kraken was calming down. Its tentacles lay still and quiet, spread out across the ocean's surface.

The chariot was coming closer. I could see Neptune, rising out of his seat, holding his trident in the air.

"We've done it," he cried as the dolphins

brought him to my side. "Bring it here. Bring it to me now. Only when it is right in front of you can you bring it fully back into my power."

I swallowed. Here? Right in front of us?

"Now!" Neptune repeated.

I cleared my throat as I glanced at Shona again. Her face was white, her eyes wide and terrified.

I closed my eyes. *Come to us,* I thought, half of me praying it wouldn't work, the other half knowing that if it didn't we were all lost.

Nothing happened.

"You have to *mean* it!" Archie said. "I've *told* you that."

I took a deep breath and closed my eyes. Then, forcing myself to concentrate totally on my thoughts, I let the words come into my mind. *Come to us, now. We can end this. No more rage, just calm . . . come to us now.*

Something was happening in the water. Movement. I could sense it. I kept my eyes closed. *It's all right,* I said in my mind. *No one's going to hurt you. Just come to us now and we can work it out. Calm. Stay calm.*

"You're doing well," Neptune said. His voice sounded as though he was talking right into my ear. "Now, open your eyes. You have to come face to face with it, both of you. You need to hold it with your minds until the rage has completely gone."

"How will we know when the rage has gone?" I asked.

"It will come back to me."

I counted slowly to three, and then opened my eyes. It was all I could do not to scream at the top of my lungs. It was there! In front of me! A face as tall as an apartment building: lumpy and dark and pocked with holes and warts, tapering toward huge white eyes streaked with blood-red veins. Enormous craggy tusks pointed up, disappearing into the clouds, it seemed. Tentacles lay still all around it, like a deflated parachute.

I could hear cheering coming from the ship! The danger had passed. We'd done it. We'd really done it! I grabbed Shona's arm. She was laughing.

"We're not finished!" Neptune barked. "Beeston, get ready. Archie, ready?"

"Yes, Your Majesty," Archie replied, swimming away from me.

"Ready for what?" I asked. No one answered. Mr. Beeston and Archie were swimming toward the ship. I grabbed Dad. "Ready for what?" I asked again. "What's going on?"

Dad shook his head. "I don't——"

"What do you think?" Neptune growled. "It's time to put it back to work."

A queasy feeling stirred inside me. Something wasn't right.

"You don't think this is all merely to save your lives, do you?" Neptune asked. "Don't you think there is more to my kingdom than that?"

"I—I don't know. I don't under——"

"The kraken is getting back to work, as I've told you. It's been nearly a hundred years, and now it will return to what it knows best: relieving humans of what they do not need. It will bring me riches in quantities I haven't known for many years."

What did he mean? He couldn't possibly——

"And that"— he pointed to the ship—"is where we start."

"But you can't!" I yelled. The kraken stirred as I shouted, a tentacle hitting the water with a splash that covered us all. "You tricked us! You made us do all this, just so you can destroy everything!"

Mr. Beeston turned in the water. "We're not going to destroy everything. That's what the kraken would have done without you. We want to regain the control that is rightfully ours."

"And the riches," Neptune added, stroking a gold sash around his chest.

"Exactly, Your Majesty," Mr. Beeston added with a creepy smile.

"Why didn't you just let it sink the ship, then?" Shona asked.

"It will sink it for *me*! When *I* am ready. Otherwise, it is wanton destruction."

"Wanton destruction?" I spluttered. "And this isn't?"

Neptune's face bulged red. "Without me, the kraken will destroy everything in its sight, losing it forever into the chasm. I will *not* suffer that waste!" He waved his trident in the air. "Now go to it! I want every jewel from that ship!"

"But you'll kill them all!" I screamed, tears streaming down my face. "My mom's on that ship!"

"Did we ASK her to be there?" Neptune boomed. "Did we ASK you to start this?"

"But you can't just *kill* her! And Millie — all of them!"

Mr. Beeston looked at Neptune, then me. "Your mother's on the ship? What the—"

"I want my mom!" Mandy was crying next to me. "I want to go home."

"You can't!" I screamed at Neptune. "Make it not happen — it can't be happening."

The kraken twitched in the water, lifting a tentacle, tipping its head to the side.

"DO NOT lose it!" Neptune bellowed at Mr.

Beeston. "We're too close. It's getting confused. We mustn't lose it now. Beeston, we need to sort this out."

"Please don't do it!" I cried uselessly.

Mr. Beeston wouldn't look at me as he set off toward the ship. "I'm sorry, Emily," he said.

Dad lunged after him, grabbing his arm. "My WIFE is on that boat!" he screamed.

Mr. Beeston's left eye twitched. "That—it's not our concern," he stammered.

"Not your concern? Don't you care that people are going to die when you sink their boat?"

"Tough tails!" Mr. Beeston suddenly exploded. "They shouldn't stray into Neptune's kingdom. He is the ruler; everything in the ocean is his. He is only regaining what he's owed. Humans have stolen from him for centuries, poaching his seas for their own needs. We're just redressing the balance."

He was crazy. They all were.

Something was happening in the water. The kraken's tentacles were twitching, batting the water, spraying us all.

"OBEY ME!" Neptune screamed. "It's caught between your control and mine. We have to combine them or it will go insane."

"We won't!" I yelled back. "We WON'T obey you!"

I grabbed Shona and Mandy. "Come on!"

Mandy pulled away from me. "Look what you're doing!" she shouted. "You're making it *worse!*"

She was right; the kraken was coming back to life, tentacles rising to smash against the water.

"It's going to kill *everyone!*" Mandy yelled. "You have to stop it!"

"Then what? If we obey Neptune, it'll go back into his power again, and he'll make it sink the ship anyway!" I cried. "What can we do?"

It was ahead of us. Mr. Beeston was calling it to the ship. No!

The kraken lashed forward, tearing a hole through the sea as it spun toward the ship. The Triangle's surface was opening up again!

And then. And then.

I saw it in slow motion.

A tentacle, rising into the air, water spiraling off around it in an arc of color and light. It came crashing down onto the water, hitting out, thwacking at the surface, swiping at the ship. The ship! It was so close. I could see people lined up along the decks, running madly, but there was nowhere to run. The tentacles rained down. It had the ship! It knocked at it, hungry for destruction. The ship was tilting, people tossed from the deck—hundreds of people in the water, screaming for their lives.

"MOM!"

I whirled toward the kraken, edging toward the chasm; I could feel it pulling me — something holding us together; I couldn't fight it.

For a split second, everything stopped. The calm came back. The kraken had disappeared under the water. In silence, I watched the chasm close up, covered over again with the glassy surface of the sea.

Just one brief moment of calm, before a screeching wail split the air around us. Lights flared. The glassy surface splintered and cracked. The whirling sea raged below. And the kraken rose. It burst through the water, screaming up from deep below the surface, its long face stretched wide by angry, gaping jaws exposing daggerlike teeth as its tentacles scrambled madly like a mass of giant maggots, smashing the still surface of the sea. As we watched, the water fell away, pouring like a waterfall, leaving just the kraken, surrounded in its fury by utter, black emptiness.

"We've lost our power," I said feebly to no one. "It's not listening."

I was being dragged toward the kraken. I could feel its mind pulling me toward it. Nothing I could do.

I couldn't save anyone. This force pulling me was too strong. No energy, no power to do anything.

I let myself slip toward the chasm.
And it closed behind me.

Down, down, into complete darkness. Nothing to see. No water, no land. Nothing. Falling through nothingness. Spiraling down, whisked around in a vacuum of whirling blackness, twisting me, throwing me around and around.

It grabbed me.

Lashing at me, scorching my face, my hands, my body, the kraken's tentacles screamed across me, again and again. I writhed and struggled, but it was impossible. I couldn't keep out of its clutches.

I touched something that felt like jelly. With shuddering, horrified disgust, I realized it was the edge of a sucker the size of a dinner plate. I gripped my body, trying to curl into a tight ball of nothingness.

"Why are you doing this?" I shouted uselessly as sticky, slippery tentacles slithered across my body, creeping around my tail, around and around, pulling me into a locked coil. I couldn't move a single thing. Brown hairs brushed across my face, writhing like a nest of worms. Terror sucked my breath away.

What could I do to stop it? Beg? What could I say? Why wasn't it *listening*? I'd woken it up! It should be in my power!

My thoughts rambled uselessly as tears streaked down my cheeks.

The tentacles reached higher and tighter, wrapping me up, trapping my arms, climbing up my body, finally closing around my neck.

This was it. This was where it ended. No one to save me.

The darkness slowly grew darker.

The ship's safe! It's all stopped. The monster's gone. But the people are still in the water. Lots of them. Someone's got to save them.

"What have you done with her?" Emily's dad is screaming at the really tall merman in the throne. "What have you done with her? Give me my *daughter*!"

The big merman waves this great big fork thing around. "Do you DARE question me in this manner?" he yells at the top of his voice. What is his *problem*? Can't he see people are in *trouble* here?

"Give her back to me!" Emily's dad howls, his voice cracking. "Give her *back*!"

"We can't," the big merman answers. "The kraken has her."

There's uproar after this. The merman's yelling. Some of the people from the ship have broken away. They're swimming toward us, shouting, calling things. They're coming closer.

"MANDY!"

It's Mom! My mom's in the water! I try to paddle my raft toward her. I can't get away. Mr. Beeston's tied it up to that stupid chariot thing.

"Mom!"

What if that massive hole opens up again? What if it sucks us *all* in?

Someone's calling Mom from one of the life-boats. She hovers in between us.

"Get in the boat!" I yell.

"Stay there, Mandy!" she shouts to me, swimming back to help the others. "I'll get them to come for you."

I nod, swallowing hard as I cling to my raft.

I can't stop thinking about Emily, in there with that thing. I can't let it happen. Was she honestly that bad? What did she ever really do to me?

Maybe I was wrong. Maybe she never had it in for me. It was always me who had it in for her. It was me who tripped her up in swimming, and called her names and stole her best friend. What did she do wrong, exactly? So a few people liked her more than they liked me. Could I really blame them? *I* like her more than I like me at times.

I edge toward the big merman in the chariot.

"Please," I beg. "You have to do something. She's going to die in there."

He turns slowly around toward me, looking down on me as though I'm an ugly beetle that's just crawled out of the sea. "What am I expected to do about that?" he says, his eyes flickering toward the chasm. He looks away from me. "I didn't cause it. She brought it on herself."

"But can't you end it? Make the monster stop?"

"I cannot and I WILL not. Now leave me al—"

"HOW DARE YOU!" Someone suddenly shouts from the other side of the chariot. "Give me a leg up, will you, Jake," she says in a quieter voice to Emily's dad. Then she hauls herself up onto the chariot. Millie! It's Mystic Millie!

The merman glares at her. "Don't you know who I am?" he asks, his voice rumbling like an approaching typhoon.

"Yes, of course. You're Neptune," she says. "But that—"

"KING Neptune!" he booms.

Millie presses her lips together, sucking on her teeth. "Look, you could be King Kong for all I care," she says, squeezing out her long black skirt over the sea. "That still doesn't give you the right to let a poor innocent child get eaten by your precious monster." She stares into his eyes and pulls something out from under her cape. It looks like a gold pendant. "Now are you going to do something about it?" she asks in a low drawl.

He stares back, his eyes flicking to the pendant. No one says anything. As he glares at her, something changes in his eyes. It's as though a flame starts to flicker behind them.

"Well, I . . . ," he says.

Millie moves closer to him. "You know, even the greatest among us are allowed to change our ways if we want to," she says quietly.

Then there's splashing in the water behind me.

"Mandy!"

It's Dad!

He's panting hard. He grabs me, clutching onto the raft. "Thank God," he says. "Thank God." He's crying. I've *never* seen my dad cry. "We've got to do something," he says, his words coming out in rasps. "Too many people in the water—not enough boats— someone's got to help."

"Where's my *wife*?" Emily's dad gasps. He reaches up to grab Millie's hand. "Make him do it," he croaks. "Get my daughter back. Promise me!"

Millie folds a hand over his. "We'll get her back, Jake," she says. "I promise."

He dives under the water and heads toward the ship.

I pull away from Dad. "PLEASE!" I scream at Neptune. "There has to be something we can do."

He lifts his fork thing in the air again. "Leave me alone, all of you," he says. "I do not need this. I will make MY decisions. I will NOT be influenced by ANY of you. If I choose to change my mind, it's not because of anything that you have said to me. Do you hear me?"

"Yes, yes, anything!" I scream.

Millie rolls her eyes, slipping her pendant back inside her cape. "Whatever you say," she says with a frown.

"Well, then," says Neptune, "there is one last thing that may calm its rage and release the child. It comes from an ancient rhyme. It has never been used."

"Why not?" I ask.

"Once its magic is invoked, I lose my power over the kraken forever. It will never return to its old ways. It will be a passive, weak shell of its former self." He scowls in disgust.

"But the old days are gone," I say. "Surely you can see that! We can't cause death just to bring you jewels." Then I add more quietly, "Not that you're likely to even find a whole lot of jewels on that ship anyway."

"So your ways are *better,* are they?" he snaps. "Only the guilty die in your world, do they? Only for 'good' reasons?"

"No, but . . ." My voice trails off.

He waves me away. "But I will not stand by and see this happen. You may be right. Perhaps we will find a different way. Let's get that girl out of there."

"What's the rhyme?" Millie demands.

Neptune lifts his eyes to the sky.

"When old hatred's rift is mended,
Thus the kraken's power is ended."

"That's it?" my dad yells. "A *nursery* rhyme? That's ridiculous! You said you were going to sort it out."

"It's not just a nursery rhyme, you fool!" Neptune bursts out. "The rhyme itself is not the solution."

"Why tell us it, then?" I ask.

Neptune turns his angry eyes to me. "You asked how to mend the situation. The rhyme will do it—but only once its words have been acted upon. Only when the hatred ends, when the rift is mended, will the power of the kraken finally cease. Do I make myself clear?"

For a moment, there's silence, then they're all shouting again. But I move away. Can I do something? *When old hatred's rift is mended.* I've hated Emily Windsnap for years. Maybe I don't have to anymore. I could change this, do something good. Can I?

She communicated with the kraken just with her mind, didn't she? Maybe I can do the same, somehow. I'm going to try it!

I close my eyes and think of Emily, then I force a thought into my mind:

442

I'm sorry.

I say it over and over again in my thoughts. And then I wait.

Nothing.

What was I expecting? More flashing lights? I should have known nothing would happen. Nothing ever does when I try to do something good.

She's dead. The kraken's killed her. And I never had the chance to say I'm sorry.

I can see her in my mind. A picture from years ago. We used to play on the pier together. We were almost best friends. Why did I let her slip away?

Years of sorrow well into a tight ball, pressing against my throat.

But then—

I forgive you.

What was that? Who said it? I look around. No one's near me. They're all too busy shouting at each other, arguing over where to find the old hatred that they have to mend. I swipe a hand across my cheek, wiping away tears and seawater as I listen hard.

I forgive you.

It's Emily. It's her voice. I can hear her, again and again.

And then the chasm opens. It's starting again. It's whirling, throwing water around everywhere, splashing us all. A giant wave heaves toward us, knocking me off the raft.

"MANDY!" Dad yells, lunging for me. He swims away from the current, grabbing the raft and heaving us both back onto it.

"Please, no!" he sobs. "Don't let me lose you." He holds me tight, clutching my face to his chest as we kneel together on the raft.

When did my dad last hold me like this?

Over his shoulder, I can see the ship—but it's on the other side of the chasm. How will we ever get back to it?

As I stare into the raging water, all thoughts are suddenly swept from my mind. The monster's coming out of the sea again. Its head bursts out through the surface, scratched and veined with black lines, pus oozing out of craterlike holes in its skin. Piercing sounds of agony fill the sky.

Tentacles lash everywhere—it's out of control, screaming, on and on, the screeching siren sound. Roaring with anger, the monster lashes out again and again. And then I notice something in one of its tentacles. Emily! It's got her, holding her tight, throwing her into the air, crashing her back down to the surface. She looks so tiny, like a little doll.

Please don't kill her. . . . She's my friend.

Instantly, one final piercing scream shoots out from the water, exploding like a bomb, sending color and water everywhere.

And it gradually quiets, slows. Stops. The giant waterfall stops raging. It's just a giant hole, spreading and cracking in a line through the ocean.

The monster crashes down onto the water and lies still, tentacles like bumpy highways, bridging the long well, jerking slightly, its head half-sunk in the water. The sea fills with color, purple lights flowing out of the kraken, seeping into the water all around us.

No one speaks. We hover in the sea, in silence, focused on the sight in front of us: the monster lying still, no one moving an inch.

We've done it. We've really done it.

Chapter Ten

I was having the cruelest dream. It started off as a nightmare. The kraken had me. Trapped and half strangled, I was in its clutches under the water. Then I heard a voice: Mandy, apologizing. I thought, *Yes, let's make friends. I'm going to die any second now anyway.*

And then it changed. I was above the water, in the air, thrown high by the kraken. But it let go of me and I came crashing back down onto the water, sinking, then rising back up to the surface.

The worst part was what happened next.

It was the best part really, but so cruel.

I dreamed my mom and dad were there. They'd come to save me. Shona was with them.

We were best friends again. Even Mandy was there, and they were all asking if I was OK. No one was angry with me. All those eyes, looking at me with concern, helping me, carrying me somewhere, forgiving me for all the awful things I'd done. I wanted to call out to them, touch them, but I couldn't move; I couldn't speak.

I can't remember what happened next.

"Emily?"

"She can't hear you."

"She's opening her eyes!"

Mom? I blinked in the sunlight. "Mom? Is that really you?" I asked shakily.

She leaned over me, rocking as she held me tight. "Oh, Emily," she whispered into my neck, her voice choked and raw.

As she pulled away, I rubbed my eyes to see Dad's face next to hers. He was leaning out of the water, reaching up to hold my hand.

Shona was in the water next to him, smiling at me. "You're OK!" she said.

I looked around: gold and jewels beside me, dolphins at the front. I was in Neptune's chariot! And I wasn't on my own. Millie stood at the front, talking in a low, deep voice. I knew that tone. She was hypnotizing someone! But who?

"Now, moving your tentacle very, very slowly, lift another person out of the water," she said softly, "and carry them across the chasm, placing them gently on the deck of the cruise ship. Good, good. . . ."

The kraken was doing what she said.

I shuddered as I remembered being in its clutches, the horror of its tentacles around my neck. . . .

"We did it, then?" I asked numbly.

Shona beamed at me. "You're a heroine, Emily. How could I ever have been angry with you? I'm such a jellyfish at times. Do you realize what you've done?"

"I — no. I don't know."

I knew one thing, though. Whatever I'd done, I hadn't done it on my own. I pulled myself up. "Where's Mandy?"

Shona pointed out to sea. "She's on her way back to the ship," she said. "I think they'll be setting off soon."

I got up, shakily. I had to see her. My legs wobbled.

Mom grabbed my arm. "Emily, you need to rest."

"Later," I said. "I just have to do something."

Before she could stop me, I dived into the sea. I waited for my tail to form. It wobbled and shook just like my legs had, but I could move it. I could get there. I had to see Mandy.

"I'm coming with you, then." Shona swam over to my side.

We made our way toward the edge of the Triangle. I gasped as I saw what lay ahead: a gulf of utter black emptiness. My body shuddered violently as I looked down. Across the chasm, the kraken reached a tentacle from one side to the other and out toward the ship, carrying people carefully across.

"I can't!" Mandy was screaming. "It's HOR-RIBLE!"

"Quick! Come on. It's the only way across." Her dad held his hand out to her. Mandy climbed up onto the awful slimy bridge. My body shuddered. I couldn't go near it!

She tiptoed along the tentacle. It was so huge it almost looked like a road, bridging the emptiness below. By the time I got there, she was nearly across.

"Mandy!"

She turned. The tentacle was starting to slip. Two more steps and she'd be there.

"Emily," she said.

I swallowed. "Thank you."

Two steps away. She paused, stared at me. And then she smiled. I'd never seen her smile before. Not like that anyway. The only smile I'd ever seen from her was a sarcastic sneer. This one suited her better. It looked nice. Made her look like someone I might want to be friends with.

"Yeah, well," she said. "I didn't really do anything."

"No, you're wrong." I smiled back at her. "You did a lot."

Then she lurched across the tentacle, making her way back to the ship.

They'd gone. All of them back on the ship.

As the kraken lay still, I noticed someone in the water beside it. Tall, proud, and silent, Neptune bent forward to stroke a tentacle, holding it sadly. Then he turned and looked around him.

"Beeston!" he called. Mr. Beeston swam toward us from the ship.

"Have you completed the memory wipes?"

"Every last person, Your Majesty."

Neptune nodded. "Good work." Then he clicked his fingers. Instantly, his dolphins squirted

water into the air and dived down to pull the chariot through the water. Neptune clambered aboard.

"It's over," he said. "The kraken is falling back
into its sleep. Who knows when it will wake now,
or if it will even wake at all." He beckoned Mr.
Beeston. "We need someone to take on the
responsibility of watching over it."

Mr. Beeston's mouth twitched into a crooked
smile. "Do you mean . . . ?"

"Who else could I trust with such an important task?"

Neptune looked around at us all. "The rest of
you will return to your lives. The kraken keepers
will join you at Allpoints Island and you'll live
together. The Triangle shall be sealed when I have
left. Now, back to your island, everybody, and try
to keep out of trouble this time."

The ship was almost out of sight, a silhouette
slowly gliding along the horizon.

Dad put an arm around me as Shona caught
up with us, linking an arm in mine. Mom and
Millie smiled at me from inside the lifeboat.

"Hang on," Mom said. Then she pulled her

dress off. She had her swimsuit on underneath. Pinching her nose, she jumped into the sea and swam over to join me and Dad.

"I've been practicing," she explained simply as we stared.

Dad kissed her, then turned back to me with a wide grin. "Come on then, little 'un." He nodded toward Allpoints Island as he pulled me close. "Ready to go home?"

Home. I thought about our bay, about *Fortuna,* Barracuda Point, the Grand Caves, mermaid school, the million things I hadn't yet discovered about Allpoints Island—and everyone waiting for us. Althea and Marina, and all my other new friends.

"Yes, I'm ready," I said eventually. Then I turned to Shona and smiled. "We've got a party to go to."

LOCAL HEROES SAVE BRIGHTPORT PIER

The Brightport Town Council voted today to retain and modernize the town's historic pier. The decision came after local residents Jack and Maureen Rushton made a substantial donation from a recent windfall.

The Rushtons came into the money due to their stunning photographs of a raging sea monster on the open ocean. The photographs have been sold to newspapers across the world.

The photographs were taken while the couple was on vacation with Mermaid Tours. Bizarrely, they have no recollection of their vacation. "We were as surprised as anyone when we got the pictures developed," Mrs. Rushton said.

The Rushtons plan to expand their amusement arcade on the pier and are currently in negotiations with planners about a theme park, which they will open later this year. The star ride will be a massive roller coaster with a multitude of twists and turns along tentaclelike tracks.

The ride is to be called the Kraken.

ACKNOWLEDGMENTS

Once again, I can't claim to have done this all on my own. Lots of people have been involved in the process. I would especially like to thank:

Jeanette, Andrew, Alex, and Amber, for two incredible weeks in Bermuda;

Ben and Sam, for the day out on the pirate ship (even if it didn't go anywhere);

Fiz, for sharing so many special moments, and crying at most of them;

Kirsty, for being so proud and excited, and so good at sharing champagne;

Fiona and the fab team at Orion Children's Books, for being so behind Emily;

Sarah, for all the beautiful artwork;

my family, and lots of other friends, for all sorts of help along the way.

With extra special thanks to:

Kath, for 100 percent spot-on editorial feedback and for sharing the agony of second-book syndrome;

Lee, for again being a complete inspiration and a central part of helping this book to take shape;

Catherine, for doing all the right things for Emily and for me, and doing them with patience, friendship, care, and skill;

and Judith, for being such a thorough and brilliant editor that all my writer friends are jealous.

The Tail of Emily Windsnap text copyright © 2003 by Liz Kessler
The Tail of Emily Windsnap illustrations copyright © 2003 by Sarah Gibb
Emily Windsnap and the Monster from the Deep text copyright © 2004 by Liz Kessler
Emily Windsnap and the Monster from the Deep illustrations copyright © 2004 by Sarah Gibb

The Tail of Emily Windsnap first published in Great Britain in 2003
by Orion Children's Books, a division of the Orion Publishing Group
Emily Windsnap and the Monster from the Deep first published in Great Britain
in 2004 by Orion Children's Books, a division of the Orion Publishing Group

First U.S. edition in this format 2014

The Tail of Emily Windsnap:
Library of Congress Catalog Card Number 2003065284
ISBN 978-0-7636-2483-5 (hardcover)
ISBN 978-0-7636-2811-6 (first paperback edition)
ISBN 978-0-7636-6020-8 (second paperback edition)

Emily Windsnap and the Monster from the Deep:
Library of Congress Catalog Card Number 2005054261
ISBN 978-0-7636-2504-7 (hardcover)
ISBN 978-0-7636-3301-1 (first paperback edition)
ISBN 978-0-7636-6018-5 (second paperback edition)

ISBN 978-0-7636-7452-6 (paperback bindup)

15 16 17 18 19 BVG 10 9 8 7 6 5 4 3

Printed in Berryville, VA, U.S.A.

This book was typeset in Bembo.

Candlewick Press
99 Dover Street
Somerville, Massachusetts 02144

visit us at www.candlewick.com

Dive in and read the
New York Times *best-selling series!*